Cheron, former rebel leader and newly crowned king, comes to Wren Gardens on a holy mission to free his goddess from exile and bring peace to his kingdom, but he's distracted by an unholy and very beautiful concubine, Ekos.

Ekos may be more than a simple love slave, though. The King of Wren Gardens seems afraid of the strange and often blasphemous concubine and swears the man is cursed. Cheron agrees, especially when Ekos mocks and taunts Cheron's sense of honor. But the urge to distance himself from Ekos can't compete with the desire to remain close. Nor is it as strong as the urges in his body—urges he hasn't felt in years.

As Cheron tries to refocus on his mission, Ekos throws him off again—this time by offering to help him in his holy quest. Cheron knows he shouldn't trust a man who's in the employ of a rival king, particularly not one who seems to know all Cheron's deepest secrets. But he can't ignore the signs from the goddess telling him to entwine his fate with this tricky, captivating man.

He prays the signs aren't simply wishful thinking, manifestations of his very unholy desires. Time is running out, and Cheron is falling deeper for Ekos—and deeper into danger of another betrayal. One that could cost him his life.

THE DRAGON'S REBEL

Jacqueline Rohrbach

A NineStar Press Publication

Published by NineStar Press
P.O. Box 91792,
Albuquerque, New Mexico, 87199 USA.
www.ninestarpress.com

The Dragon's Rebel

Printed in the USA
First Edition
June, 2019

Print ISBN: 978-1-950412-99-0

Also available in eBook, ISBN: 978-1-950412-98-3

Warning: This book contains sexual content, which may only be suitable for mature readers, graphic violence, dark themes, and threats of rape.

To the amazing Anna Kaling, a merciful goddess who uses her awesome powers to help mortals achieve their dreams. Thank you for everything you've done for me. This journey would have been impossible without you.

Chapter One

HALF PARTED IN invitation, the concubine's painted red lips teased the possibilities for Cheron's sole benefit, for his sole pleasure, for his sole use. At least that was the intended impression, but who knew the actual number of men the concubine had truly pleasured? Many, Cheron assumed. Undeniably gorgeous, the pampered little house pet had all the markings of a palace favorite. Jewels hung from his earlobes, fine silks concealed his thin but muscular frame, and his body had been rubbed down with musky oils. Minus the golden, diamond-studded collar at his throat, he appeared to be a member of court.

"Is Ekos not to your taste, Majesty? He is personal stock, in case you are worried. No *low-born* has touched him."

The emphasis had Cheron grinding his teeth. While Sinnac politely used the proper title while addressing him, there was always a lilt to his pronunciation, a gentle reminder that Cheron had only recently became a king. Before, he'd been a lowly soldier—a servant. To men like Sinnac, men who'd been born into power, he would never be anything other than a lucky usurper playacting at greatness.

Sinnac continued, "Perhaps His Majesty would like to see him from a different angle?"

King Sinnac tilted the concubine's face upward to give Cheron a better look. Ekos lowered his crystal-blue eyes demurely, as was proper, but Cheron swore he saw a flash of mocking defiance in the depths before his lashes lowered. In a second, the brazen glare vanished. Ekos bowed his head, allowing his golden-yellow hair to fall over his shoulders. The posture gave Cheron a clear view of the concubine's long back and the enticing dip of his ass.

Suppressing his disgust, Cheron kept his response to King Sinnac formal. "He is most pleasing. I am recently sated and do not require sexual services just now, Your Excellence. Perhaps later."

"I heard you Northern men needed no pause between sessions. That you were an insatiable lot." Sinnac, a severe man who resembled a long tendril of smoke with his long white body, steel-gray hair, and gray eyes, raised his bushy eyebrows and took a drag from his hookah. Foul-smelling mist coiled around his head, momentarily canceling out the masculine, sweet smell of the concubine's body oils.

Cheron gave the characterization a breathy laugh. "I'm afraid all men must submit to biology."

"Of course. Of course."

Truthfully, Cheron's carnal needs hadn't been satisfied recently or even in the past year. His aversion to touching Ekos had nothing to do with lack of desire. Perhaps the young concubine served freely now, but at some point in his life, he'd been brought here in chains and trained in the arts of pleasure. The very thought made Cheron's skin crawl. Not too long ago, he'd been enslaved under the reign of a cruel king who raped and tortured to stay in power. He had no intentions of following the same path.

After he took control of Broken Maw, servants continued to exist, but they were compensated for their work. No one was compelled to offer sexual services. Those who sold themselves demanded money, certainly, but also equal pleasure. Ekos's circumstances were much different.

Sinnac, as if stressing those differences, commanded the concubine to attend to Cheron's needs. "Show our guest your skills, my pet. Seduce him."

The concubine pouted. In a spoiled voice, he said, "My treasure, I do not believe he wants me."

A hard glint in his eye, Sinnac returned, "Nonsense. Help him settle in to Wren Gardens. I'll not have my guests frustrated. And if the rumors I hear are true, he is quite congested with lust."

Gossip between courts wasn't uncommon. Certainly, Cheron heard his fair share of stories from Sinnac's lands, especially tales of the financial troubles of Wren Gardens. It didn't upset Cheron to learn he was the subject of discussion among Sinnac's people, but his temperature rose at being so directly contradicted by another monarch.

"What do you know of my frustration, Excellency?"

His laughter croaked as he took another puff from the hookah. "I hear you haven't had any pleasure since Aethel. His betrayal must still sting, yes?"

Honesty roughened his voice to an almost inaudible, harsh whisper. "Betrayal burns more than it stings, Excellency. Afterward, the smoke blinds us."

Sinnac raised an eyebrow. "Dramatic. Betrayal also chokes us, apparently, though I heard your lover made good kindling for fire."

Cheron swallowed down the memory before it overwhelmed him. Sometimes, in the dead of night, he still woke to the sound of his lover's screams as he twisted on the pyre and the king's executioner's grim pronouncement that justice had been done. Now that Cheron had overthrown the king in a successful rebellion, there would be no such burnings. Never again.

Cheron kept his voice level. "His crime was nowhere near as severe as the punishment."

"Hm," Sinnac responded. Supposedly, the price for his displeasure ran higher. This marked Cheron's first time visiting Wren Gardens, but his father told tales of a ruler obsessed with revenge to the point of madness. If the stories were true, Sinnac's gardens grew on human blood.

Cheron tried to smile. "At any rate, that is in the past."

"Well, then. My pet can make you forget the traitor existed. Perhaps he can make you forget your own treason."

It would be unwise to answer the bait, so Cheron kept quiet on the matter. "I have no doubt of Ekos's skills, but they are wasted on me at the present."

"We'll see." Sinnac waved his graceful fingers, an order for Ekos to proceed.

The concubine's crystal-blue eyes lowered again. Looking into their depths was akin to jumping into ice-cold water. One could drown, but he'd feel the sting of cold as he sank. Just the same, Cheron barely kept from gasping out loud as Ekos's long fingers stroked the outer folds of the long robe he wore. Beneath the clothes, his body was taut, ready for a lover's touch.

"Majesty," Ekos simpered, his full, round mouth set in a pout. "I can't please you through so many layers of clothing."

In Wren Gardens, sex servants weren't allowed to remove the clothing of nobility. Such a task was reserved for only the most trusted of servants, those who'd been with households for generations. Poisons that seeped through the skin were common here; the precaution made sense.

Ekos's own dress confused Cheron. Station required servants to wear only thin scraps of fabric that advertised their wares and marked them as slaves. The concubine was swathed nearly head to toe in a loose-fitting, semitransparent silken frock that was embroidered along the hem by a skilled hand. Somehow, this enticed Cheron's interests far better than any scant loincloth.

As if sensing his increasing desires, the concubine formed his full mouth into an aware smirk. The arrogance took Cheron aback and made him worry for the concubine's safety. The man's voice was strong and confident when he said, "Perhaps His Majesty would like to undress me first?"

Sinnac guffawed at Cheron's horrified expression. "Forgive Ekos, my royal brother. He is overeager to prove his affections."

Once again, Cheron ignored the overt slight. For now, Cheron had to be content another monarch had even stooped to meet with him. Smiling, he said, "He hasn't been tested already?"

Sinnac's countenance darkened. Without thinking, Cheron had insulted the other man's virility, which he touted with great pride. In the short time Cheron had been a guest at Wren Gardens, Sinnac boasted as many as fifty lovers, all of whom couldn't get enough of their lord and master.

"My apologies, Excellency." Cheron spread his hands in contrition. "I understand your prowess is legendary."

Sniffing, Sinnac got to his knees and began undoing the knot keeping his robe together. Seconds later, he was nearly naked except for his white linen undergarments. Covered in a network of impressive scars, his body flaunted a lifetime of war. "Turn around," he commanded Ekos.

Immediately, Ekos obeyed. Cheron swore he saw a flash of disgust in the man's crystal-blue eyes. Soon enough, the meaningless and practiced smile fell back into place. The young man dipped forward, raising his hips. "Enter if you dare," he mocked.

Sinnac growled at the challenge.

Stomach lurching, Cheron realized the other monarch's intent. Baring witness to rape immediately quashed his previous desires. He knew it was a typical practice in Wren Gardens, but Cheron failed to control a wave of pity. This was no way to treat another human being.

"Excellency," Cheron said, interrupting the looming sexual encounter. "I have been an ungracious guest. I would love to indulge in Ekos's sweet attentions privately. But how can I enjoy him if you put me to shame? Will he even consider me adequate after you?"

"I'm sure I would, Majesty," Ekos softly assured him. "A man as magnificent as you must be bliss to touch."

Sinnac ran his hands up and down the length of the concubine's body, slapping and prodding as he went, but eventually sat back against the cushions without penetrating, much to Cheron's relief.

His gaze hooded, almost fully concealed, Sinnac said, "Please retire to your quarters, Majesty. We'll attend to matters of state after dinner. I will have Ekos sent to your rooms. Treat him gently. I paid a high price for him."

As equals, they stood and formally bowed. The concubine, head still bent toward the ground, his expression concealed by a long flow of honey hair, remained prostrated. His fists clenched and unclenched. When he lifted his head, he smiled serenely and said, "You have yet to pay the full price for me, Excellency."

Chapter Two

CHERON PRACTICED WHAT to say on his way to the chamber. He'd offer the young man alcohol, the strongest on reserve, and lavish a few expensive treats on him. He'd compliment the beauty of his body, the lush swell of his lips, and possibly his intellect if he proved good at games. With any luck, the concubine would pass out, and Cheron could claim to have possessed him. Before he could guard his tongue and keep on script, Cheron blurted, "I won't hurt you."

He couldn't suppress a wave of pity. Someone had bound Ekos to the bed. His delicate wrists pinched in the rope's coils. Flashes of red marred his pale skin where he'd clearly struggled to free himself. The same collar, made of gold and diamonds, still graced his throat. Far from enticing, the man's eyes now had a wild gleam. His chest rose and fell beneath the silken tunic. His undergarments had been removed, and the bulge of his sex lay flat between his thighs. Unaroused.

"I won't hurt you," Cheron repeated.

Ekos didn't respond, but his breathing evened out. "Do what you came here to do, rebel."

Cheron spoke as though he were calming a spooked mare. "I didn't come here to hurt you, only to get you drunk. Would you like me to untie you?"

"Yes," Ekos said in a way that suggested, *obviously.*

When Cheron sat on the bed, Ekos involuntarily flinched away, but he tried to hide the fearful gesture behind a fierce snarl. Cheron clucked at the noise but understood the vehemence. Placed in a similar situation, he would have seethed and turned to murderous intentions to escape. To preserve the man's modesty, Cheron used one of his personal furs scattered on the bed to drape the concubine's midsection. This calmed Ekos enough for some of the ice to melt from his crystal-blue eyes. There was a faint splash of warmth. Not enough to dip a toe in but encouraging nonetheless.

"There," Cheron said once he removed the final binding. "You are free."

"Not quite that," Ekos snarled back. Seeing Cheron purse his lips at the harsh tone, the concubine added, "But thank you for this, at least."

Cheron shook off his previous ire. He had no right to expect politeness from a man in Ekos's situation. "Are you hungry?"

Frowning, Ekos rubbed his wrists. "I'd eat an entire cow if you'd let me."

Small in frame and narrow in waist, Ekos didn't look like he could eat a grape, let alone an entire farm animal. Cheron said, "None of those here, I'm afraid. But I do have some lamb if you'd like."

Moments later, Ekos gnawed on a meaty leg with rigorous greed. Cheron was forced to swallow his previous assumptions regarding the man's appetites as his entire week's food supply vanished down the concubine's gullet.

Cheron, his voice dry with amusement, said, "By the twin moons, you are quite a bit different outside of Sinnac's chamber."

"I suspect we have that in common, rebel."

Coming from the servant's mouth, the insult didn't have the same sting. Cheron, a solider by birth, was accustomed to how men talked about those in power behind their backs. In some ways, it was refreshing to hear his role as usurper so frankly addressed.

"So you've heard how I came to power?"

"Indeed. Who hasn't heard the tale of Cheron the Devourer, Scourge of the Green Sea, Deflowerer of Maidens, *Dragon* of the Broken Maw?"

The odd emphasis on the word *dragon* caught Cheron's attention, but he didn't comment. "Is my reputation as bad as all that?"

"Savage. And I must say you fit the part. You're very much the big, hulking bear."

War hadn't weaved a pleasant tapestry from the threads of Cheron's face. His features, though angular and firm, were marred by a long, jagged scar that trenched from his temple to his chin. But he knew his stature to be impressive. Broad-chested, tall, he cut an imposing figure on the battlefront. Men flocked to his standard, eager to spill blood for the Dragon of Broken Maw.

Helpless as he was, Ekos didn't seem bothered by Cheron's physicality. Rather than keep a leery eye on him the way most other men did, the concubine met his gaze directly and with an odd humorous glint. Those full lips of his continually pulled up in a satisfied half smirk, as though the man had received news of his greatest enemy's demise.

Goading a reaction, Cheron said, "And you look the part of a whore. You're very much the pouting, simpering pet who'd topple over in a silken pile after lifting a feather."

Rather than bristle at the insult, Ekos chuckled. The melody of the noise was light and musical. The humor didn't ebb from his eyes. If anything, more flooded in, turning them from ice to air.

Ekos poured them both some wine. Elegant hands skipped right over the mugs, comfortable in Cheron's monstrous paws, and plucked up two flutes with slender, easily broken necks. He filled one only a quarter way full and used two fingers to push the crystal glasses in Cheron's direction.

Brow knitted in a manner Cheron knew made him appear as a contemplative savage, he asked the concubine, "Are you mocking me?"

The half smirk twitched upward, showing Ekos's increasing amusement Ekos said, "Maybe. Or maybe I want to see if those preposterously large hands of yours can handle tender burdens. You said you wanted to get me drunk. To what end? Can you not perform if your lover isn't inebriated, Majesty?"

Adding the title to the insult, the first the concubine had used it outside of Sinnac's chamber, chaffed Cheron's already frayed nerves. He didn't have much use for honorifics, but he disliked his new status being the butt of jokes. He'd prefer the man address him as an equal rather than mock his title. "You truly are testing me."

"That doesn't answer the question."

Ekos took a sip of his wine and gestured for Cheron to do the same. He studied the delicate glass, so tiny and frail, and thought of how silly he'd look sipping from it. "I'm not thirsty. And I had no intention of pleasuring myself tonight. I wanted to get you drunk so you would sleep and leave me in peace."

"Hm, and why is that?"

Ekos guarded his expression and shut off the light of humor shining there. Surprising himself, Cheron admitted he missed the smug playfulness and hated the dark suspicion. He enjoyed the view of the sky, limitless and breezy, more than he did sinking in ice water. But could he be honest with this man who served the court of Wren Gardens? Here, sexual slavery was the norm. Denouncing the practice as barbaric to the wrong person would put him at odds with the entire court.

Cheron lied. "Because you are not to my taste."

Ekos's slender fingers toyed with the wine glass, pushing it around on the table. Through narrowed eyes, he considered the response. Finally, after taking a slight sip, he passed judgment. "I don't think that's the truth. Tell me, why didn't you want me? Wasn't I all you desired in a lover?"

"Are you so eager to be abused?"

"Curious word choice there. *Abused.*"

Trying to play Ekos's astute observation off as unimportant, Cheron snapped back, "I don't sit around much and think on my word choice."

"That I believe. You don't play a very good game do you, Majesty?"

Ignoring all the slights and barbs became an increasingly difficult task. Normally, Cheron prided himself on not being the brash, hotheaded savage who used violence to clean up his messes the way others used rags. Defying such expectations helped him win the war and his crown. Right now, he struggled to remain calm. He'd never strike the much smaller man—especially not when his bond with the mercy goddess Kalin gave him additional strength—but he'd love to pick Ekos up and fling him out into the hall.

"Thinking about punching my face in, are we?"

"No."

"Why not? Is it against some code thing you have?"

Cheron frowned at the dismissive hand wave Ekos gave to his "code thing," which he did indeed have. Grinding his teeth, he said, "No."

"Oh, my hulking rebel bear, you are a terrible liar."

Cheron grunted. "If you are so eager to be worshipped in bed, seek out Sinnac."

"He hasn't touched me. He doesn't dare."

"He gave you to me to use. He can't think that highly of you."

Ekos smirked. "He thinks my asshole is cursed."

"What?"

The burst of laughter caught Cheron off guard. Ekos, face red with amusement at his own private joke, eventually ceased his howling laughter. Sobering, he took another sip of his wine and said, "I told him if he dared to penetrate me, his dick would squirt blood and eventually rot off. I guess he doesn't think too highly of your cock, my friend."

Cheron thought back on the stern Sinnac, who was renowned for being brutal and no-nonsense. Not the type to believe in curses or magic. "Why would he believe such a silly tale?"

"Because, my dear rebel, I am not what I seem."

"What are you, then?"

Instead of answering, the concubine grabbed the entire flagon of wine and guzzled it down. His Adam's apple bobbed as he chugged; the corners of his lips tugged ever upward, fighting the gravity of the situation. He wiped the excess liquid away from his mouth and said, "So, you came here for the Hell's Echo?"

Cheron, rising in haste, accidentally swiped the delicate flute to the ground. The fine crystal shattered everywhere.

Chapter Three

THEY STUDIED THE broken fragments of the fragile crystal goblet. Only the rounded lip remained intact; a single drop of red wine clung to its tip. Cheron's own heavy, uneven breathing filled the chamber, drowning out all other noise. Always mocking, or at least that's how Cheron saw the wry twist of Ekos's mouth as the concubine studied the wreckage with a raised brow. Sweetly, he said, "Your hands seem unsuitable for tender burdens, after all."

"Perhaps."

Ekos raised his glass in salute. Cheron expected the man to gloat more; blackmail wouldn't be outside his nature either, Cheron suspected, but he sat there sipping on what remained of the wine. There was little left. He should have been drunk from the copious amount he consumed thus far.

"Are you...?"

"Behind the cork? Not at all, I'm afraid."

Whores probably drank their fill every day; the man's tolerance must have rivaled a dragon's. Cheron grumbled. Ekos's sweet smile spread ever upward. The pleasure on display rekindled his urge to grab the man by his scruff and throw him out of the chamber by force.

"You'll need me," Ekos said. "For your little quest."

Ekos's ability to guess his thoughts rankled Cheron further. Heat spread from his chest upward to his face. No doubt he'd appear flushed, like a schoolboy who'd been caught in the middle of a childish depravity. Why did he feel so out of sorts around the strange concubine? Certainly his beauty commanded attention, but Cheron knew many alluring men and had lain with several over the course of his lifetime. But none put their finger on his pulse the way Ekos did.

Ekos tipped his head back and took the rest of his wine. "Think out your problems."

Without responding, Cheron did just that.

He'd been sent here by the goddess Kalin, who only gave him a vague notion of his mission—to obtain Hell's Echo. The journey was to be one of faith and one she asked him to make alone. She'd promised to guide him along the path and had given him the gift of considerable strength to aid his endeavors, but so far, her interference had been minimal. Cheron didn't know what the Echo was, what it did, or even what it looked like. He only knew an apostate had betrayed her and condemned her to a prison in Yellow Sky, and she needed a true follower to release her.

A ruse to mask his quest, the trade agreement needed to conceal Cheron's true intentions until he was able to escape, hopefully with the item in tow. The servant knowing didn't bode well for his odds of lasting long.

Ekos, as if guessing his thoughts, said, "Yes, if I know what you came for, Sinnac does as well. What are you to do?"

There was nothing wise to say, so Cheron said nothing.

"Yes, you don't want to confide in a whore. I understand. Yet you must wonder what harm might come from telling me your secrets. I can't tell Sinnac more than he already knows, but it's possible I could tell you how to wiggle out of your noose."

"From what I gather, he's not the hanging type."

"You gather correctly. His depravities extend far beyond mere execution. I know where he keeps the relic." Ekos put his slippered feet up on the table and tapped them together, raising his eyebrows mischievously. The silken frock fell down well below his knee to show off his shapely calves. Through the dim candlelight, Cheron saw the outline of the man's sex, now partially aroused.

"Are you enjoying my circumstances?"

Far from being ashamed, Ekos stood so that Cheron saw the full length of Ekos's arousal. "A bit. Admittedly."

"I'm not your plaything."

"No, not yet."

ONCE HE'D CALMED himself and saw beyond the red haze clouding his vision, Cheron admitted the folly of having the concubine dragged away from his chamber. Rather than take the episode personally, the young man had the gall to say, "I'll see you at the gate to Yellow Sky, then!" He was, of course, referring to the realm where souls were banished after they died.

Despite his anger with the quarrelsome whore, Cheron felt responsible for Ekos's rough treatment at the hands of the guards. They'd slapped him across the mouth for his remark. Even if they didn't understand the meaning, it was enough that someone as lowly as a concubine would dare speak such a way to a king.

"I'm sorry," Cheron had said to the unfortunate concubine as they dragged him away.

He'd responded by spitting out his own blood and shrugging.

Alone with only his thoughts, Cheron struggled to formulate a new plan. He wasn't incapable of advanced deduction as many assumed, including the frustrating Ekos. His options were simply limited, and he knew it.

Near frantic, he turned to the divine. "Kalin help me. I need your guidance."

Warriors, and Cheron considered himself such, habitually prayed to Atyx, the god of war, vengeance, and greed. But he prayed to Kalin, the goddess of wisdom, temperance, and mercy. Kalin's amulet, a two-headed dragon with necks entwined, warmed against his chest. He felt a slight, tingling vibration to let him know her interests had been piqued.

Gods didn't directly communicate with mortals; such a feat would be impossible now. They'd been locked away in Yellow Sky, a region of heaven well above the blue dome the residents of Ulara knew. Twin moons, supposedly Kalin's lovers, marked the division. Beyond their light, the universe turned a sickly yellow.

Dragons, their servants, had also been imprisoned. No one knew where, but there'd been no sign of the creatures since the fracture. Supposedly, possession of Hell's Echo could bring them back, at least the ones who served the goddess.

The gods still offered signs to the worthy through the earthly symbols: statues, amulets, relics. Cheron's amulet came from his mother, who'd been a priestess in the old world in the time of the gods.

Cheron clutched the amulet, prostrating himself. "Kalin, I seek your wisdom. It was your will that I should lead Broken Maw and the Northern kingdoms away from the barbarity of the old king. Please tell me how to keep the peace. How should I proceed in my undertaking?"

The warmth on his chest seeped through his heart, slowing the beat to a peaceful lull akin to sailing on calm waters. He imagined himself in a small boat, held up in Kalin's care, set to drift on a vast ocean. In her hands, he felt safe, loved, cherished. He'd never known such a feeling in any other's embrace.

The amulet came unfastened from his neck and fell to the floor. Cheron studied the talisman intently, waiting for the goddess to make her sign clear. Light poured from the diamonds symbolizing the dragon's eyes. They glowed a clear, icy blue with vague hints of sky.

"Your mercy binds me," he said to his goddess.

Calm left him. He looked at the ajar door and remembered how roughly they'd treated Ekos. Would the concubine's offer to help still stand after all that? Cheron hoped so. "I am to be a plaything after all. Of the gods and of man."

The last, he found, didn't actually bother him so much.

Chapter Four

WHISPERS CAUGHT CHERON'S ear. Although he caught little more than a few words of the gossip, he knew himself to be the subject of much speculation. Nobel men and women lingered on the outer edges of the garden's periphery. Behind fans, they observed him the way they might a zoo animal. The more daring of the lower-born, those who had access to the court, drifted closer, hoping to score themselves points for bravery among the nobility and perhaps a juicy drip of gossip to sale.

A plucky boy came nearer and nearer.

Cheron, acting the part of the savage, gave him a cutthroat grin. He knew the dark ink tattoos on his pale skin were unlike anything they'd seen before. Men and women of Wren Gardens didn't mark themselves after battle. Winking, Cheron leaned toward the boy and said, "I got this one from killing a bear. That's worth at least a dule, a just compensation for such valuable information if you ask me."

The boy took the information and vanished into the crowd.

Acting as though he hadn't a care in the world, Cheron dipped his fingers in the reflecting pool and flicked the water playfully toward the new concubine they'd sent to please him. Lion was the young man's name. Although he had the type of immaculate face—high-browed, delicate, and charming in its symmetry—

that appealed to base instincts, Cheron longed for the sardonic tilt of Ekos's mouth.

"Your Majesty," the new concubine said with manufactured breathlessness. His wide, innocent brown eyes shone, and he played with one of his soft curls. Like the other concubines, he was clothed only in a thin strap of cloth over his groin. "You killed a bear! What a devious scoundrel. You must be punished."

Nearby, perched on a mound of cushions and eating a pear, Sinnac grinned as if he found the prospect of punishment especially agreeable. Cheron did his best to ignore the queasiness in stomach and returned the concubine's good-natured flirt. He swatted driblets of water into his sweet face again and said, "Perhaps you'd like to take a switch to my back?"

"If it pleases you. I'd be gentle." His grin widened. "Or rough if you prefer."

"Gods help us all," Ekos said. "Let me die before I hear more of this."

In the middle of the garden, he stood on a marble pedestal. Arms bound behind his back, he remained perfectly still; the noose around his delicate, pale neck ensured some measure of docility from the mouthy concubine.

Punishment for insolence, Sinnac had said, but Cheron wondered if the concubine had failed at some other task, like spying on Cheron. *No*, he decided. *The goddess would not mislead me.* Somehow, Ekos was key to his quest.

"Quiet, you," a guard commanded Ekos, tapping the pedestal with his foot until it wobbled. Unable to regain his balance, Ekos pitched forward. The rope tightened around his neck, making the sound of an unbroken pair of riding gloves when it snapped taut. The chains they draped him in pulled downward, adding weight. Cheron thanked the twin moons that Ekos's head didn't pop off.

Cheron forced his expression to veer toward amusement, overriding his natural reaction of revulsion at the cruel display, as Ekos's legs twitched and he gasped for air. To his credit, he never begged mercy or even looked in Sinnac's direction. Indeed, he bore death with serenity greater than most soldiers Cheron fought with.

Sinnac waved his long, slender fingers. "Now, now. That's enough. Help him stand."

Cheron's own tensions eased as Ekos once again stood on solid ground. He hadn't realized he'd been so worried. *It's because you need him. Not for any other reason.* Despite his own internal assurances, he extinguished a near-unbearable urge to wrap Ekos up in a swath of furs and kiss his golden head until the coughing fit that gripped him eased.

Sinnac asked him, "Are you contrite for your inability to satisfy our guest, my pet?"

Ekos let loose one more hacking cough. "Not nearly as sorry as I am to see his brutish face again."

The nobility of the court tittered.

Lion, the concubine not hanging from a tight rope, took this as his cue to offer Cheron his slavish devotion. "Your face is so strong, Your Majesty. I have never seen eyes so fierce. They are the brown of a hawk on the hunt. In your elevated gaze, I feel but a small rabbit caught in a snare of pure bliss. I long for—"

"Yes, thank you, lovely one." Cheron cut Lion off. Had he not, the young man would have gone on forever with his over-the-top praise. Rather than make Cheron feel exalted, the speech made him feel silly, like some over-puffed simpleton whose intellect was so easily bought with glib flattery.

Using that strange ability of his, Ekos detected Cheron's discomfort. "Oh goodness, *lovely one*, you've offended him."

The young man froze. Panic made his pristine features pallid and dull. He stammered more compliments. They rolled out of his well-shaped mouth one after another until he finally broke off and searched Cheron's face for the sign of approval he needed to be safe.

Ekos winced. Cheron got the sense he regretted throwing the other young concubine to the fires. He tried to undo the harm. "I'm sure, though, you can ease His Majesty's troubles in the bedroom."

The entire courtyard's attention was riveted on the exchange. Murmurs went through the crowd. Sinnac, his bejeweled fingers propping up his chin, observed in a detached, cold manner. His gray, predatory eyes remained locked onto Cheron, studying his every move.

Not knowing what else to do, Cheron grabbed Lion by the nape and pulled him forward to lock their lips together in a seemingly passionate kiss. The young man yielded to his attentions, allowing Cheron instant access to his mouth. Relieved, he placed his hands against Cheron's chest and kissed back with an ardor born from terror, not pleasure.

Cheron couldn't stomach the ruse any longer. He broke away and gave the young concubine a shaky smile. "You excite me beyond measure, lovely one."

Holding his breath, Cheron waited for Ekos to expose him as a fake and to declare the fit of passion a ruse. Tight-lipped and for once not smiling, Ekos looked on with open hostility until he eventually said, "Your code of honor breaks so easily, then."

Sinnac laughed heartily at that. "What a sour whore you turned out to be."

Cheron laughed as well. Soon, the rest of the court echoed the merriment.

Had Cheron's kiss fooled Ekos? Oddly, he found the thought unsettling rather than gratifying. He didn't have time to dwell. Sinnac stood from the dais. His long, blue robe flowed behind him. Servants scuttled after him to make sure the long train didn't touch the ground.

"I will walk with my guest. We have a trade agreement to discuss and then a feast to celebrate our accord. Afterward, some light entertainment!"

Polite applause broke out on the patio. The nobility continued to talk behind their fans. Cheron knew their mutterings were not in his favor. He guessed, judging by their pinched brows and their worried glances, that the thought of entering into any sort of deal with a savage like him vexed their sensibilities.

He wanted to tell them not to worry. There would be no deal.

Chapter Five

"LET US TAKE the air." Twitching them gently in a circular motion, Sinnac used two fingers to command a guard. "Bring Ekos along. Come, come."

Cheron didn't know what was ordered until they yanked Ekos from his pedestal. Still in chains, dragging them behind him in what was clearly a struggle, he stumbled forward without assistance. One of the guards stepped on the dangling lead. Ekos pitched forward and landed roughly on his face. When he stood, Cheron saw that a patch of shredded skin marred his beautiful flawless skin. The contusions didn't appear deep, but they'd sting.

"Unshed his chains. Instead, put our pet on a leash and bring him here."

The guards did as told and handed the chain leash over to Sinnac, who pressed the leather handle into Cheron's hand. Refusing would have been a grave offense, so Cheron gripped the handle in a tight fist and did his best to calm the surge of bile rising in his throat.

"You honor me, Excellency. I do not feel right disciplining your servant, as a humble guest."

"Don't want to get your hands dirty?" Ekos sneered.

Sinnac ignored the outburst. "He offended you, not me. I do hate to punish one so beautiful in this crass manner, but his actions merit an admonishment. Be rough as pleases Your Majesty."

"Of course, Excellency. Thank you."

Too little force and he'd appear lenient, as though he didn't value his honor. Too much and he'd actually lose his honor. Striking a balance proved a difficult task to manage. At least the concubine made the task easier. Being wise for the first time since they'd met, Ekos trailed behind and said nothing contrary or snide. A hard glint to his eye teased an inner world rich with revenge fantasies. When he looked too long, Cheron swore he saw himself on a pyre. Ekos smiled, showing all his straight white teeth.

Cheron gave the lead a slight tug, pitching him forward. Guilt pinched his heart uncomfortably when Ekos's skin under the leash puckered. Cheron's constrained pulls were not rough enough to do any serious injury, but the taut snaps would remind Ekos of the chain.

"How do you feel about your surroundings, my royal brother?"

"Glorious. The tales I'd heard do not do Wren Gardens justice, Excellency."

That much was true. The garden did hold many cruel wonders.

Animals Cheron had thought long extinct wandered freely, with the exception of predators. Anything with long, pointed teeth paced restlessly in a cramped cage. On display, the animals grunted and roared in frustration and fury. Cheron pictured Ekos in a similar situation. Curiously, it wasn't difficult to imagine the concubine with sharp, pointed teeth.

Cheron and Sinnac strolled further through the pleasure garden, walking over narrow bridges that spanned over vast ponds filled with bright yellow fish. Money littered the bottom of the pools, enough to pay for improved livelihoods for hundreds and thousands of peasants. The food one could buy with the sunken fortune would make a spectacular feast.

If the servants shared similar thoughts, they kept their expressions blank as a snowdrift.

Sinnac continued, "And have you enjoyed your stay here?"

"Yes, Excellency. Thank you."

"Wonderful." Sinnac stopped suddenly. "A small detour, Majesty. This way please."

Uneasy with the turn and the slight smile playing about Sinnac's lips, Cheron followed but instinctively kept his hand where his sword normally rested. He'd been disarmed before entering the palace, but old habits died hard.

They went under an arched bridge. Vines tangled over the structure and small flowers shaped like hearts dripped down and brushed the top of Cheron's head. A sweet fragrance, almost like honey, filled his nostrils. Lovely. So why was he so unsettled?

The leash tugged. Behind him, Ekos—pale and trembling—tried to back away. When his eyes met Cheron's, he swallowed and gave his head a slight shake. *This is bad*, he mouthed.

Sinnac, a shadow caught between worlds of light and darkness, called back over his shoulder. His tone playful, he asked, "Coming, Majesty?"

He had no choice. Mastering his fear, Cheron sent a silent apology to Ekos and pulled him forward. Colder under the massive bridge, the air around them congealed. Cheron swore it stuck to his skin, leaving an oily film behind. Avoiding any action likely to be misconstrued as an insult, Cheron maintained a pleasant smile and walked with a calm, light stride.

"Turn back, you fool." Ekos's voice was a harsh whisper. He must have been terrified to risk saying anything at all.

Cheron couldn't turn back now. He'd never get out of the palace alive.

Once again, he pulled Ekos forward. They stepped out of the cold shade of the arched bridge and into the light.

The pleasant fragrance curdled into something horrific. Bright light momentarily blinded him, but he could tell by the horrified gasp from Ekos that he wasn't going to like what he saw once they'd adjusted.

"Here it is," Sinnac said with pride. "My true pleasure garden."

Tropical flowers that Cheron had only heard of lined the flowerbeds. Their elegant heads bent downward, as if heavy with grief. At first, it seemed as if nothing were amiss and the concubine's panic was unwarranted. Cheron looked closer. Whatever his other faults, Ekos had proved to be no coward.

"I am inclined to agree to your trade negotiation. I must warn you, however, I take a rather dim view of betrayal. See for yourself."

The flowers in a nearby bed bent upward. Perhaps vermin, Cheron thought. A low moan dispelled that notion. Disgusted but compelled forward nonetheless, Cheron leaned toward the flower bed. Instantly, on instinct, he reared back. The manufactured pleasant smile he'd plastered to his face fell away.

A living man served as the soil in which the flowers grew. His chest cavity, filled with rich dirt, was split open. White, jagged, the bones of his rib cage poked upward. His mouth opened and closed. His eyes begged for the merciful touch of death.

Unable to bear the sight any longer, Cheron turned away. "This is...an abomination."

Sinnac said, "Magic keeps them alive."

"Sorcery."

"Same thing, Majesty."

No, it wasn't. Magic was controlled by Kalin and brought life and peace. These incantations were dark. Cheron knew of only one god who would allow such perversion. Domination through any means necessary was his creed and that of those who served him.

"You are a worshiper of Atyx?"

"His glory binds me," Sinnac said.

Ekos had turned his head upward, looking anywhere but at the living corpses nourishing the vast array of plants. Pinched lines appeared at the corners of his eyes, making him seem much older. A single tear ran down his smooth, pallid skin. "Behold the powers of the mercy goddess," he said.

"This is not Kalin's doing," Cheron replied.

Ekos turned his face away. One of the damned mumbled his name. "Ekos," he said in a croaked whisper. His agonized cry accused betrayal.

Cheron understood why Ekos's courage had failed him. He knew these people.

Chapter Six

THEY CELEBRATED THE impending treaty with a lavish feast, but Cheron's mind dwelled on the images from the garden, no matter how many tasty morsels servants shoved toward him.

Most people took a dim view of betrayal. Cheron couldn't think of a single person who delighted in being taken advantage of, lied to, or discarded. Sinnac had taken his disgruntlement to a whole other level. Reminding himself he'd come here for a purpose other than to make peace with the despot, Cheron donned the expression of a jovial guest and made small talk with Lion, the concubine who'd played with him in the fountain earlier.

Face ashen, Ekos sat at the bottom of the dais with his head bent, once again letting his cascade of golden hair hide the map of his features. Was he fierce or resigned? Cheron wondered which expression he'd find if he stroked the hair out of his face. For his own sake, he hoped the former. He needed a fighter.

"Majesty?"

The sweet concubine placed his small hand on Cheron's large arm muscle.

"Hm?"

"I asked if you were enjoying your supper?"

Truthfully, he hadn't tasted any of the fine cuisine placed in front of him on large silver platters. Though the array of meats, cheeses, and wines were impressive, he wasn't much in the eating mood after witnessing the spectacle of Sinnac's pleasure garden. The smell of decay clung to his skin. Dimly, he wondered if he'd ever forget the odor.

"Help me enjoy the feast more," he invited the young man.

"Yes, Majesty."

Lion's instant happiness sent waves of guilt through Cheron. Using him as cover might later have dire consequences. Forgiveness didn't appear to be one of Sinnac's finer qualities, and he couldn't bear the thought of the young man suffering a horrible fate. Still, sentimentality was a decadent, not to mention deadly, luxury in his present circumstances.

Smiling, Cheron said, "One of the dates, perhaps?"

Lion plucked one up and nearly placed the sweet fruit into Cheron's mouth. His master's harsh voice interrupted him. "Stop. I'd like Ekos to redeem himself to our guest." To Ekos he said, "His Majesty has requested to be fed. Are you up to the task, my pet?"

Without responding, Ekos crawled on his hands and knees toward the spread of food at Cheron's feet. The loose silk garment he wore dipped downward, giving Cheron a view of his long, slender body. He took the date from Lion and fed the fruit to him rather than Cheron as instructed. In response, Lion looked at him with a sort of bemused helplessness. Ekos leaned forward and licked his own lips.

"Thanks," Lion stammered, wide-eyed in panic, and he jerked his head toward Sinnac, checking his reaction.

Sinnac's bushy silver eyebrows slanted together. "Last I checked, Lion was not our royal guest."

Ekos grinned rakishly. "I thought His Majesty might enjoy the taste of sweet and sour."

Clapping his hands merrily, Sinnac shouted. "Quite so. What say you, Majesty?"

Refusing was another luxury Cheron could ill afford. Never before had the foreign clothes felt so cumbersome. The long silk robe bunched around his waist, his arms, his chest. Squeezing him in their bind. Feeling more suffocated than turned on, Cheron said, "Indulge me," and hoped the breathlessness of his voice would be attributed to desire.

Lion rushed to obey. Fumbling in his haste, the young man dropped a grape into Cheron's lap. Red-faced, he stuck his hand out to snatch it away, but Ekos caught it. Clucking his tongue in mock chastisement, he pushed Lion aside. "Watch and learn," Ekos told the younger concubine.

Had Cheron known what Ekos had planned, he might have stopped him. But it was too late. Ekos bent his head toward Cheron's lap, rubbing his hands up and down the length of Cheron's thighs as he bent forward. To get the grape, he had to press down and work his mouth against the soft material of the robe, which—as if in on the whole tease—kept swallowing the fruit in its folds.

"Tricky little devil," Ekos chuckled.

"Indeed," Cheron mumbled. "His only virtue, I fear."

"The grape is a *he* now? Curious."

"I don't know. *Is the strange fruit* a man or something else entirely?"

Ekos's amusement only increased at the implied slight. "Something else entirely, I'm afraid."

Lion sat back and watched the show. Cheron figured the younger man might be glad to be free from the burden of playing host to a savage, but then he screwed up his features in a worried frown. Arms folded across his chest, he darted glances between Cheron and Sinnac.

"Come over here," Sinnac bid the young man. "Teach Ekos manners. He desperately needs to learn them."

Ekos pinched his thigh. The sharp burst of pain told Cheron that this was a game and Lion wasn't invited. Stifling a peeved groan, he took Ekos by the shoulders and forced him upward until their eyes met. The worried, haunted expression was back in full force.

He leaned over and whispered, "Leave Lion alone." To make the gesture appear sexual, he took the lobe in his mouth and sucked. Cheron stifled another type of moan.

Sinnac said, "What, now you don't want our poor Lion to play?"

"Later," Ekos said. "Right now, he only need observe."

That seemed fine by Lion, but he was keen to know if the plan suited everyone else.

"Yes," Cheron said. "I'd enjoy that. I want to hear his delightful praise."

"Hm. Or perhaps a dance?" Sinnac snapped his fingers at Lion, who hopped up like a trained dog.

"I'll dance for our savage bear," Ekos said.

Sinnac, his teeth showing, said, "I gave an order."

"You do want me to please him, don't you?"

Fingers tapping, the wisp-thin man considered. "Just so. But come here, Lion, keep your king company." Sinnac patted the plush cushions by his side. Gulping, the boy crawled his way up there on hands and knees the way Ekos had done earlier. Sinnac gave him an affectionate pat and a plum but never broke his gaze from Ekos. He said, "Dance for us. And it had better be an exemplary show."

Graceful, fluid, Ekos strolled to the stage-like area beneath the dais with a confidence of a man who knew his own abilities. He stole candles from the tables of the attending noblemen with a wink and a mock apology and set them in locations that seemed strategic.

And then he danced.

The reason for the candlelight became clear when the soft outline of Ekos's body beneath the loose garment revealed itself. He writhed in time with music only he heard. After a while, Cheron swore he was listening too. In his mind, they dipped and swayed together, slaves to the same mysterious beat.

Except Ekos was an actual slave. Cheron reminded himself of this to fight back the salacious excitement goading his body to response. "Enough," he said.

"Is the show not to your liking?" Sinnac asked.

"Too much so for present company."

Sinnac guffawed, as did several nearby nobles. "One can't control the flow of blood, eh?"

"It goes where it will."

Sinnac waved Ekos back up to them with one flick of his wrist.

Ekos knelt beside Sinnac and said, "Your royal guest has aroused me beyond my previous misgivings. I was wondering if His Excellency would indulge me one more night with his most cherished guest?"

A pleased smile smeared across Sinnac's features. "Nothing would delight me more. I trust you'll give him everything he needs this time?"

"Everything and more," Ekos promised.

"Would that delight you, Majesty?"

"Yes," Cheron replied automatically.

Chapter Seven

TITTERS OF LAUGHTER broke out through the court. Cheron's enthusiastic acceptance of Ekos's seduction genuinely delighted them, especially those who also had pleasure slaves by their sides. Those gave him conspiring winks and nods. Turning his grimace to a benign smile, Cheron met each eye with a good humor becoming of a guest.

"Very good, very good," Sinnac beamed.

Cheron assumed the night's festivities were concluded and stood to leave. Gently, he took Ekos's slender hand and began to guide him back toward the guest chamber.

An amused guffaw stopped him in his tracks. Sinnac said, "My dear royal brother, before you indulge your sexual appetites, first witness and relish in some blood sport!"

Massive cheers erupted. Cheron had never heard such a cacophony, not even in the din of battle. The faces of the nearby nobility were rapturously murderous. Mouths open in battle shouts, they pounded their chests and tables. When a slender woman with long chestnut hair strolled to the stage where Ekos had danced, they began to whoop.

Ekos's grip on his hand tightened. Cheron risked a glance in his direction and saw the elegant features were once again pinched. Whoever this woman was, she and Ekos had some type of history. And it wasn't good.

"You all know the reigning champion, Isali the Scourge of Wren Gardens!"

The applause indicated they'd already witnessed her battle prowess. She accepted their cheers with a serene smile. Her eyes, the color of absinthe and nearly as intoxicating, flashed at their adoration. She raised her battle-ax up high and made a lazy, unconcerned circle around the arena to showboat her confidence. The applause continued unabated.

"Today her challenger comes from the Northern realm of Ice Sea. A frozen wasteland where only the pitiless savages survive!"

"Home sweet home," Ekos whispered in Cheron's ear. "Do ruthless ones survive as well or truly only pitiless ones?"

Severe, Cheron bit back, "You'll find out one day."

When the purported savage hiked to the stage wearing an obscene amount of battle armor and furs, Cheron wondered if Sinnac was really even trying to hide the parallels. The other king's smoky-gray eyes gleamed at his own little drollery.

The boos heaped on the challenger, who remained unnamed, were almost as loud as the earlier acclaim. Apples were thrown at his head along with other food items from the nearby tables. Ashen-faced, clearly afraid, he smacked the debris with his sword. With as much dignity as he could muster, he crouched in a battle-ready position.

"Kill for glory!" Sinnac declared.

The battle began.

The two circled each other in a dance very familiar to Cheron. He watched their feet glide over the smooth tile and felt his own twitch in response to their movements.

Each searched for an opening in the other's defenses. Cheron saw the Northern man's sword drop—nothing more than a slight dip. In the blink of an eye, Isali lunged. She was fast. Unnaturally so.

Although the Northerner was able to parry in time, deflecting the battle-ax in an upward arch with the flat of his blade, the woman warrior opened a large gash in his arm. The wound bled freely, cementing the conclusion of the battle unless he somehow ended the flow of blood before he got too weak to hold his blade.

"Ah-ha! Yes!" Sinnac shouted, as if the blow were his own. He licked his lips and leaned forward on his throne.

The crowd went wild as blood hit the ground. A portly gentleman even went so far as to sneak inside the ring to mop up splatters of gore with a white silk handkerchief. Triumphant, he returned to his seat, stood on the table, and raised the handkerchief above his head, waving it like a flag. "Glory, glory, glory," the man chanted to the screams of his peers.

"Nothing close to it," Ekos whispered, echoing Cheron's thoughts. His eyes were distant enough to be with the gods in Yellow Sky but too blue to stay there.

Before long, the Northern man began to pant. Blood loss drained him. Instead of closing in, Isali observed from a distance, never allowing him to close the gap.

Caution, an admirable battle strategy, didn't set well with the onlookers. "Come on!" someone from the crowd jeered. "More carnage! Don't let him die without suffering!"

The crowd joined in on his call. "More, more, more!"

Others chanted, "Glory, glory, glory!"

Bowing to the request, Isali dropped her battle-ax and took a pair of bejeweled daggers from the sheaths her side. The handles were the curved necks of dragons reminiscent of the ones in Cheron's amulet. Absinthe-colored, like her eyes, the jewels representing its scales glinted in the light.

The crowd oohed and *aahed* at the brazenness of the play. Using daggers against the Northerner's wickedly long blade was just the type of cheeky pageantry they'd hope to see from her.

For the first time since the altercation began, the Northern man displayed signs of hope. He lifted his weapon with renewed purpose and charged. Like a dancer, Isali faded backward, falling in a squatting position. As the Northerner went over her head, she rose up and stabbed both daggers into his stomach. She pulled both blades outward.

Expecting to see the man's innards plunge to the ground, Cheron was surprised when he staggered forward, still very much alive. Moaning, he clutched at the wound. When he pulled back his hands, blood saturated them, dripping to the ground.

Flaunting the victory, Isali raised the daggers above her head and took the same circular path she did at the start of the fight. This time, she walked closer to the onlookers and allowed a few lucky ones to lick the blades. Glistening red, their tongues lolled from their mouths like they were sated dogs rather than humans.

The Northern man, now on his knees, stared at the crowd as the wound along his stomach opened farther. His eyes sought out a friend among the jeering crowd. Dying alone was more dreaded than actual death in the Northern realms. Souls lacking guidance to the underworld were doomed to wander the earth as ghosts. Powerless to enact their own vengeance.

Cheron rose from his seat.

"Going somewhere?" Sinnac asked.

"Yes, I'd like to congratulate the winner. Your blessing?"

"Granted."

Concealing his true intentions behind a delighted smile, Cheron strode up to Isali and wrapped her in his massive arms. The woman stiffened but didn't push him away.

"Congratulations," he said loud enough for the entire court to hear. "Quite a battle! Quite a battle! Allow me to honor you in the tradition of my people."

He bent down next to the Northerner. "Fear not," Cheron told him in a low voice. "I will make sure your soul makes its journey when I am able. Die in peace, brother."

He couldn't linger. He smeared his fingers with the dying man's blood and quickly walked back to Isali before suspicions arose.

On her forehead, he drew the symbol of virulence, an empty sun, but said, "There, the mark of courage for this realm's bravest warrior."

She thanked him, but her eyes were void of warmth. She twisted her mouth, as cruel as it was beautiful, into a thin mockery of a smile. "Thank you, Majesty."

Cheron climbed the steps of the dais while ignoring the cries of the Northern man, now increasingly pained. Giving Ekos a gentle tap on the nose and a salacious grin, he sat back on the cushions with a flourish. He ate a fig as if the scene before him were of no consequence—just a slave dying. In reality, his mind was filled with turmoil.

Ekos stroked Cheron's leg as they watched a man die. There was nothing sexual to the intimate contact, though it was meant to appear that way to others. The gesture bordered on comforting, as if Ekos understood his pain and needed to ease the grief of seeing a fellow Northern man fall.

In his mind, he saw the blue eyes of the dragon amulet glowing once again. Somehow, Ekos was key to his plans to get Hell's Echo. Was he the key to something else as well?

Chapter Eight

NO, JUST HIS plans.

That's what Cheron decided the moment he and the concubine were once again alone in his chamber and the insufferable creature freely dined on his personal food. Unmindful of his place, he even had the gall to use one of Cheron's furs as a napkin. As an afterthought, he licked his fingers, then wiped the spittle on Cheron's bedding.

"You understand I'm a king, don't you?"

"No you're not, not really. You're a rebel. A usurper. Not even from royal blood from what I've heard."

"Above you in station, nonetheless. And I won't stand for your insolence anymore."

"By the twin moons, what are you going to do? Hit me?" He had a mouthful of chicken. Speckles, and some globs of half-chewed poultry flew out of his mouth as he spoke. "I know you have some type of code thing. Don't pretend."

"No, I won't hit you. I might leave you for Sinnac's garden."

The barb hit its mark. Ekos paled and dropped the chicken bone he'd been gnawing on with such delighted zeal. "You wouldn't," he said. "You need me."

"Not really," Cheron lied. "I need Hell's Echo."

"Which I can help you obtain."

"Theoretically. Tell me how you propose to deliver."

The smug smile made its reappearance. Ekos's eyes flashed; a glimpse of clear sky amid all the fog. He nibbled on the chicken bone again and licked it for good measure—just in case Cheron didn't fully comprehend how bad his table manners were. "I'll need reassurances first."

"Of what type?"

"I need to hear you'll take me with you when you leave. Me and Lion."

The addition of the other concubine took Cheron by surprise. Previously, he had assumed Ekos's interference in the young man's attempts at flirtation were competitive rather than protective. Learning otherwise humbled him. He'd been ungracious to peg Ekos as selfish simply because he was a whore. Had Cheron already become so disconnected from his own servant roots? The thought troubled him.

"I don't know if I can promise to rescue either of you, only that I'll try," Cheron said.

"But you'll endeavor to save us?"

"Yes. Kalin's grace binds me."

Cheron struggled to interpret the face Ekos made. His eyes squinted shut into reptilian slants and twisted his compressed mouth at an awkward angle. The mention of the goddess had clearly hit a raw nerve. Cheron opened his mouth to ask about the curious response, but Ekos held up his hand to ward off any attempt and said, "Good enough. Not like any better offers are coming along anytime soon. First, you'll need to do what Sinnac expects. Take pleasure from me."

"You want to have sex?"

Guffawing as though the very thought were ludicrous, Ekos said, "Don't be nonsensical. I'd rather jerk myself off in front of my mother. This is a no-other-option type of affair."

"How can I withstand such flattery?"

With an unconcerned shrug, Ekos tossed the chicken bone aside. It clattered on the silver platter. Eyebrows raised in an expression of resignation, he dipped down to grab the hem of his silken frock and pulled the garment over his head, exposing his chest and impossibly long torso. Plain linenundergarments concealed the rest of his body. He didn't remove them. Instead, he flopped down on the feather bed face-first and said, "Okay, get it over with. Stick your dick in."

"What?"

He looked over his shoulder. "You do know how to do this, don't you?"

"Yessss," Cheron hissed.

Ekos slapped his ass in invitation. "Well, then, work your magic, rebel."

"Using anyone in such a way is dishonorable."

Ekos sighed. "Honor is stupid."

"Honor is not—"

"Oh, shut up, and take off your pants."

"I am—"

"Still wearing your pants. Yes, I can see that."

"No. I won't do this. You haven't even told me why."

Childlike, Ekos screamed into the pillow and beat his hands against the mattress until his rage subsided. Afterward, he sat up, calm and collected as though nothing had ever happened. "You insufferable, do-gooding idiot, Sinnac sent me here to spy on you. If you don't fuck me, we'll both be part of his garden."

Through gritted teeth, Cheron asked, "Why not just kill me now?"

"Strange as it seems, he wants this trade agreement to be real. His finances are not in order, as you know. The Northern realms love you. Killing you makes negotiations with them difficult."

"Then he won't kill me. You, maybe. Me, no."

"Well, if trade doesn't work out, he can always try conquest now, rather than later. He wanted the North to bankroll his war against them, but patience was never a virtue he possessed."

What he said made sense, but Cheron still didn't know if he could force himself to rut on another man who clearly wanted nothing to do with him. It wasn't rape, as Ekos had consented, but taking pleasure from his plight wasn't honorable, either. Much like Ekos, the situation was base and crass.

"Is my asshole really all that disagreeable? I assure you it's not actually cursed."

"You...made it clear you won't enjoy me."

"Do you need me to?"

"Yes."

Ekos's face twitched. His eyes rolled into the back of his head. Expecting another round of fury, Cheron straightened and prepared for the onslaught to come. Hand over face, Ekos paced the room, considering.

Cheron said, "How will he even know? Can't we just lie?"

Ekos stopped pacing to say, "You impossible idiot," and then resumed.

"Really? You seem quite apt at deception."

"I am, my dear rebel. But Isa—Isali to you—is not what she seems. She can tell when I'm lying."

"How?"

"As I said, she's not what she seems."

"The same way you're not?"

Ekos fiddled with his golden collar as if it chaffed. "The exact same way, rebel."

Further details were not forthcoming from the looks of Ekos's hooded eyes. Simultaneously rubbing his fingers along his barely visible stubble, Ekos resumed his pacing. None of the conclusions he came to seemed to please him much. Eventually, he stopped and said, "What if you were really drunk?"

"That hinders performance in other ways."

"No, no. What if I get you really drunk, and you tell me your secrets while inebriated? I'll have to confess to the failure at seduction, but I would have served my purpose otherwise. That should buy us some time at least."

Cheron, feeling beyond exasperated, said, "Why can't I simply tell you my secrets? Better yet, tell them yourself. You seem to already know."

Equally vexed, Ekos responded, "Because she can tell when I'm lying. If I say, 'Yes, he told me as part of our own little side plot to fool you,' I imagine Sinnac might take that poorly. Don't you?"

Cheron didn't dispute the point. "Very well," he said. "I have some mead. That should do the job quickly."

When he brought out the flagon, Ekos sniffed the Northern brew delicately and immediately passed judgment, as was his habit. "I have been nose-deep in ass cracks that smell better."

Cheron ignored him and chugged down the fiery liquid. It was a pleasant taste of home that, for a moment, took him away from his troubles. He drank and drank until he felt a pinch of Northern cold on his skin. No, an actual pinch.

"How much more of that foul bilge do you need to drink?"

"I'm a big man." Cheron hiccupped. "Big! Like a bear!" He stood and posed with his hands raised like claws. "Grrr...rawr!"

Ekos blinked. "Okay, you're corked. Tell me about your plans."

Chapter Nine

LAST CHERON REMEMBERED, he'd been babbling to Ekos about how Hell's Echo was believed to have the ability to summon Kalin's dragons from where they'd been imprisoned. Late one night, after he'd conquered the North, he'd received a message from the goddess in his dreams. When he woke, his amulet burned as if to stress the importance of obeying Kalin's will. And so he'd traveled south intent on completing a quest he didn't fully understand but trusting the goddess to guide him.

That was not where he was now. Ekos was gone, and Cheron had been chained to a wall—shackles on his wrists, his ankles, around his neck, pinning him with zero wiggle room. Beside him, as if in mockery, someone had placed a piss pot. Cheron groaned, realizing he did indeed need to relieve his bloated bladder.

A light, melodic voice greeted him. "Good. You're awake."

His eyes snapped on the source of the noise. Just outside the bars, Isa leaned against the wall. She inspected her nails, and a nasty smirk compressed the corners of her lips. The thought she'd been waiting for him this entire time did not bode well. Hoping to find some weak point, Cheron strained against his bonds.

Isa laughed. It sounded more like a short bark. She grabbed hold of one of the iron bars and shook his cage. "Do you imagine you can bend these, you stupid, savage brute?"

He could, actually, but he wouldn't give such information to an enemy. Let her discover the blessings his goddess gave him in time. "Ek—" he rasped. His throat was oddly dry. He swallowed some of his own spittle and tried again. "Where is—"

"Ekos? Betrayed you. Yes, he does that."

"Why are you here, not Sinnac?"

The titter of laughter, this time sounding genuine, frayed Cheron's already-wrecked nerves. She said, "He wants information."

"I will say nothing."

Snorting at his bravado, Isa waved a hand. A guard rushed forward to unlock the cell, and she swaggered inside, her gait naturally loping and indolent. Her hips swished in a manner that might have been sexual in any other context. Perhaps it was sexual for her in this one. After seeing the excited gleam in her odd green eyes up close, Cheron wouldn't rule out that she was aroused by the prospect of torture and bloodshed.

She bent and whispered in his ear. Her breath tickled the hairs on his neck. "Dear pet, I know you labeled me as quarrelsome with your little battle marking. And you're right. I am going to make you scream for for the affront, though. Oh, and I also burned the body of your Northern friend. I'm afraid his soul is forever lost, your oath to him meaningless."

He had every intention of keeping his dignity throughout whatever abuse she forced him to endure. Steel-faced, proud, he lifted his chin and met her cruel gaze.

She placed a clawed hand over his heart and said, "Let's begin."

He didn't understand what was happening. He'd withstood torture for weeks when captured during battle. His own toe had been cut off and fed to him, and he hadn't even leaked his name, let alone the position of his army. In Isa's strange thrall, he wanted, no, needed, to tell everything. His very body screamed the urgency—like the urge to eat, sleep, drink, piss.

Terror unlike Cheron had ever known seized hold. Thirty seconds into the ordeal and he was already stuffing words back down his gullet and beating his head against the wall behind him in the hopes he'd render himself unconscious, thus preventing a betrayal.

"You're stronger than most," Isa congratulated him. "But my sorcery is powerful beyond mortal comprehension. Yield to me."

"No!"

Isa cackled. "So I've heard many times before, savage, and I'll hear such denials again after you're gone."

Mouth frothing with the glee from his agony, Isa jabbed her fingers directly into his flesh and twisted. Fresh pain wove through his body.

Cheron cried out. He couldn't contain his wails of agony any longer. Whatever sorcery she worked was unlike anything he'd ever experienced.

Her only response was to dig in deeper and twist again.

His eyes rolled into the back of his head. His body began to seize, his muscles tensed. The shackles pinched into his flesh. A warm wash of blood flowed down his wrists and neck. Then Cheron told her everything he'd told Ekos. The information came out of him along with a stream of piss as his body, sure it was dying, thrased in death throes.

A puzzled frown marred her smooth forehead. "We already know that, savage. The whore informed us. Tell me more. What is your plan to retrieve the Echo?" She resumed her torture.

"I have no plan!"

She guffawed. "You came here with no plan at all? You thought to simply arrive here and hope the path would show itself to you?"

"An act of faith. Her grace binds me."

"How delightfully stupid."

Actually, Cheron found a genius in the goddess's strategy. Had she told him her design, he would have been compelled by Isa's magic to reveal the goddess's intentions. How could he divulge information he didn't possess? Kalin had been wise to make him blunder along. He hadn't seen the merits of blind obedience at first. He'd doubted. But now here he was witnessing the effect.

To Isa, Cheron said, "I trust in Kalin's wisdom."

"Yes," Isa said with a smirk. "I'm sure that will work out for you."

WHEN HE NEXT woke, he was no longer alone. Ekos had been chained on the wall next to him.

"What now?" Ekos asked.

Cheron squeezed the amulet at his neck. Isa's scorn for Kalin was evident in the fact she let him keep the powerful talisman. To her, it was a bauble of no consequence, nothing more than gaudy jewlery given by a powerless deity, but the prayers he muttered into the amulet reached Kalin's ears. His,wounds began to heal. Cheron thanked her grace that none of his injuries were life-threatening. The goddess's touch only cured light ailments.

Beside him, Ekos twisted in his bindings and griped, "Really? No plan?"

"None."

"You have considerable talent for being stupid."

"And you for being a pain in the ass."

The two had little else to say to each other. Their long period of silence was only broken by the sound of dripping water and the *clank, clank, clank* of Ekos struggling against his binds. Occasionally, he seemed to forget his own dire pronouncement that the situation was hopeless and that they were doomed.

"Well, do you know what to do now?" Ekos huffed, slumping back against the wall in defeat. "Tell me you have some type of idea going forward. Some goddess thing or honor or whatever."

"No, I thought you did, and that's why I ended up tortured at the hands of Isa. You said you were like her? Surely you have some power?"

"Limited powers," Ekos said. "Courtesy of my gift from Sinnac."

"The collar?"

"Yes."

Helplessness combined with frustration had Cheron gritting his teeth. He shouldn't have expected anything different from Ekos, yet he did. He had anticipated that his ploy was part of a larger scheme. Now that it wasn't, he felt simply betrayed. At least they ended up in the same predicament; that outcome was a small sort of justice. "I take it Sinnac was displeased by your method of obtaining your information?"

"He is a purist, that one. Information through fucking only."

"Did you assume he'd leave you untouched after you gave me up? Hedging your bets but risking nothing?"

Ekos took a long time answering, which, in itself, was an answer. Finally, he sighed and said, "I was going to help you if you got in too deep. Like I said, I thought you had things under control."

"I see."

"Look, if I wanted things to go to Yellow Sky just for you, I would have simply spied as Sinnac demanded. I got you as close to Hell's Echo without putting you right on top of it."

"Hell's Echo is here?"

"Nearby. Below us in the vault."

The amulet on Cheron's chest vibrated, growing warmer. Through the talisman, he knew the goddess's happiness. Ekos was serving his purpose after all.

Chapter Ten

CHERON DIDN'T REALIZE he'd been grinning ear to ear until Ekos cleared his throat and said, "You seemed happier for a moment. I thought maybe that might mean you had a plan. I guess I should have known better."

Ekos's tone irked Cheron, but then so did everything else about him. "I know where Hell's Echo is now."

"Yippee."

Cheron ignored the heavy-handed sarcasm and focused his mind on the task. "I can break these chains," he said. "I just need a bit more slack."

Ekos mumbled something under his breath that sounded an awful lot like *Stupid fool bears.*

Cheron ignored the insult.

The goddess had brought him this far and twined his and Ekos's paths together for a reason. It was up to him to play his part in her design, even if that meant dragging along the insufferable concubine for the rest of his days—on his back if he had to. He hoped that wasn't what Kalin's vague directives meant. *Goddess, please let that not be the case. Let me be rid of this insufferable fool after this,* Cheron thought.

The amulet glowed hot on his chest. He swore he felt a faint amusement radiating from it.

"What's that? She tell you what to do?" Ekos asked.

"You sensed her presence?"

Appearing uncomfortable with the question, Ekos scooted as far away as his restraints allowed and said nothing. For added measure, he stared at the wall as though it had the answers.

Amazed, Cheron exclaimed, "You did! Does her grace bind you?"

"At one point," Ekos said bitterly. "Until I realized my devotion to her was greater than hers could ever be to me."

"She is a goddess," Cheron reminded him in case he'd forgotten.

"What does that even mean?"

"She lives on our worship, not the other way around."

Pure resentment twisted Ekos's features, making the attractive lines squeeze into a grotesque mask. Before he answered, he turned away, "Easy to say when you have her talisman around your neck and she communicates directly to you."

"Maybe she stopped speaking to you because you stopped listening."

"Maybe I stopped listening because she failed me horribly."

"Kalin can't solve all your problems. We all fail those we love in one way or another." Shuddering, Cheron thought about Aethel, his lover, twisting on the pyre, and his own inability to intervene. "I lean on her to guide me through times of trouble rather than blame her for the state of the world."

Ekos was still addressing his replies to the wall. "You're an inspiration to all apostates."

On his cool skin, the amulet warmed again. Cheron, remembering an apostate had confined Kalin to Yellow Sky, blanched at the other man's use of the word. But the goddess spoke to him, sought contact with him. And Cheron knew Ekos must have felt Kalin's presence. He hunched down into a tight ball and buried his head so Cheron only saw a long stream of golden hair, which was only a little bit marred by the dirty surroundings.

Over time, Cheron had loosened his chains to the point he could at least move his arms in a limited arch. He used his scant mobility to place the amulet on Ekos, who flinched at the touch of cool metal on his back. First, Cheron thought he might have misunderstood the goddess's directive, but then a warm, golden light began to emanate from the relic, bathing Ekos in a gentle, loving glow. The goddess had lit a candle for him. In the North, the gesture was meant to help weary travelers find their way home.

"She loves you still. Let her."

Tear-streaked, Ekos turned back to him. "You loosened your chains, and you use that advantage to give me a trinket?"

"To give you salvation."

Fresh tears spilled over on his cheeks, catching on the fine hairs on their path to his chin. Those ice eyes of his were melting bit by bit. Voice shaking in emotion he wasn't yet comfortable sharing, Ekos said, "Seriously, though, can you break your restraints?"

"Probably."

Chains clinked together as Ekos twisted back and forth in them. During his struggles, he wiped his head against the dirty wall, right over a mud clot. Clearly irate, he yelled as loud as was prudent, "Then why don't you, you dumb, hulking bear?"

"I was waiting for the goddess to give me a sign."

"Didn't you just say she can't solve all your problems? Did you imagine she wants you to camp here until they come to kill you?"

"Perhaps."

"If you think that's her plan, worship a new goddess." Ekos sucked in air to launch into what was probably a lengthy tirade. He paused. "Your shoulders are shaking. Are you...are you laughing at me?"

He was. And couldn't stop.

"What, may I ask, is so funny?"

Cheron sputtered, spraying a fine mist of spit in front of him. On Ekos's forehead, there was a smudge of dirt that looked exactly like a giant penis, balls and all. Telling him right away would ruin the fun. If Cheron had to die in this miserable place so far from home, he'd have some laughs at the rude whore's expense.

Cheron said, "It's just I'm receiving a sign from the goddess."

"And it's...funny. What is it?"

"I believe she's calling you a dickhead."

Ekos blinked his big, blue eyes. "What?"

"I'm afraid the signs are quite clear."

Ekos sniffed in distain. "That's rather gauche for a divine being. Is she the goddess of the tavern brawlers now?"

"She might be."

"Well, I'm glad you two have time for such merriments!"

Refusing to be ashamed of his own childishness, Cheron gave one last chuckle and said, "Me too. Here, let me take the amulet from you."

"Gladly."

Ekos dipped his head forward just enough for Cheron to push forward and lift the amulet over his head. He grasped it between his two massive paws, loving the way the metal calmed him. *Kalin,* he prayed. *Grant me your boon and give me the strength to break my chains.*

Prayers augmented the unusual strength Kalin had bestowed on him as a gift long ago. Power coursed through his body, igniting his aching muscles with the heat of the goddess's flame. The shackles surrounding his chest heaved and broke. With a snap, he pulled the ones binding his arms away from the wall. The same for his legs. He'd have to carry around the shackles, which was less than ideal, but he was free.

"Damn," Ekos said. "You really are a giant bear."

"Yes. Yes. Here, now yours."

Cheron broke Ekos's bindings from the wall. Cement crumbled around them. A fine coating of disintegrated rock dusted both their faces. Ekos spit out the grime, which turned a dirty brown on his lips, and gave the manacles on his delicate wrists a fierce glare. "I don't suppose..."

"No, those will have to stay for now. Sorry."

"Hm."

Cheron pushed him off to the side and prodded at the wall where Ekos had been chained. "The rock is softer here. Maybe I can..." Cheron reeled his leg back and gave the wall a savage kick. The block moved a fraction, crumbling loose pebbles in its wake.

"Now the plan is to pummel things?"

"Uh-huh."

Waving his elegant hand, Ekos bid, "Smash away, my good bear."

Cheron did just that.

Chapter Eleven

THEY BROKE THROUGH to a passage lined with glowing torches. Thinking they might need light later, Cheron nabbed one from the wall and held the flame out in front of him. As he moved, dirt fell from his bare shoulders. The light caught on the metal of their shackles, making them glow. The reflection of the blaze in Ekos's pupils buckled and twisted. The playful flicker reminded Cheron of Ekos's dance in the courtyard.

"Your face is flush. All that wanton destruction wear you out?"

"Yes," Cheron said. "Do you know where we are?"

Forever unhelpful, Ekos responded, "In a hall."

"I gathered as much."

"Then you know what I know."

"You said the Hell's Echo was nearby?" Cheron snapped. "How do you know that if you've never been down here before?"

"Pillow talk."

The thought of Ekos living the life of a whore left a sour taste in Cheron's mouth. He imagined Ekos *willingly* in the arms of another man without too much anger, only a sharp jab of jealousy he didn't want to admit to. But the thought of him as an unwilling slave, as a puppet, a toy to rich men, induced a near-manic anger.

"Thinking about how to ditch me?"

"No," Cheron said. He hated that Ekos thought so little of him.

"Good. Because you made a promise to save me *and* Lion. Remember?"

"Of course. I'm not a savage," he bit out. "No matter what you think."

"You just demolished a wall...with your foot."

"I had Kalin's blessing."

"A blessed savage with an especially blessed foot."

"Says the man with a cursed asshole."

Ekos smiled. Cheron admired the way merriment lightened the blue in his eyes. Water to air in seconds. His smile dipped a little bit as a cobweb brushed the top of his head. "As much as I enjoy banter, do you think we should worry about where we're going?"

"Down," Cheron said. "We're going down."

"Sarcasm doesn't suit you. It's not honorable."

Cheron guffawed. His laughter was rough, growl-like, which did make him somewhat resemble a bear, he supposed. That and other things. They'd taken all his clothes except for his buckskin trousers, and he was uncomfortably aware of his bulk as the walls closed in and his flesh scraped the sides. Ekos's narrow frame had no trouble navigating the passages. He slipped through like a ghost while Cheron remained behind, a giant bit of flesh stuck between the doorway's teeth.

"Are you stuck?" Ekos asked him.

Cheron tried to push through again. The force of his efforts rubbed his skin raw.

"Turn sideways."

Cheron supposed he earned the dryness in the other man's voice. Internally sighing at himself for living up to the stupid savage stereotype, Cheron tried to do just that, but his shoulders wouldn't slide back around.

"Yeah, you're stuck. Pray to the goddess to make your shoulders weapons of destruction."

Grunting, Cheron wiggled back and forth, trying to get through on his own merits. "That's not how her grace works."

"That's exactly how it worked last time." Ekos took the amulet, which dangled from Cheron's neck, into his slender hands. Arranging his features into mock prostration, he said, "Oh goddess, please make your hulking bear man thing smash through this wall."

The goddess didn't respond. Not a single light flickered.

"Don't mock Kalin."

Ekos made a sour face but dropped the amulet back against Cheron's chest. The light touch of his warm fingers against Cheron's cool skin worked a different kind of alchemy. Blood turned to magma. Soft flesh stiffened. The oxygen inside his lungs turned to water, drowning him and choking off sound. He needed to press his lips against Ekos's for air.

"Are you...are you aroused?" Ekos asked and held his hand to his chest like a fainting maiden.

"No," Cheron denied through gritted teeth.

Letting out a disgusted snort, Ekos rolled his eyes and said, "Here, scoot forward while I push from behind."

Cheron couldn't hear anything over the blood, flowing freely from embarrassment and desire, pounding in his ears. "What about stuck confuses you?"

The concubine took the torch and darted under Cheron's legs. He came up on the opposite side and placed the torch back up on the wall. None too gently, he pressed his shoulder against the small of Cheron's back and pushed—harder and harder, his feet sliding on the loose gravel of the floor—until Cheron finally yelled, "What are you trying to accomplish?"

"The miracle the goddess failed to provide: getting you through this door! Now shut up and wiggle while I push."

"This is ridiculous!"

"You have only yourself to blame. You and your dim view on planning."

"The goddess—"

"Guides you. Yes, I *know*. Now if only she'd seen fit to slather your thick pelt with butter, or, you know, to give you the sense to turn sideways."

Cheron growled in indignation but did as Ekos asked and wiggled forward while he pushed from behind. The cuts on his arm stung, and he swore the concrete walls had to be coated in salt.

"Forward! Scoot! Scoot!"

The way he carefully pronounced each word, as though Cheron had difficulty understanding basic language, almost drove him over the edge of insanity. Why was he so attracted to someone with such boorish manners? The goddess must be punishing him. That was the only reasonable explanation.

Ekos didn't help matters. He kicked Cheron in the butt and yelled, "You're not trying hard enough!" Strain was evident in his voice. The arms pushing against him were slick with sweat, and Ekos huffed in his ear. Cheron doubted he ever had to endure much physical exertion.

"I can't help that the architecture here doesn't accommodate—"

"What? Bears?"

"I'm not a bloody bear!"

Saying nothing in retort—for once—Ekos doubled his efforts. This time he took a running start and collided against Cheron, pitching him forward into the room below. He hit the wall with a thud and staggered backward, completely disoriented.

"Prayer and honor are both overrated," Ekos called from behind. "Is it safe down there? Are you getting eaten by anything?"

He was not. At least not at the present moment. Heavy breathing—not his own—did cause some concern, but Cheron wasn't about to tell Ekos that. "Seems perfectly safe. You should head on down."

Cautiously, holding out the torch in front of him and whipping the light back and forth scanning for threats, Ekos entered the room with a great deal more grace. Seeing no immediate enemies, he sighed in relief. Then he must have heard the same heavy breathing Cheron had before. His brow furrowed, and he turned his dark glare on Cheron. "We need to revisit your definition of perfectly safe. What is that thing?"

"I—"

"Right, you don't know."

Worried Ekos might take off, preferring to take his chances with Sinnac instead of braving the unknown with him, Cheron prepared to go it alone. A solo adventure was what he'd expected the entire time, but now the prospect daunted him whereas before, he had accepted the assigned task as his sole burden.

"I will find you and Lion. Assuming I make it out alive."

Rather than answer, Ekos held the torch up high and led the way.

Chapter Twelve

THE HAND GRIPPING the torch trembled, but Ekos maintained a steady pace and Cheron never got the impression he was near to bolting. He bore terror with the same pinch-lipped silence he used to face death. Biting back words of comfort, which he knew would be unwelcome, Cheron did his best to stay right behind—close enough to offer support, far enough away as to not intrude.

Thankfully, the doors widened as they made their way down the catacombs, allowing Cheron easy access to the different rooms and winding passageways. The structural changes unnerved him. Whatever lurked inside the inner rooms was bound to be large, unfriendly, deadly, and possibly magical.

"Maybe it's a big, fuzzy dog," Ekos said, directly addressing his thoughts as always. "His name is Duke and he likes cheese snacks."

"I doubt we'll be so lucky."

Ekos agreed and added, "Maybe it's afraid of bears."

Cheron was pretty sure people five kingdoms over heard him grinding his teeth. Ekos certainly did. Pleased by his ability to get under Cheron's skin, he chuckled.

Whimsical thinking wasn't going to get them out of here alive, unfortunately. Cheron reflected on what Ekos had said previously, how he and Isa were similar. He didn't want to press the secretive man, but if his ability matched that of the warrioress, then they they'd be better for the added help. Powerful magic would make a great ally in present circumstances.

"Earlier, you said you were special the way Isa—"

"I don't have access to my power," Ekos snapped. He pointed to the collar around his neck, which Cheron assumed was decorative. "We'll need to unlock this first."

"How?"

"Key. Sinnac keeps it in his bedchamber."

Sighing, Cheron discounted receiving any help once the battle started. Perhaps Ekos had mastery over his fear and faced battle like a soldier but he lacked proper training and physical strength to brawl. By the way Ekos shuffled his feet and tried to hide his panting, Cheron determined he wasn't fit either. Irritation wouldn't get either of them through the situation, so Cheron tried to think of a way to say what he needed without invoking the other man's temper.

"Whatever's down here is—"

"Big," Ekos supplied.

"Right, and you are—"

"A pipsqueak. Got it. We can't all be bears playing at human dress up."

By Kalin's grace, he made everything so difficult. "Then hide when the battle starts."

"Well, what did you imagine I was going to do? Run into the fray? Perhaps if I clanked my manacles together—"

Something slithered along the wall, halting the argument. On reflex, Cheron placed his hand against Ekos's chest and pushed him backward out of harm's way. Nearly naked and lacking a weapon, he wasn't quite sure how he'd manage to defend himself, let alone another person, but honor demanded he try. Honor and something else he didn't quite care admit to.

"What's wrong?" Ekos asked.

"I don't know," Cheron whispered back, lying to keep the situation calm. "Raise the torch. Make sure. Shine the light ahead of me."

"Are you sure that's a good idea? Won't that make us easy targets?"

Cheron bit back the impulse to say that they were already sitting ducks without the benefit of the light. He knew what creature lurked in the darkness—a basilisk. Such creatures were renowned for their sense of smell and human cunning. They were also known for their cruelty, for keeping their prey alive for decades if they weren't hungry. Knowing Sinnac, this basilisk had been well fed.

Basilisks also horded treasure in a manner similar to dragons. If Sinnac had to keep the creature happy to ensure it guarded the relic, there might be something nearby to use as a weapon. Metallic clatters as the serpent's body slid over its trove confirmed Cheron's suspicions.

"You're going toward the horrible noise," Ekos said.

"I know. I have to find a weapon. Give me the torch and stay near the exit," Cheron said. "Feel no shame running if you need to."

Ekos pursed his lips into a thin line and kept quiet. Cheron got the sense he resented the implication, but he didn't have time to soothe ruffled feathers. He took hold of the torch and scanned the immediate area, hoping the light would catch the metal of a sword or something equally useful, but there was nothing in the room but skeletons and the remaining tatters of clothing the deceased had worn when alive.

Cheron steeled his resolve and walked toward the next chamber. With some amusement, he noted that Ekos followed close behind; his eyes were large, his marble face ashen white.

"You can stay behind," Cheron reminded him. "There's no shame in staying out of the fray. You're not trained for battle."

"I'm every bit as blooded as you are."

Cheron remembered the man's smooth skin, unbroken and flawless, and he sincerely doubted the claim, but he said nothing and continued forward.

Rubies, diamonds, gold coins, and various bobbles glittered in the dim glow of the torch. Cheron dug his toe through one of the mounds of treasure by the door. His foot uncovered a metal plate. The creature hissed when he bent to pick it up.

"I don't think our friend liked that," Ekos told him in a flat voice. "Find a weapon. And fast."

Light illuminated the room, and Cheron saw a sword hanging on the far wall, deep inside the chamber. Relief at being able to see didn't last long. The source of the brightness turned out to be a fireball. Too fast to dodge, the molten-hot orb blazed in their direction. Unnatural heat singed his belly hair, curling like the tips of a maiden's eyelashes. The smell clogged his nostrils as black smoke choked his lungs and vision. Oddly, though, his flesh didn't burn. Expecting his skin to bubble and agonizing pain to follow, Cheron marveled at how painless death truly was.

"Move, you big ninny! The shield won't last forever! Stay inside the treasure room! The basilisk won't use fire there. It cares too much about its loot!"

The shield? Cheron opened his eyes and saw a yellow dome stretched above and around him, protecting him from the blast. Behind him, Ekos—his face strained and furious—channeled. "Move!" he yelled again.

The betrayal of Ekos telling him he was powerless stung. The lack of trust between them would need to end if they were going to survive together.

"Do you see a weapon?" Ekos yelled.

The initial blast of the fireball had tapered, leaving the room only dimly illuminated. Cheron ran to where he'd seen the sword previously and searched along the wall. His hand glided across something sharp, splitting open his palm. The momentary flash of pain couldn't quash his elation. He'd found a sword.

Chapter Thirteen

BLOOD RUSHED IN excited waves through Cheron's body, lusting after battle the way he'd previously lusted after flesh. The cold of the metal hilt morphed into an extension of his arm. He didn't know this blade's name, or if it had one, but the weapon had the signature of the goddess. It was hers and he was meant to wield it. The amulet on his chest warmed in confirmation.

"Are you going to eye-fuck that thing or swing?"

Ekos's jeer cut through his reverie. Although Cheron couldn't see him anymore—the glow from the fireball had abated, leaving the room dark—he imagined the concubine standing with his hands on his hips, the clouds in his eyes swirling into a storm.

Cheron didn't have time to jibe back. The basilisk's scales skittered across the room; gold coins jangled in its wake. Nearby, goblets clattered on the ground. One of the gaudy cups rolled against Cheron's foot. He swiped it away, along with anything else in his path, to keep from twisting an ankle during the heat of battle.

Sword poised in front of him in a defensive position, he backed out toward the exit, thinking he could better control its movements in a narrow passageway.

"Stay in there with its loot," Ekos advised him. "The basilisk loves its treasure too much to use fire again."

"An expert on basilisks, are we?"

"Practically cousins," Ekos said. Then, far less calmly, he shouted, "To your left!"

Heeding the warning, instinctively trusting Ekos's warning, Cheron fell to the ground. Above him, the wall shook as something massive collided against it. The creature's tail, Cheron guessed. Debris rained down on top of his head. Larger fragments cut into his flesh, leaving trails of scratches that bled freely.

"Keep moving!" Ekos warned him. "To your right."

How is he seeing anything? Cheron couldn't even make out vague shapes in the pervasive darkness.

"Down!" Ekos shouted.

"Stop yelling!" Cheron needed to concentrate. Without the benefit of sight, he had to rely on his ears and other senses to tell him where the enemy would strike next. "You're disrupting my focus!"

Ekos growled at the harshness of Cheron's tone but fell quiet. Thankfully.

Now blessed with silence, Cheron isolated the sound of the creature's breathing and the way its scales slid across the room. The brief flash of the fireball awarded him a quick peek of the room's layout. He knew treasure filled the left side and that the trove was piled nearly to the ceiling. Only a narrow strip from the doorway to the next chamber remained barren.

Cheron remained still until he heard the beast charge toward him. Then, with all his strength, he hit the nearest wall. Gold coins clanked together. The cups, platters, and various other treasures rattled. Cheron hit the wall again and kept up the assault until he heard the treasure slump downward.

Enraged, the basilisk hissed in indignation as its own horde rolled over its body.

Cheron wasn't sure his plan had worked until Ekos shouted, "The beast capsized! Attack!"

Cheron lumbered in the direction where he heard the thrashing. Not being able to see made his advance difficult to maneuver. One wrong move and the creature's tail would snap his spine. He moved forward cautiously, but also too slowly to press an attack, he realized.

"Get back! It righted itself."

The warning almost came too late. Cheron heard jaws snap right where his head had been just moments before.

Ekos let out a tired sigh as though the life-or-death ordeal were an especially boring play.

Cheron felt a tug of magical power in the room. At first, he suspected the goddess might be trying to communicate with him. He clutched his amulet, but it was cold, unresponsive. She wasn't speaking. Then who was?

He got his answer soon enough.

Light burst from around Ekos. His fine yellow hair floated in air, framing his face in a golden burst. His strange eyes swirled, the white in them darting across the surface like clouds caught in a breeze. Enraptured, Cheron stopped to gawk. Luckily, the basilisk was similarly befuddled and preoccupied. Otherwise, the fight would have ended rather abruptly, not to mention poorly, for Cheron.

The light radiating from Ekos filled the chamber. With a satisfied smirk, he said, "There, now I trust you can handle the rest?" When Cheron continued to gape, Ekos said, "That's your cue to jab that brutish, clunky thing inside the beast. You can pretend I'm a quivering maiden if that helps you along."

The sour pronouncement jarred the basilisk into motion. The creature lifted its tail and flung the appendage full force toward Cheron's head. This time his reactions, aided by Ekos's magical light, were sharp. The creature's attack missed him by a mile.

Cheron recovered quickly from his dodge. Sword in hand, he lunged toward the beast while it tried to coil its body, readying for another strike. He raised the blade high and plunged the sharp tip into the basilisk's side. Greenish-black blood oozed from the wound. To open the gouge farther, Cheron dug the blade side to side before pulling it out.

Reeling from pain and surprise, the beast roared. It released the tension in its body and sent its tail hurtling toward Cheron. This time, he was too close to dodge. The blow caught his shoulder. He heard a popping noise. A sharp, nauseating pain followed. He hadn't realized he was flying through the air until he hit a wall. His teeth clanked together, and he tasted red-hot, coppery blood.

"Cheron!" Ekos cried. His voice sounded pained.

Dazed, Cheron staggered to his feet. He realized he had some assistance when someone gave his upper arm a squeeze. "Ekos?"

"Yes, Ekos, you dithering rebel bear."

Ekos picked up the sword as easily as Cheron might have, which didn't make any sense at all, given how slender his arms were. Chin tilted stubbornly, he stood in front of Cheron, blocking the creature's kill shot.

Tentatively, weary of the strange humanlike figure who summoned light, the basilisk held back another attack. It blinked its serpent eyes and slithered forward at a crawl. Strange blood trailed behind it. Only half-conscious but feeling triumphant, Cheron realized the blow he'd dealt would eventually be fatal. Having the thing die from blood loss rather than chopping off its head wasn't as glorious, but a victory was a victory.

"Stay back," Ekos warned. Oddly, Cheron found menace in his voice.

Basilisks could not speak in human tongue, but jaws open and poised ready, the wounded creature let out a mocking hiss and continued forward.

Although he didn't budge an inch, Cheron saw the fear in Ekos's eyes. No doubt, he hoped his strange magic would be enough to deter the beast, which was known for cruelty more than bravery. "Stop," he said again. This time the word trembled from his mouth.

Of course, the beast paid him no mind. It leered with its yellow eyes and reared back its massive head. Snakelike, it coiled backward, readying for another lunge.

Ekos swallowed. From his position on the floor, Cheron swore he heard the other man's stomach churn. Once again, he faced death with a soldier's grace that Cheron admired.

"Get the Echo!" Cheron told him and snatched the sword from his hands. "Save yourself."

He pushed Ekos out of the way as the basilisk snapped downward. He'd thought to stab upward with all his might as the jaws closed in, but a sticky substance clogged his lungs and dulled his senses. Blackness enveloped him, and Cheron didn't see the fog ever abating.

Chapter Fourteen

OUTSIDE, IN THE dying world, Cheron heard a fierce battle cry. Around him, the beast's flesh trembled, shaking as though caught in a massive earthquake. Sudden light blinded his eyes. Befuddled by the turn of events, he realized he was peering up at Ekos, who stood above him like some sort of avenging angel from lore. Flesh hung from his hands. Saliva dripped from his mouth. Upon reflection, Cheron noted he appeared more demon than seraph.

"Did you…" Cheron was about to ask if he'd ripped the basilisk apart, but he wasn't sure if he wanted to know the answer. "What are you when you take off the collar?"

Instead of answering, Ekos bent down to examine Cheron's injuries. Still illuminated by his strange, magical glow, his hair fluttered around him as if underwater, an otherworldly vision.

Cheron was pretty sure he'd actually died until Ekos lightly slapped him and said, "You're not allowed to quit on me, rebel bear. I need you—" He grew quiet for a bit, then added, his voice quiet, tentative. "—to escape from here."

Cheron wasn't so sure if that last bit were true. Ekos seemed to be doing fine on his own. He gazed up on the concubine, whose full lips hovered near his own, and said, "What are you?"

"Pissed," Ekos replied.

"No, what are you?"

"A pissed-off none of your goddamn business. Now get up."

"I'm not sure I can," Cheron confessed, groaning.

"Well, try."

Doing as instructed, Cheron lifted himself from the ground with Ekos's assistance. The other man's tone might have been severe, but his hands were gentle enough as he helped lift him to a standing position. "Watch my finger," he said and zipped the damn thing around like an intoxicated fly. The erratic movement made Cheron dizzy. Exasperation evident in his voice, Ekos snapped, "Are you trying?"

"Yes," Cheron hissed back. "But do it again."

Huffing, Ekos once again lifted his finger and twirled it around Cheron's head. This time, he was able to follow the twisting path. Satisfied with the result of the test, whatever it was, Ekos nodded. "Good. Let's walk. That thing was probably guarding Hell's Echo."

What he said made perfect sense, but Cheron didn't want to move. His stomach lurched at the thought.

"Go ahead and vomit," Ekos said. "It'll make you feel better."

"Yeah," Cheron agreed and then did just that. Afterward, he did feel better but also pretty disgusting. He glanced at Ekos's silken blouse with an arched eyebrow.

Horrified, Ekos clutched the fine garment and said, "Absolutely not!"

Well, asking was worth a try. Using the back of his hand, Cheron cleaned himself enough for the task, at least by the standards allowed.

They continued their journey in silence. Cheron wanted to bring up the topic of Ekos's strange power, but the set of the other man's jaw all but demanded he keep his thoughts hidden. That didn't stop him from sneaking glances at the ethereal halo of light surrounding Ekos's body.

"Watch where you're going," Ekos scolded him. "It would be a pity to break your neck on stairs after defeating a basilisk."

Cheron chuckled. "But kind of funny." Ekos shot him an irate glare. Shrugging and grinning widely, he amended, "In a dark sort of way."

Ekos muttered something under his breath, but Cheron swore he saw the man's lip quirk upward slightly. Contradicting the gesture, he sourly said, "Good thing you have Kalin's love. Otherwise, I'd fear your quest never would have made it past the shipyard. It's a wonder you checked the schedule for departure."

"When you're king, the boats leave when you tell them to."

"Is that why you overthrew the previous monarch? So you wouldn't have to plan travel?"

"Or meals," Cheron added, patting his belly. "Kitchen is open twenty-four seven."

Ekos rolled his eyes but finally outright laughed. "Kalin bless you with a lodestar, Cheron. You'll need him to help you find your pants in the morning."

"Maybe she sent me you," Cheron said, pleased to finally hear Ekos say his name. "To keep me north, and to...uh...find my pants."

All merriment dropped from Ekos's features. He didn't like that one bit, judging by the sudden downturn of his full mouth. "If that's true, she favors you even less than she does me."

Before Cheron asked him what he meant, they entered a chamber unlike any Cheron had ever seen before. Its walls were composed of pure metal. Under Ekos's magical light, they gleamed a fierce, fiery orange but still reflected their dazed features.

"What is this?" Cheron asked, suspecting Ekos might know the answer.

"The Chamber of the Trudid."

Cheron waited for him to elaborate, but to no avail. Ekos, open-mouthed and staring as though he didn't quite know how he'd gotten there, surveyed the room with the same confused wonder Cheron felt. Reverently, he folded his arms inside the long sleeves of his silk shirt. Poised this way, he seemed more akin to a cleric than a palace whore.

"Is the Echo nearby?" Cheron asked him.

"One would assume."

Cheron tried to walk forward, but Ekos took him by the arm and pulled him back.

"This is no room to blunder. Let me go," Ekos said.

The amulet on Cheron's chest heated, nearly to the point of burning. The goddess was warning him against the course of action. "No, this is my duty." The discomfort abated, and Cheron knew he'd interpreted her sign correctly.

"Don't be mad. Within lies a test of mind, not brawn. And, to be frank, you didn't exactly nail the test of strength. Also, you got *stuck* in a door. I'd hate to see what mess you'd get yourself into without me."

Cheron didn't want to get into a protracted argument. In a move that perhaps proved Ekos's point, he pushed the other man backward and hopped inside. The metal shelling vanished, and he stood on top of a snow-covered mountain.

The entire range spread out before him, and he recognized the terrain instantly from the cragged red rocks peaking out from snow drifts. The Hungry Peaks, so named because they claimed the lives of many so-called faithfuls who traveled there to prove their worth to whatever god or goddess whose favor they wished to earn.

A booming voice greeted him. "Cheron Ashborne, King of Broken Maw. Welcome."

"Thank you," he said. "What may I call you?"

Cheron winced at his own assumption that the keeper of the chamber would want to exchange pleasantries like a houseguest, but there was really no known protocol for dealing with this sort of thing. As the silence stretched onward, he began to worry he'd offended.

Then the same booming voice said, "I am the Echo. Are you ready to begin?"

Expecting Hell's Echo to be an item of some sort, as he was taught in lore, Cheron momentarily forgot where he was and who he was addressing. Fearing retribution if he stammered or lost his poise, Cheron shook off his surprise and said, "Yes, I am ready to begin."

Chapter Fifteen

ALONE ON THE mountaintop, Cheron staggered through the knee-deep snow, not feeling the cold, only the anxiety from getting in over his head as Ekos foretold. Doubt unlike he'd ever known before pursued him. Although he tried to remain chipper, his dark thoughts persisted. Then they intensified.

"Kalin guide me," Cheron whispered. No one responded. Normally, even if she were silent, he'd still feel warmth through his chest. The lack of her presence distressed him. Was he truly abandoned to wander in this forsaken place? He'd never felt so far away from home or missed it so much.

The sun began to set. Orange light reflected on the underside of the clouds; the glow was reminiscent of the metal room but not quite. No heat radiated from the sun. No cold from the snow. Wind rustled his hair, and he wished for a tempest. The landscape provided zero creature comforts but also no real hardships. Struggling was better than nothing at all.

"What is this place?" Cheron asked himself.

He expected to hear Ekos's snide response, something about his lack of preparation or perhaps a dig at his body. When a rebuke didn't come, he missed the sarcastic concubine's sharp, but shapely, tongue.

"Why the hell would I miss that scorn monger?"

He knew the answer, he realized.

Cheron shook his head at his own ridiculous thoughts and walked because there was nothing else to do. Continuing the theme of his journey thus far, he had no real idea where he was going or what to look for. All he knew is that the goddess had asked him to serve a purpose here. That's what he intended to do.

"I am here to serve you, Kalin," he said and kissed his amulet. "No matter the cost. Your grace binds me."

The sound of pebbles falling from one of the steep ridges caught his attention.

Ahead of him, a lone figure crouched in the snow. Furs hid his features and his body from view, but Cheron knew the profile the way he knew his own heartbeat. Aethel. His lover. He smelled the sandalwood on him and tasted the cinnamon in his mouth. Although he knew it couldn't be true—the man was dead, he'd watched him burn—Cheron needed closure too badly to second-guess his appearance.

"Cheron," Aethel said without turning. He knew him too.

"Aethel."

"You've been gone a long while. Was your hunt not successful?"

"You betrayed me."

Aethel finally looked at him. The surprise in his face took hold of Cheron's soul and cut its strings to his body all over again. Where Ekos's eyes were a clear, light blue reflecting the air and light around them, Aethel's were dark, pitiless things that warned those who couldn't swim that the waters were too deep. Cheron hadn't heeded the dangers.

"What do you mean, Cheron? How did I betray you?"

"You spied on me for the king. He lured me out using you afterward. Why would you do that? Why would you help a tyrant who killed your family?"

Aethel shook his head in confusion. None of this made any sense to him. Cheron understood this version of his lover hadn't lived those moments. Still, he hoped he had some explanation to offer. He must know his own mind, if nothing else.

Cheron tried again. "Why *would* you betray me? I love you."

"I wouldn't. I love you too. Always have. Always will."

Cheron wanted to believe him. Certainly, he said the words with such sincerity, his eyes wide and guileless, that Cheron momentarily forgot the hellish torments he had endured due to Aethel's loose tongue and even looser loyalties.

"Stop looking at me like that," Aethel said. "I don't know of what you speak. Why don't you come here and have some stew? I'm cooking your favorite. Rabbit. Well, minus the rabbit since you didn't catch one."

Cheron sat and forgot the end and remembered the beginning. The two were young servants in their master's household, cloaking themselves in the shadows of dark corners where their lips would meet for brief moments. Later, up in the loft of the barn, they'd talk rebellion and true change for people like them.

Such talks ended with their mouths pressed together. Their hands tore at the other's clothes until they had access to the flesh beneath. Cheron remembered the urgency of their sex most of all. The way they went from kissing to penetration in the beat of a wing like they were birds about ready to fly away.

And then they'd been enlisted in one of the king's wars. Everything followed after that.

"Do you know where you are?" Cheron asked him.

Aethel glanced around. "Of course. The Hungry Peaks. We came here searching for a sign from Kalin. You wanted to confirm her desire for you to rule Broken Maw."

They'd never made such a journey together, though Cheron had often suggested such a trip many times. The goddess's blessing meant everything to him, but he was never to have it formally. He settled for his mother's amulet.

"How long have we been searching?"

"A great time," Aethel said. "I'm starting to think this mountain is our new home."

The thought appealed. In this strange world, the life he left behind was his to choose: his lover, his blessing, his freedom. There were no masters on the mountain, no kings or princes. The rugged world judged men by their utility.

"We should get moving," Cheron said. "Before nighttime."

"Do you even know where you're going?"

Cheron twisted back in the direction of the voice, which no longer belonged to Aethel. Ekos, still wearing his silken frock from the palace, stood in his spot.

"No," Cheron confessed. He wanted to explain more, but he wasn't sure he could, not to this stubborn, infuriating man. "The goddess bestows the path."

Lips twisted in a grimace, Ekos cocked his head to the side as if that amused him. "Then follow me, rebel. I have something to show you."

Without so much as second-guessing the order, Cheron obeyed. Deep down, the trust felt right, natural. He knew Ekos, unlike Aethel, would keep him from danger. But not from pain, apparently.

In front of him, a massive fire burned. The flames licked the underbelly of the sky. On top of the pyre, a man twisted and begged for his life. Aethel. First, before it consumed his lover, the flames would have to eat the ship they'd built together to sail to their new life.

"Save him if you must, rebel." Ekos's voice stirred the hairs at his neck. "But then they'll have you, and the rebellion will be over."

This had happened. Ekos hadn't been there, and no one whispered the choice in his ear. Another face in the crowd, he'd watched as his lover begged for his life. Most likely, the king had told Aethel he'd be spared if Cheron showed himself. But Cheron knew such ppromises weren't true, and so he'd watched as the spark that set off their war died.

Was that the wrong choice? Why was it being offered again?

On the pyre, Aethel twisted and screamed. The flames were closer now. "Cheron!" he called. He scanned the crowd, his eyes red from the smoke. Despite the great distance, Cheron swore he saw them and he was equally sure they returned his gaze. "Cheron!" he said again.

People in the crowd laughed, pleased by Aethel's desperation. People who'd never been to battle enjoyed the spectacle of death. They wanted a sanitized version of the suffering real warriors endured on the field.

In this moment, Cheron hated the people he might one day lead.

"Save him," Ekos said again. "You can."

"No," he said. Tears ran down his cheeks, and he hated every breath of air he took while his lover choked and sputtered. "I can't."

When the fire's fingers eventually entangled itself in Aethel's long chestnut hair, it pulled his head sharply against the mast. As he'd seen him in a fit of passion, Aethel reared back and howled. The tattoos they'd earned together blackened and seared away. Cheron remembered touching the spot on his arm that Aethel had promised to ink once they were married.

"It's over now," Ekos's voice called to him. "You can open your eyes."

That was right. He had closed them at some point. He remembered now. "Thank you," he said but kept them shut.

Much later, Cheron had risked sneaking to Aethel's grave, which was left open for display. No guards awaited him, as he halfway expected. The king must have assumed his sentimentality would be his downfall, not his need to hold on to the past.

"I'm sorry," he remembered saying to Aethel's burnt-out husk. Turning to ash, Aethel's face leaned into his for a kiss, but his lips disintegrated before they met one last time.

Chapter Sixteen

WARM LIPS PRESSED against his in a commanding manner. Cheron recognized they weren't Aethel's; instant surrender had been his way of doing things. This person challenged him, molding Cheron's lips to his desire the way a potter shaped clay into a suitable vessel.

"Open your eyes."

Cheron did and looked into the sky. In this man's gaze, he was buoyed up rather than dragged down. "Ekos?"

"Bear," he said, smirking in that arrogant way of his.

"Don't call me that."

His smirk tilted, letting Cheron know—without saying anything—that he had every intention of using the nickname until he died. To his surprise, Cheron realized he really didn't mind. Ekos could call him whatever he liked. Not that he needed permission.

"You kissed me," Cheron said. His body still tingled where they'd touched.

"Did you enjoy yourself?"

Not quite understanding, or trusting, the man's sudden lust, Cheron admitted he had...but. "Are you real?"

As he spoke, Cheron searched for signs of either the mountain or the busy town square. Finding a chamber filled with sweet perfume and silks instead, he rubbed the back of his neck. Obviously this was some type of illusion, but what was the goddess—or whatever entity had him in its thrall—trying to show him? What was the test?

"Would you like me to be real?" Ekos asked and plucked a strand of hair from his shoulder.

"That's not an answer."

"There aren't always answers. That holds true in worlds both real and imaginary."

Cheron felt thoroughly lost. Maybe he was just a big, dumb bear who was ill-equipped to handle tests of the mind. Just as Ekos had said.

Licking his lips, Cheron patrolled the chamber, searching for some clue to his purpose, any sign of the goddess's will. Ekos's eyes followed him as he lazily dragged his hand through a small fountain. Guiltily, Cheron realized he'd forgotten where he stood moments before and what he'd witnessed. Though the memory was an old one, the pain still had power over him. "What happened to Aethel?"

"Who?"

The coyness infuriated Cheron. "You know him."

Ekos flicked water from his long, graceful fingers and said, "He died a long time ago. You chose not to save him. Do you regret that?"

The situation demanded honesty, so that's what Cheron gave. "Yes."

Ekos nodded as if he knew this was the answer. "And yet you did the same again."

"Yes."

"Why?"

"I had promised the people following me a shot at a better life. I could no longer be a servant to my own desires."

Ekos pursed his lips, considering his answer. "You do not worship Atyx, god of war and warriors. Why is this?"

"He does not speak to me."

"You are a warrior, are you not?"

"I do not seek bloodshed for my glory."

"Why, then?"

"For a greater good. To end oppression, hatred, bigotry."

Ekos nodded. His golden hair swished around his delicate face. "All noble causes. But you killed to achieve them. That is a warrior's path to victory, not a wise man's."

Lifting his chin, Cheron defended the rightness of his actions. "The sages of the realm sat in their temples, studying books, while their king destroyed villages, raped to forward his bloodline, and set fields of children on fire in order to quell uprisings. I do not question the need for knowledge, but I do not laud its lack of use in times of great suffering. Such is not wisdom. Such is cowardice. Sometimes, wise men need warriors to kill in order to end the tyranny of the cruel."

"There now. You do have spirit. Follow me."

Tired of playing whatever game had him in its grip but not knowing what else to do, Cheron trailed the creature wearing Ekos's likeness. Part of him worried he'd be forced to once again witness the death of Aethel. He didn't think he'd withstand the torment one more time, not without breaking.

The inside of the lavish bedchamber melted away. In its place, there stood a cave where drops of water echoed as if traveling through time. Well lit by some unknown source, the stones gave off an eerie red glow. His guide smiled. "This is the end of your journey, Cheron Ashborne. The goddess asks one more thing of you to prove your worth."

"Anything."

"Step aside."

Cheron didn't understand what he meant. Step aside from what?

Sensing, or perhaps directly knowing Cheron's confusion, Ekos elaborated by gesturing toward an open pit. Wind whistled upward from the black maw. The chill made Cheron shudder.

Cheron didn't have to look to know the fall would kill him. Merely asking him to step inside a ditch wouldn't be much of a request. His instincts fought against obeying the order. Hadn't he served her will in all he'd done? He'd earned a better reward for his devotion.

"Prove you did not kill for your own glory," Ekos said. "Step aside."

Cheron walked to the edge. His feet sent pebbles hurtling the same forsaken path he was being asked to hurtle. He never heard them hit the bottom, only plunk against the sides. Up close, the blackness was even more daunting.

"For whom am I abdicating my throne? Is he or she just and kind?"

The question made Ekos smile. "Perhaps there will be no more thrones. Perhaps the time of kings is done."

Oddly, the thought gave Cheron some comfort. In their musings, he and Aethel had envisioned such a world where men and women would live on their merits rather than the status their birth accorded them. "And I must die for such a world to exist?"

Ekos nodded.

And so Cheron jumped.

He didn't hit the sides of the abyss as the pebbles had done. He fell straight downward, plummeting at a speed that made his stomach's contents rise up in his throat. He thought that alone might kill him. But eventually he saw the bottom, the true end to his journey. Jagged red rocks, pointed at the tips, peaked from the ground. Death, at least, would be quick.

"Kalin keep me," he prayed and shut his eyes. The sound of an unfurling sail snapped them open again. A ship? In this forsaken place? No, not a ship. Wings. Beneath him, a massive golden dragon readied to catch him. To devour or to save? Cheron wasn't sure. He prepared for either outcome, grateful that the goddess had at least given him a glorious exit.

Then he stopped falling and began gliding. Beneath him, the dragon beat its wings and soared higher until they'd climbed out of the abyss and entered a clear blue sky. Cheron had never felt so free. Or terrified.

When the creature finally landed, it slid him off its back without comment or warning and flew off. Cheron watched its withdrawal, feeling like a kid who believed in magic again. Caught up in his wonder, he failed to notice a figure behind him.

"You are judged worthy," the same booming voice from the start of his journey said. "You may possess Hell's Echo."

Cheron whirled at the sound but just in time to catch a mere glimpse of the strange figure who'd overseen the trial. The images had already begun to turn to a dark mist and swirl toward Kalin's amulet. The jewelry glowed a brilliant white, then went dim and cold. Cheron clutched at the talisman and prayed his thanks to the goddess. "I understand," he told her. "I will do what you ask me."

But her charge would be difficult for him. What she demanded went against his nature and what he'd fought so hard to become. The goddess wasn't asking him to lead. She was asking him to follow.

Chapter Seventeen

THE MOMENT HE woke, drawing in a breath so deep his belly grew ten sizes to accommodate, Ekos slapped him and called him a stupid bear. Cheron'd ask if the concubine were real, but so far he'd acted perfectly in character. Signs pointed to this being the true Ekos.

"What happened?" Ekos asked after he was done with his lecture. "Did you pass the trial? Do you have Hell's Echo?"

"Yes," Cheron wheezed because Ekos was leaning on his stomach.

"Good. I'd hate to think you'd done something so unforgivably stupid for no reason at all." He paused. It might have been Cheron's vision, but his eyes appeared red. Certainly his hair was mussed. Some of the strands were wet and clung to the sides of his cheeks. "Sorry," Ekos eventually said. "About the slap. You were flopping around so hard I thought you might be having a seizure."

"And so you hit me?"

"Well, I'm not a damn medic!"

"Obviously." Cheron pushed to a sitting position. "But for future reference, try a bucket of water or..."

He was about to say a kiss but stopped before the words escaped and condemned him to a journey of scorn. Ekos had made his lack of interest quite clear, and Cheron needed to respect the boundary.

"Or what?" Ekos prompted him, his eyebrow raised nearly to his hairline.

"I don't know. I'm not a damn medic, either."

"Right. Where's the Echo?"

Cheron touched his chest where the medallion rested, only it had slid off to the side and his hand rested on flesh.

Ekos snorted. "Seriously, after all this, I will kill someone if that's the case."

Cheron looked down and realized his hand covered his heart. "Oh, no, not in my heart. Here." Cheron held up the amulet by its chain so that it dangled in Ekos's face.

"That's almost as bad!"

"What did you want?"

Ekos gritted his teeth. Then, as though having second thoughts about his anger, he let his lips fall to a pouting frown. "I don't know. Something shiny." His eyes gleamed.

"I think you spent too much time with the basilisk."

"As I said, we're practically cousins."

"Hm," Cheron said without comment, but he mulled the idea over. There was an odd ring of truth to the statement.

The two sat on the ground face-to-face. Ekos was so close Cheron smelled the sweetness of his skin, that odd mixture of sky and water that translated throughout his very essence. Cheron wanted to taste his lips for real, not as part of some strange test.

Cheron leaned toward Ekos, who, encouragingly, did not pull back. He slanted forward, too, pressing his temple against Cheron's. Then, sweetly, he said, "Can you walk?"

"I believe so."

Less sweetly, he said, "Then do it."

CHERON WALKED, BUT his sore limbs made him pay for the effort. His entire body felt like a child's toy he'd outgrown and since discarded. Now he was being forced to play with it again, and the joints were quarrelsome. Sensing Ekos's growing ire, he did his best not to moan out loud when his joints popped and his muscles contracted. Asking the other man for a massage was obviously out of the question.

"We need to move faster. I told Lion no more than a few days. If he's found…"

"You told him to hide?"

Ekos's lips pinched. "Hurry" was his only response.

Now that Cheron knew the stakes, moving faster was easier. Despite his name, Lion wasn't a fierce creature; more like a house cat whose claws were for climbing tall trees. So, Cheron hobbled and tried not to think about the sounds his body made in protest.

He placed his hand on the amulet for reassurance. Cold, unresponsive, its texture resembled ordinary metal.

As they neared the exit, Cheron felt a change in the air, how it went from musty and heavy to floral and light. The garden was ahead. Combined, their anxieties bent the world to stillness. But they had to keep moving.

"Almost there," Ekos said. Cheron got the impression the observation was more to break the silence than to make notation of their progress.

"Yes," he said for the same reason.

Something wasn't right. Cheron wondered if Ekos felt anxious, too, or if he was alone in his unease. Ekos's breathing changed from even to ragged, hinting at some discomfort. Whether it was tiredness or fear, Cheron didn't dare ask.

They'd escaped the catacombs and stumbled into the garden. Around them, bees buzzed and zigzagged across the sky. Hummingbirds fluttered flower to flower. Brooks babbled. Flowers reached toward the sun. Everything appeared perfectly normal. Except the absence of people.

Pale, lips pulled to a taught line, Ekos said, "There's a boat in the harbor floating near where the delegation greeted you. You'll know the ship by its dragon head. Lion waits inside the hull. Remember your promise to save him. Follow me."

Sinnac waited for them on the dais. As usual, he'd planted his chin against a curled-up fist, and he seemed thoroughly bored by everything. He did grace them with a slight smile. Much like the man, it was a wisp of a thing.

Beside him, Isa postured with her hand on the hilt of her weapon.

"Greetings," Sinnac said. His tone was light, pleasant. "Did you manage to secure the relic?"

Ekos stepped forward to answer. "Yes."

"What are you doing?" Cheron said. "Tell him nothing."

The pitying and apologetic look Ekos shot him told him all he needed to know. Cheron had blundered again and trusted someone he shouldn't. No wonder the goddess hadn't communicated with him. She knew her missives were not private.

Sinnac waved him forward. "Good. Good. Bring it to me, my pet."

Infuriated, Cheron braced for the betrayal to come, but Ekos did not take the necklace to his master. Instead, he pulled out an extremely large diamond from a hidden pocket in his silk frock and presented this to Sinnac's eager hands.

The man studied the relic, turning it side to side. "How does Hell's Echo work?" he asked.

Ekos shrugged. "Leave the question for your scholars. I fulfilled my part of the bargain."

Sinnac raised his eyebrow. "So you did. Well done. Seize them both."

Guards closed in around them, pressing long, curved blades up against their backs. A trickle of blood skidded down the length of Cheron's spine. Ekos dropped to his knees. Blue eyes opened wide in terror, he begged for his life. "Please, I did everything as instructed. You have the relic and the savage."

Sinnac gave the display a tired yawn. "Take them back to the dungeons."

Isa placed a hand on Sinnac's shoulder, which he grabbed and squeezed. Apparently, he'd made promises to her too.

"Yes, of course. Prepare the savage for battle. Take Ekos to the dungeons."

Isa's eyes were hard, her smile cruel. The promise in both was that Cheron would suffer. Not because torture served a function. No. It would be because she enjoyed bloodsport.

Chapter Eighteen

EXPECTING THEM TO cheat, Cheron gaped in surprise as he was handed his preferred weapon: a long-handled ax. This one was especially beautiful. Ornate carvings of dragons graced its handle, and its blade was diamond tipped. Cheron tested the sharpness with his thumb, marveling at the painless, effortless cut.

"Satisfactory?" a squire asked.

"Yes," Cheron said and flicked the edge. "It will taste marrow."

The young man left him without another word, pulling up the ladder behind him. The room itself, more of a pit, kept sufficient guard. The steep sides stretched upward as far as the eye could see. Unless Cheron suddenly sprouted wings, he wouldn't be able to escape.

Ekos's plan, whatever it was, better come with its own ladder. *Please have a plan*, Cheron added to himself.

Because there was little else to do, Cheron practiced his swordplay. Confident in his own abilities but mindful of the spectacle Isa had made of her last opponent, he focused on the task at hand. His muscles, sore from the journey, refused to cooperate at first. Soon, the familiarity of the movements settled in and Cheron lost track of time.

"Magnificent."

Cheron whirled to see Sinnac's appreciative eyes raking over his body, which was slick with sweat and coated with a fine crust of white dirt. Although he felt grimy, he knew city men like Sinnac tended to romanticize such things.

Sinnac tilted his head to the side. "Must you look at your weapon in such a way?"

Cheron didn't know he'd been staring at the blade of his ax so intently. Realizing that Sinnac would most likely be heavily guarded, Cheron let his weapon fall to his side. Briskly, he said, "What do you want? To gloat over my upcoming demise?"

Sinnac held his hand to his chest as though affronted. "I come to offer terms of peace."

"What terms?"

"A union. Yours and mine."

Cheron couldn't believe what he heard. After shaking his head to clear out the buzzing, he bent to pick up his weapon. Sinnac, judging by his ringing laughter, thought this marvelous. He clapped his hands together and said, "Our two kingdoms together would be a force. Losing you would be costly."

"You mean a war would be costly?"

He bowed, acknowledging the truth of the statement. "It would advantage you as well."

"I'm sure."

Hands clasped together behind his back, Sinnac paced a small area. His ebony robe breezed across the dirt, stirring dust around him in elegant swirls. "Come with me," he finally said after a period of quiet. Immediately after, he snapped his fingers. Isa appeared. To her, he said, "Transport us out of here."

The sour expression loudly declared she'd rather not, but she obeyed. In a swirl of magic far more powerful than Cheron had ever witnessed, they left the arena and stood on the balcony of a lavish room. Isa bowed and departed.

"My private chamber, my sanctuary. Very few ever enter here," Sinnac said in a way that suggested Cheron ought to be impressed, possibly humbled.

Playing the part of the polite guest no longer, Cheron said, "There will be no marriage between us. Changing my accommodations won't entice me."

"Of course. Of course. Noble to the last. This way." Sinnac dipped his two fingers, beckoning him deeper into the chamber.

Once inside, he pulled back the rich hanging fabric from his massive bed. Resting on the mattress, bound head to toe, was Ekos—unconscious and possibly drugged. His eyes fluttered as though he sensed Cheron's presence. He groaned something that sounded close to *run*. Things, then, were not going according to plan. And wasn't that the problem with scheming?

Sinnac studied Cheron's reaction, which he tried, but failed, to control. "Why must you torment him this way?"

Sinnac gave the question one of his ghostly, wispy smiles. "Because I think you are fond of him. I have a good sense for these things." He tapped the bridge of his nose. "And you'd very much like to introduce him to at least one peak in the North, no?"

Cheron waited for the man to be done laughing at his own joke before he said, "I don't want him that way."

"But you do want him. Willing, yes? Begging you to let him swallow the mountain whole? Well, Isa can see to his change of heart, just as she saw to him telling the truth about your amulet." Delicately, he picked up the diamond from a nearby nightstand. "Beautiful, but useless, yes?"

Cheron remembered Isa's skills. There was little sense in denying the truth. "Yes."

"It was a clever attempt, but Ekos should have known I'd confirm." Sinnac clucked and shook his head at the unconscious man.

Cheron agreed but kept that to himself.

"Normally, I'd put him in my garden for such insolence and trickery, but I feel inclined toward mercy. For him and for his little cub." Once again, Sinnac snapped his fingers and a swirl of magic brought Lion to stand before them. He blinked his terrified brown eyes and gaped at the room around him.

"Where..." he stammered.

"Enjoying the boats, were we?" Sinnac asked him. "Planning to sail away without saying goodbye?"

Caught, Lion could do nothing but swallow down his terror and flinch. He rolled his hands into tight fists and wrapped his arms around his body. Moisture gathered in his eyes. When he saw Ekos, they took on a different glint—harder, sharper. "Please don't hurt him."

To someone like Sinnac, such horror appealed on several levels. Cheron swore he saw the start of arousal press the fine fabric of the man's robe forward. Certainly, he licked his lips and his dark eyes gleamed. He said, "I won't have to hurt you if our good Cheron here agrees to my terms. You see, Lion, I need money, resources. Our Cheron here has those things. I'd take them from him, but wars are costly. And then a foreigner keeping those Northern territories. My goodness. I'd have to kill them all. Practicalities are monstrous things, really.

"Marriages, on the other hand, solve things quite nicely. And I do appreciate my guest's beauty. Do you not think him lovely, Lion?"

The young man gulped. "I do, Excellency."

"Yes, I saw you admire him, despite yourself. His muscles. His kind eyes, so gentle, like a cow's. And those tattoos. My, my. I especially love this one." Using one finger, Sinnac trailed the serpent's crest along Cheron's forearm. "It's an attractive bundle, minus that hideous scar on an otherwise noble face. But even that adds some appeal, yes? A bit of danger?"

Lion merely nodded. Sinnac could have declared Cheron was a three-headed dragon that farted hordes of treasure, and the young man would have nodded along in agreement.

Sinnac must have known this as well. He bent to cup Lion's chin and dragged his gaze upward. "And because he is so kind, so brave, so gentle, and so noble, he will agree to my terms, and he will protect you as Ekos wanted. Don't you think?"

Lion directed his focus on Cheron, which was no doubt intended. Wide, innocent, the brown eyes begged affirmation and to spare him whatever torments Sinnac had planned.

Cheron stole a glance at Ekos again. One of the last things he'd asked was for Cheron to keep the young man safe. Honor demanded he keep his word. "Yes," Cheron said, hating himself after.

"Good. Excellent. Now hand me your medallion."

Cheron did that too. Oddly, he hated himself less for that.

Chapter Nineteen

INSISTING WAS SOMETHING Sinnac did the way other men buttered toast in the morning. He spread it on thick, too, playing to the court of nobles gathered in a way that made them all chuckle appreciatively. He insisted they attend through royal decree. He insisted they laugh through his posture. He insisted they accept his foreign groom with eager arms.

"One is not enough for my virile Northern man. Our Lion will have both his hands busy as our concubine!" Kalin's amulet hung from his neck. It swished as he spoke.

Lion giggled nervously, but lifted his hands up as though gripping something massive between them.

The number of references Sinnac made to Cheron's dick were truly staggering. Cheron suppressed an eye roll, but the joke—as intended—played well to the crowd. Women fanned themselves. Men chuckled and boasted of their own endowments. Sinnac wasn't a fop or a fool; he was an apt showman. Cheron, and his foreign otherness, served as a good bit of theater. That was why Cheron hated the arts.

"Come," Sinnac said after the crowd dispersed. "I have a treat for you before the wedding, my precious."

Whatever the surprise was, Cheron doubted it would please him.

They entered a room tiled in decorative glass—blue, white, and reflective. Steam rose from the center, coiling upward like long tendrils of rope Cheron couldn't climb to escape, though he'd almost be willing to try. Guards snapped and came to attention as they passed. Although they called him by his proper rank, they stiffened and turned up their noses at Cheron.

Sinnac noticed too. "You." He pointed to the nearest guard. Cheron got the sense the choice was at random. "Impale him."

"Your Majesty?"

"Impale the guard next to you. Obey."

He did.

Cheron knew brutality, but the sudden burst of violence took him off guard. Slack-jawed, not appearing very majestic, he watched as the other man disemboweled his fellow soldier without so much as a blink. Judging by the other man's confused, pained expression, he thought they were friends up until his dying moments. He'd been wrong.

"There," Sinnac said and turned to the guards. "The rest of you are pleased with my chosen mate, are you not?"

They all enthusiastically agreed they were. Seemingly satisfied, Sinnac waved them off and continued forward, lifting the hem of his robe as he stepped over the pool of blood.

"My apologies, love. They'll show you proper respect from now on."

"I prefer to earn my respect," Cheron bit back. "You made them hate me more."

"Fear is its own currency. You can spend it anywhere in the world."

"I don't think our views align."

"They will. Ah, and here is our surprise."

Ekos stood naked in the center of the bath. Although the water hid the lower reaches of his body from Cheron's view, his mind filled in the blanks. "Your Majesty," Ekos greeted him. The anger in his voice took Cheron aback.

"Now, now," Sinnac chided him. "Remember what we talked about. Think of what poor Lion will feel if you disrespect us."

Tight-lipped but smiling serenely, Ekos repeated the title and gave Cheron a full bow. The eyes betrayed him. They were hard and cracked like ice. His voice was sweet enough when he said, "I am to ease Your Majesty's burdens before the wedding."

"Go on, enjoy yourself," Sinnac told him, as though indulging Cheron's desires. "Stay with me, and you can have him whenever you like."

"I will n—"

Sinnac cut off Cheron's refusal. "Perhaps you are shy. I can remove the rest of the guards."

The way he said *remove* left no doubt to his intentions. Resentfully, but not wanting more bloodshed for his sake, Cheron stripped to his undergarments and entered the water.

Ekos bathed him. They weren't alone. Nearby guards, close enough to hear even the slightest hint of a whisper, clutched their weapons and probably thought about the folly of letting them be together. But Sinnac had insisted, and he was a man to whom pettiness appealed more than security. Besides, they'd recently learned not to question decisions regarding the strange foreigner.

"Remember to wash his privates," Sinnac called, reclining lazily off to the side on a plush chaise.

Ekos's face flushed an angry red. But, then suddenly, a mischievous smile brought the corners of his mouth upward.

Cheron tried his best to focus on anything other than the gentle touch of the sponge as Ekos dripped water against his shoulders. Occasionally, the smooth planes of the other man's belly brushed against his back. Cheron's burdens increased tenfold, as did his temper.

"Stop," Cheron said. "This is…"

Ekos pressed his erection against Cheron's butt, and the noble things he was about to say fluttered from his head. He almost forgot his own name or what he'd come here to do. What was the Hell's Echo? Who even was Kalin? Some type of fruit perhaps.

"Your Majesty wants me to stop rubbing his back? He'd like me to rub something else? Very well. Turn around. Turn around, *I* said," Ekos emphasized when Cheron didn't obey. "Do it for *me*."

Cheron turned. Immediately after, Ekos took hold of Cheron's cock and pulled upward, released, and then repeated the process until he let loose a small gasp. For the guards, Ekos made a point to act as though he were merely soaping Cheron's chest. Meanwhile, underwater, he continued to tug in a coaxing rhythm. Cheron, repressing the urge to drag him out of the water and take him then and there, gently pushed him away.

Ekos, his blue eyes more black now, gave him a disappointed frown. "Was Sinnac right? Are you shy?"

The audience didn't bother Cheron. During war, men had to find their pleasure in more awkward moments than this. But he didn't want Ekos to feel compelled.

"You don't have to—"

Ekos kept him quiet by pressing their mouths together. Uncertain at first, exploring Cheron's body in short bursts, he gained confidence as their erections swelled and pressed together. More like himself, Ekos grabbed again, taking what he wanted and going where he pleased.

But was this passion or something else? "Ekos..." Cheron said. "I..."

"Give this to *me*," he panted. As usual, he guessed at Cheron's inner thoughts. "I want it. Not him. Me. Something to remember when I'm..." His voice trailed off. "Just shut up and kiss me."

Wonders would cease eventually. Until then, they had each other in this moment.

And it would end soon. Already one of the guards kept clearing his throat, trying to catch Sinnac's attention without outright saying the monarch's little amusement had morphed into something that would most likely piss him off.

Cheron decided to make the best of the time they had. Greedily, he worked his tongue inside Ekos's mouth, exploring each corner and tender fold with a determination to make the other man moan in frustration.

Ekos had ironclad will, unbendable control. He didn't verbally indicate his pleasure, but his grip on Cheron's cock tightened uncomfortably, and his eyes narrowed into languid slits. At least his breathing, which came in ragged gasps, indicated strain. That was no good. Cheron wanted him begging, panting, clawing—utterly on the brink of desperation.

"That's enough. Separate them," Sinnac commanded. His ghastly white face, red now, bloated in anger. Perhaps realizing the gossip would reflect a loss of control on his part if he continued to seethe, he forced his voice back to its sweetness. "You'll wear yourself out for the wedding night."

"I'm sure he'll give it to you good, Excellency," Ekos assured him, every bit as sweetly.

The two glared at each other, both testing the other's resolve. Cheron stood aside and let Ekos convey his scorn through a simpering grin and a secretive hand job. He was making this punishment into his own triumph, and Cheron wouldn't get in the way of his revenge.

Fear was a currency that could be spent anywhere in the world. But Ekos apparently didn't give a shit about money.

Chapter Twenty

AFTER THE INCIDENT in the baths, Sinnac called for an immediate wedding. They'd gone from betrothed to wed in the span of a few days. The timeline didn't allow for Cheron to scheme his way out of the predicament, which was likely the intent.

The reception made him more uncomfortable than the event itself.

Cheron wore a blue-and-white wedding robe trimmed with gold thread. On his head, they'd placed a garland of white lilies. They'd even painted a batch of blue lilacs where his scar cut a jagged path down his face. Cheron had never felt more ridiculous.

Outsider or not, Cheron still heard gossip about Ekos's display at the baths from nearby revelers. Of course, no one told him directly, but he overheard mutterings around the common area where the nobles ate and socialized. The word he most often heard was *humiliated*.

"They had sex right there in front of His Majesty, while he gushed about the upcoming nuptials!" a noblewoman huffed, sounding positively scandalized. "Can you imagine such a thing?"

"They're both savage!" another one said. "He should come to his senses before it's too late!"

Had he been free to fight back, Cheron would have told the gossips that Sinnac had set up the scene. The only thing that had not gone according to his plans was Ekos's unwillingness to be an unwilling plaything. But Cheron stuffed the words back into his mouth along with a piece of pungent cheese. These were the same women who'd fanned themselves while Lion held an invisible dick. Cheron doubted they were much affronted, but they talked a good game.

"Sh, here he comes!"

The two women curtsied as Sinnac approached.

Dressed in a long white robe with blue flowers embroidered on the sleeves, Sinnac lingered a moment to give each lady a small nod. If he heard the rumors swirling around him, he refused to dignify them with a response. Other than the fact his long, narrow mouth twisted downward in a perpetual frown, he appeared unperturbed.

He laughed at something one of the politicians following him said, but his ring finger tapped on his wine glass. Cheron heard the *click, click, click* and smiled, knowing Ekos would have enjoyed Sinnac's anger as well.

A servant held a golden tray up under Cheron's nose. "Would Your Majesty care for another plum pot?"

"No, thank you," he said and waved the man away. If nothing else, his bowels would be regular for a month.

Cheron distrusted the new level of deference Sinnac's subjects showed him. As Sinnac had promised, everyone now accorded him the proper respect. To his face. Behind his back was another story, but it was a tale of bigotry that—as far as Cheron was concerned—didn't merit telling. So, he graciously accepted their forced supplication as though they treated him genuine respect. Eventually, circumstances would be different. That would take time.

"My darling." Sinnac's voice roused him from his musings. "Are you ready for this evening's entertainment?"

Cheron wanted little more than to retire for the night and contemplate his grim future. He hadn't given up exactly, but being married to this monster was a resounding defeat that Cheron felt to his bones.

Cheron hid his discomfort. For now, he had a part to play. Later, only Kalin knew how long, he'd get the amulet back and fulfill his promise to the goddess. "Of course," Cheron said. "After you."

Sinnac led the way back to the dais in the pleasure garden. Isa stood in the middle of the stage area below. Her weapons were drawn, and she was in a battle-ready stance. Already, Cheron's nerves frayed upon seeing the woman.

A throne that was only slightly shorter than Sinnac's was placed on the upper platform next to it. Carved from mahogany, the intricately designed chair resembled a flowing river. Quite lovely, actually. And comfortable. Cheron sat down on the cushioned chair and marveled at the artistry.

"I had this throne made especially for you," Sinnac said. "Aligned with me, you shall not want for fine things."

"Made for me?" Cheron asked, thinking about the timeline of their nuptials. "Can you see the future?"

"No, but Atyx can. He promised me a husband worthy of my love."

Cheron assumed Sinnac had gone to the ceremony only to secure his financial interests, but when he looked into Sinnac's gray eyes, he saw an emotion he wasn't expecting: desire. Cheron didn't quite know what to make of the strange, unwelcome reaction.

He gave his husband a quick smile and said, "Thank you. It's quite extraordinary."

Satisfied by the response, Sinnac gave his upper leg a possessive squeeze and then turned and clapped his hands. This signaled the start of the event, the nature of which remained to be seen. Cheron realized the night's entertainment, as always, involved bloodshed. It was only a matter of whose. Reflexively, he looked over to the side to check on Lion. The poor young man gave him another lopsided smile that tilted his mouth until it resembled a grimace.

Cheron couldn't offer comfort without Sinnac noticing. He didn't want to make Lion more of a target than he already was, so he snubbed the gesture.

The festivities started.

Drummers beat out a battle rhythm. Dancers wearing dragon costumes—red and blue—took the stage, twisting and turning around Isa while she remained stationary in the middle of the chaos. Adults and children alike *oohed* and *aahed* at the spectacle. A few, offbeat with the rest of the group, clapped.

Looking bored as ever, Sinnac propped his head on his fist. When he caught Cheron's glance, he lifted his eyebrow slightly and held out his hand for Cheron to take. Playing the part of the doting husband for Lion's sake, Cheron took the offered hand and planted a gallant kiss on the palm. Color rose up to Sinnac's cheeks. This marked the first time Cheron had ever seen him a shade other than gray. Perhaps he wasn't playacting his lusts after all.

Lion, witnessing the exchange, allowed a slight frown to convey his displeasure.

Sinnac saw the telltale grimace. "Would our pet like to be a part of the day's event?" he asked, his voice dripping slow and thick.

In a surprising turn of events, Lion lifted his chin at a defiant angle and said, "Yes, if that means escaping you."

Although Cheron admired the newfound mettle, the young man had picked the wrong time to reconnect to his spine.

Nostrils flared, Sinnac glared at Lion in such a way that would have dismantled the bone, but Lion wouldn't backtrack. He remained steadfast in his defiance.

Cheron placed his hand on top of Sinnac's and did his best to sound like a happy, indulgent groom. "Deal with him later. This is a celebration."

Whatever his other faults, Sinnac wasn't foolish. He gave Cheron's attempt a rueful smile and withdrew his hand. He said, "I will keep my promise despite his belligerence. My hope is that you remember this, my husband. But also remember that some things can't go unpunished."

"What things?" Cheron asked, dreading the answer.

Sinnac didn't respond.

The dancing had slowed down. The music came to a sudden, jarring halt. A man Cheron instantly recognized was led, by leash, to the stage—Ekos. He wore an ill-fitting suit of armor to match his ill temper, which he expressed through a series of colorful gestures to the crowd. They, of course, loved the vulgar display.

"Are you okay, my love?" Sinnac asked, knowing damn well he wasn't.

Cheron swallowed the painful lump in his throat and tried not to think about the horror Isa had inflicted on the last poor soul who fought her. Still, the images of the

Northern man with his guts in his hands came to mind. Dry-mouthed, Cheron shifted in his seat, leaning halfway out. Compelled by his love for Ekos, he started to rise.

"Lion doesn't want you to join the fray, dearest," Sinnac said. "It would distress him a great deal.

"Yes, I do," Lion returned. "And no, it wouldn't."

Cheron ignored them both. His gaze remained fixated on Ekos, who tore at the collar at his throat. Taunted by the crowd, Ekos lashed out verbally and physically, especially to those who dared tug on his leash. The people gathered enjoyed his outbursts until he punched one of them to the gut. The man doubled forward, blood spilling from his mouth. Ekos finished him off with a savage backhand.

The crowd went silent and backed away from Ekos. Wild-eyed, spittle flinging from his mouth, he yelled, "Cowards. Fight me yourselves if you want glory!"

Sinnac let loose a dry chuckle. "He doesn't disappoint, does he?"

Cheron didn't trust himself to speak. He'd been tricked into believing whatever kept Ekos safe through his captivity would continue to bless him with immunity from Sinnac's wrath. But it hadn't.

"Kill for Atyx's glory!" Sinnac yelled.

And the battle began.

Chapter Twenty-One

CONFIRMING CHERON'S WORST fears, Ekos immediately tripped to prove he was no warrior. As he stumbled, his helmet rolled off his head and landed at Isa's foot, clattering on the tiled ground. Luckily, Isa wasn't expecting him to be such a klutz and nearly twisted her ankle on the rolling scrap of armor. Being overestimated saved him. The irony might have delighted Cheron if not for the overwhelming worry twisting his guts like dry rags. Ekos wouldn't last very long, not against a trained fighter.

"Are you okay, my love?" Sinnac asked again.

"No," he bit out, not bothering to conceal his anger. "Stop this. They are unevenly matched, dishonorably so."

Sinnac nodded vigorously as if he'd received an answer to various questions at once. Whatever vision he had for their future together went up in flames. His gray eyes ferried the smoke to the afterlife.

Cheron shifted uncomfortably in his seat while he watched Ekos scramble for some semblance of a defensive position. He crouched low to the ground and circled, letting the long blade of his scimitar drag. The noise made Cheron's teeth grind, his eye twitch, his heart race. Maybe that was the point. Maybe Ekos decided he'd die annoying as many of his enemies as possible.

"Pick up the blade and fight!" Sinnac shouted, throwing a grape toward the spectacle. "I know you can lift it!"

Ekos continued to keep distance between himself and the advancing Isa. Although she gained confidence by the minute, she held back from outright lunging toward him. She executed a series of quick darts toward his throat, thigh, and stomach, but didn't put much force into the blows. She tested Ekos's reflexes and skills with the blade, which were nonexistent from what Cheron had witnessed.

When she finally did attack, she knocked the sword from Ekos's hand. Ekos yelped in pain. Cheron didn't see blood—not yet—but he gripped his hand to his chest and hissed in pain. Bones were probably broken.

Sinnac yawned and waved in the direction of the battle. "And she was worried."

Yes, Isa had seemed more concerned than when she'd fought the Northern man. Ekos had said they were special in the same way, and Cheron had seen evidence that might be the case. Namely, Ekos's ability to summon light and his odd strength. But Cheron didn't know what good that would do him here if Isa had similar powers.

"He's done," Sinnac said, sounding bored. "Will you save him, rebel?"

Instantly, Cheron snapped back to his trial to obtain Hell's Echo. Hadn't Ekos said that exact same thing? Yes, Cheron remembered. During his trial, he'd refused. If Cheron had revealed himself to save his lover, the rebellion died and tyranny won. Now the answer wasn't as clear. He was already exposed, and Sinnac already had him in his grasp.

Cheron wanted the amulet on his chest, to feel the warm glow of the goddess's approval or the burn of her ire. Sinnac, as if guessing his thoughts, clutched Kalin's talisman and gave Cheron a thin, humorless smile.

On the stage below, Ekos abandoned the pretense of knowing how to fight and ran. As he fled, his hand kept going up to the collar around his throat. He was trying to remove it, Cheron realized.

"Glory, glory, glory," the crowd chanted.

"Will you save him?" Sinnac asked again. "Or will you be my partner in a new world?"

The decision became clear. Previously, with Aethel, the choice had been between saving his love or protecting the rebellion. Here, the choice was between saving himself or saving someone the goddess had selected to help him on his journey. Kalin had marked Ekos. Cheron needed to protect him until he fulfilled his purpose.

Cheron sprang from his seat and shoved through the crowd to the arena below. Along the way, he removed the crown of flowers from his head. Using the wadded-up fabric of his discarded outfit, he did his best to wipe the paint from his face. Scars were beautiful to his people, and he'd fight as a Northern man.

Jeers followed him. Free from the constraints placed on them by Sinnac, the people of Wren Gardens pelted him with food from their tables and spat on him as he passed. A few braced their bodies against his to slow him, but Cheron gave these men a savage growl and they immediately slunk off to the side, muttering dark condemnations but letting him pass.

Cheron stood behind Ekos and Isa. "I'm here," he told Ekos.

"Yes, I see that. Go away," Ekos screamed. "You'll only get yourself killed!"

The concern he heard in Ekos's voice heightened his bloodlust and his single-minded determination to protect him.

"Ah, here's our Northern usurper," Isa said. "I told Sinnac you'd choose honor over practicality."

"I chose love," Cheron said.

Ekos's groan was almost louder than Isa's. He added, "You unbelievably dumb shit!"

Cheron smiled at his outrage. "Get the collar off. I'll hold her back."

"You'll try," Isa snarled, but her voice lacked some of the confidence from before.

She charged directly toward Ekos, who stood rooted to the spot, worriedly looking at Cheron. In her desperation, she was clumsier than normal. This saved them both. Before she closed the gap, Cheron rammed her with his shoulder, sending her crashing to the ground.

"Run!" he shouted at Ekos. "Get your collar off!"

"You run! You don't know what she is!"

Cheron growled. "At this point, we're both dying together if that is to be our fate. Now go!"

Snarling in frustration but submitting to common sense, Ekos sprinted off. His glorious hair streamed in a rush of gold behind him. Marveling at his beauty, perhaps for the last time, Cheron prayed to Kalin for Ekos's safety, forgetting to pray for his own, and steeled himself for the battle ahead.

"Move, you fool!" Spittle flew from Isa's mouth while she seethed and tried to charge past him. When he didn't relent, she fell back and paced while she searched for a way through his defenses.

She wasn't going to find one. Eventually, she'd have to accept that and fight.

"Very well," she sneered. "Die for him, then."

Their blades clamored together. Like Ekos, she was much stronger than her slender, delicate-boned frame suggested, and the force of her heavy blow nearly knocked the sword from Cheron's hands. He recovered quickly and lunged toward her stomach. The attack didn't penetrate flesh, but it did force her to back up even farther to avoid being impaled on his blade.

She snarled, "You stupid savage. He can't take the collar off, anyway. Not without the key. Step aside."

"I'd gut myself before I let you get to him."

Isa gave his heartfelt declaration a loud, unimpressed growl. Deft with the blade and lightning fast, she sprang toward him, aiming for his upper thigh. Cheron turned sideways so her thrust only grazed the side of his leg. The thin cut she sliced into his flesh bled freely. Worse, it stung.

"Move," Isa said. "Or the next one goes through your gut."

"You aim too high."

Evenly matched, the two circled, searching for an opportune moment to strike. Isa had relaxed her shoulders and settled into the rhythm of battle. Cheron admired the sleek lines of her body and the way she controlled the blade with effortless precision.

Isa taunted him, "He's not coming back. He's left you here to die while he runs off with his little whore son."

Lion was Ekos's son? The revelation stunned Cheron, but he didn't let his guard drop. If he allowed distractions to turn his head, Isa would run him through in a matter of seconds.

"I—" Isa cut off her taunt. Eyes wide, she dropped her jaw along with her weapon. "No, it can't be. Sinnac wouldn't have given him the key."

A long shadow fell over them both. People screamed. Mothers picked up their children and ran.

Behind him, Cheron heard the sound of scraping claws and the taut flap of a sail unfurling in the wind. He recalled hearing the same noise during his trial. Then, in the fantasy, it had been dragon wings, but that wasn't possible. Dragons had vanished from the world, along with the gods.

Cheron couldn't spare a moment to check to see if it was Ekos. He had to keep his focus trained on Isa. She recovered from whatever shocked her and spared a quick glance in the direction of Sinnac's throne. Cheron thought he heard the man scream, "Atyx needs him to unleash Hell's Echo! Do not harm him!"

Isa bared her teeth and shook her head. "Last chance to move," she told Cheron.

"No."

"Be crushed like the insect you are. I don't care what use my master has for you!"

Her body shook as she collapsed on the ground. In an instant, her metal armor buckled, bent, and launched from her body. The snap from the joints breaking rang in Cheron's ears. Her limbs contorted in an odd, jittering way reminiscent of an electrical shock.

Cheron took a step forward, sword raised. At that moment, massive talons sprang from her back. Her skin transformed into scales. The white of her eyes vanished, as did the blue. Yellow now, they blinked slowly in a reptilian fashion.

Seconds later, Isa vanished. He stood face-to-face with a massive dragon. She was the color of blue veins, the red of spilled blood. Her jaws opened, and then she was nothing but blackness and the sharp white of teeth.

Chapter Twenty-Two

ISA LIFTED HER massive, scaly foot. Its shadow blotted out Cheron's and that of all other living creatures in the area. There weren't many left. Upturned chairs, some tossed haphazardly away from tables, littered the grass of the nearly empty pavilion. Off in the distance, children cried. Cheron imagined their parents pressing the small bodies against their chests as they fled.

Amidst the chaos Cheron tried to process the odd turn of events.

Dragons had vanished from the world when the gods did. This truth had been passed down along with the basics of arithmetic and how to navigate using the stars. Immutable fact. Or so everyone thought. Overcome with wonder, Cheron stared at an impossibility in motion.

As the clawed foot descended, the world around Cheron grew darker and darker. Mindful of his own state of shock, he tried to get his limbs to cooperate, to move, but he remained immobile—rapt and foolish.

Isa's foot stomped into the floor, shooting up dirt and tiles. Tremors shook the earth beneath him, sending reverberations through Cheron's body. His legs wobbled and he toppled. "Kalin, forgive me," he said and cast his eyes to the ground to pray that Ekos was indeed the other creature and that he would be safe.

"Do not kill him!" Sinnac shrieked from somewhere.

A thundering crash snapped Cheron's attention away from the other man. Isa reeled backward, shrieking in anger and quite possibly pain. A thin trail of white liquid sprayed from her neck. Another dragon, this one a golden yellow, snapped its jaws toward her head. Isa stomped backward and reared. The ground shook, rattling Cheron's teeth.

The golden dragon slung its tail, hitting Isa broadside. Massive golden wings unfurled, veined an odd white in the sun, and flapped in a display of power. The creature craned its neck and drew in air. Immediately after, white lightning erupted from its mouth.

Isa launched herself to the sky to avoid the full force of the blast, but the blow caught the edge of one of her dusky blue wings. The holes from the assault instantly seared at the edges, turning the wounds a charcoal black. Her wail of agony rang in Cheron's ears, and—for a moment—he felt a stab of pity for the amazing creature.

His sympathies didn't last.

Rather than direct her fury at the aggressor, Isa focused on Cheron. Like her opponent, she drew her head backward and inhaled a massive reservoir of air. Remembering the electrical blast from the other dragon's mouth, Cheron darted behind a nearby brick wall and hoped that would be enough to stave off the blow.

Fire erupted around him. The flames seared the rock against his back. The tips of his hair singed, and he thanked the goddess it didn't catch fire. Foul-smelling billows of smoke coiled around him. Cheron knelt where the air was more breathable, holding his hand against his mouth and nose to block the worst of noxious smell.

One of the beasts let out a bellow that sounded almost human, near to grieving.

The massive golden dragon took to the air. Instead of bolting toward Isa, pressing the advantage of her serious injuries, the creature scanned the ground beneath until its eyes rested on Cheron. When it saw him, its mouth split open into a...smile. Its yellow eyes crinkled at the edges and narrowed to slits.

The sound of wings flapping diverted its attentions. Both of them witnessed Isa fly up to the clouds, becoming a small black dot against the deep blue of the sky.

The golden dragon rumbled a noise Cheron thought resembled a deep, frustrated sigh and gave his wings an agitated flap as if contemplating pursuit. In the end, the beast settled on remaining grounded.

Heart beating against his chest, Cheron stood perfectly still as the beast maneuvered its considerable bulk around the now empty pavilion. The creature's scales caught the sunlight as it moved, nearly blinding Cheron when they reflected just right. The head, massive and wedged like a viper's, joggled as the creature sniffed the air. A forked tongue darted in and out. Close up, Cheron saw strange white veins corded over the entire body. They were most visible on the breast and wings, where the creature's skin was a lighter shade of cream.

"He-hello." Cheron fumbled over the word. "I'm... I'm going to go search for my friend. He was an enemy of the other dragon."

The dragon snorted and shook its massive head but let him pass unmolested.

Everyone, including Sinnac, had retreated. No, not all, it would seem. A curly head of hair peeped out from under the cushions atop the platform where the twin thrones sat perched and undisturbed. Lion?

To Cheron's bafflement, the boy emerged and hopped up the moment he saw the dragon. Arms outstretched as if running into an embrace, he went straight toward the beast. Cheron, remembering his promise to Ekos, intercepted him. Fierce for the first time since they'd met, Lion pushed him aside and continued forward.

The dragon's strange smile increased tenfold. He gave his wings a slight flap, a gesture oddly resembling a wave. Then, he bent low toward the ground to allow the young man to climb on.

Lion mounted him. Once perched on the shoulder blades, he let out a delighted clap like he'd just mounted a pony at a town fair. The dragon took some exception to this. It rotated its massive head and gave the man a narrow-eyed glare. Quelled, Lion gave him a tilted, sheepish smile and said, "I knew it! I knew you weren't lying!"

The dragon flipped its tail left and right as though slandered by such a consideration.

"Sorry," Lion apologized and patted its neck.

By now, Cheron suspected he knew the golden dragon's name, by the way the creature strutted around, its head high and tail thudding lightly on the stone as if it didn't have a care in the world. But he just couldn't force himself to acknowledge the truth, which both excited and terrified him.

"What? I said sorry," Lion repeated to the irate dragon, shouting this time. "Do you want me to prostrate myself before you like Sinnac?"

Mollified, the creature shook its head and strolled around the pavilion to inspect the goods and delicacies left behind. He ate the roasting pig in one gulp and sniffled at the scattered blankets. As the dragon inhaled, the fabric coiled forward.

"Should we go?" Lion asked.

The creature shook his head again and pointed a long claw at the trove of wedding gifts. Gold coins, jewels, and other valuables were heaped in a pile. Using his paws, he scooped up the entire cache and put it in a membrane pocket close to his belly.

The dragon and the young man were...robbing the place?

"Ekos," Cheron bellowed. He couldn't deny the truth anymore. "That *is* you."

The dragon snorted and grinned. Long, sharp teeth gleamed as bright as his scales.

"Come on! We must get the relic!" Cheron said, adding a battle cry. "Let us strike now while Sinnac's beast is occupied."

Ekos exchanged looks with Lion, who shrugged his thin shoulders in a way Cheron interpreted as befuddled.

"Come on!" he roared again.

Ekos shook his massive head. He grabbed hold of the two thrones and turned his head to look at one, then the other, and then at Cheron.

"Just put one down!" Cheron yelled, understanding the dilemma.

Shrugging, Ekos opened his mouth and swallowed Cheron whole.

Chapter Twenty-Three

CHERON'S PREVIOUS WARM thoughts evaporated as he became waterlogged on drool. He bobbled up and down against Ekos's tongue and the roof of his mouth. Fear didn't cinch his stomach into a tight knot, despite his hatred of heights. He could feel the buoyancy of the air beneath them and imagine the long fall. But Cheron felt safe. Ekos wouldn't hurt him.

Eventually, Ekos spat him out unceremoniously onto a rough stone floor. In his massive talons, he still clutched the twin thrones he'd stolen after the wedding. Cheron, covered in gooey slime from his time in Ekos's mouth, griped, "You could have left one of the chairs and carried *me* instead."

Still in dragon form, Ekos snorted. Afterward, he vanished deeper inside the cavern; his scales scraped against the sides of the cave, cutting deeper into already existent grooves. A few scales remained lodged in the smooth slabs of rock, jutting out like brilliant yellow spikes against the gray.

Lion crouched beside Cheron and laughed. While the boy's trills rubbed his already chapped pride, Cheron understood, or at least assumed, Lion meant no malice. He was both amused by Cheron's appearance and delighted to be free at last from his predicament.

"You made it," Cheron said. "How was your ride?"

Lion held his hands aloft as though gliding on a breeze and said, "Glorious!"

"Um-hum," Cheron said, dragon slime dripping from his chin.

Perhaps feeling a bit guilty, Lion bit his lip and added, "I was also really cold."

"But the trip was glorious, nevertheless?"

His enthusiasm returned full force. Cheron had never seen such deep dimples. Infectious as it was, Cheron couldn't help returning the smile and giving Lion a fond pat on his shoulder. He was glad to see him free and had high hopes for the young man's future.

Ekos cleared his throat. "Young for you, isn't he?"

"I'm eighteen!" Lion shouted back. "Not a kid anymore!"

Cheron jolted to his feet and gave his hands a quick, conscience-stricken inspection. He hadn't been touching Lion that way, but Ekos's tone made him feel like they'd been caught tongue tangled and pantless.

Human again, his expression pinched and furious, Ekos continued, "You are a kid. And you're going to school, and you're not getting involved with hairy bears on half-brained quests to do...whatever it is he's doing!"

"The goddess guided me—" Cheron said.

"Misled you, more like!"

"That's sacrilege!"

Ekos gave Cheron's condemnation a full-body shrug. Even his feet shuffled, propelling him forward until his outstretched finger poked Cheron in the chest. "But true. You honorable dimwit."

As suddenly as his furor started, it stopped. Ekos inspected Cheron head to toe, puckering his lips and nibbling his mouth. The black of his pupil dominated the clear blue of his eyes.

"What?" Cheron asked. He hoped he didn't have a dark smudge on his head. Goddess, that would be embarrassing. Thinking perhaps the decorative paint that Sinnac's people had smeared on him for the wedding ceremony remained, Cheron used his hand to wipe his face, vigorously scrubbing just in case. "What?" he asked again when Ekos didn't answer.

Ekos dropped his eyes to Cheron's torso and kept his focus there.

Lion followed the direction of the gaze and flushed a deep red.

Finally, Cheron saw himself. Saliva adhered the thin fabric of his wedding garments to his body. The outline of his cock protruded. To his shame, especially since they'd been arguing about the validity of the goddess's quest, he realized he was half-erect.

"Go to your room," Ekos told Lion. His voice was low, controlled.

"We're in a cave," Lion pointed out.

"Yes. Fine. Go to your cave room, then."

"Which room is mine? We only just got here!"

"Okay, go down the tunnel and keep walking. Follow the sound of rushing water. If you encounter a chamber filled with lush bedding, fantastical treasure, and wonders the likes of which you've never seen, that's my room. You can take a blanket, or two," Ekos amended after some thought, "and keep going. Your cave room is where you put those blankets. Understood?"

Lion grumbled and twisted his mouth in protest, but Ekos held firm. "Go on," he repeated.

"Okay," Lion said. "But I'm taking whatever I want."

"Fine, fine, fine," Ekos said, waving him off. "Do whatever. But go. Go, go, go."

Once he was gone, the two stood separate, staring at each other. Cheron tried to keep his voice light despite the heaviness in his chest. He said, "You're a dragon?"

"Yes," Ekos said. Some of the impatience he showed with Lion remained. "I am."

"You're not going to eat me, are you?"

Ekos kept his eyes fixed on Cheron's cock and said, "Yes. But you're going to like it."

Heat rushed through his body. When Ekos vanquished the space between them and placed his hand on Cheron's neck, stroking the blub of his Adam's apple with the pad of his thumb, the flow of blood stopped and started. His heart, along with the rest of the world, operated according to the man's whims and wouldn't beat anymore if Ekos willed it.

"Earlier, you said you didn't want me," Cheron reminded him.

"You said the same," Ekos said.

"I lied."

Ekos's lips twitched. He tilted his head at the memory, giving one of his smug smiles. "I lied too," he admitted. "I do that."

"We've got a lot in common," Cheron said, trying to chuckle, but he couldn't manage with so much pressure on his chest.

Down the hall, Lion yelled, "This place is a maze! I can't find anything."

Ekos's hand dropped from Cheron's throat. His eyebrows drew together. "Come with me," he told Cheron. "To my lair."

"Do you have to call your home a lair?"

Lights danced in his eyes as if a candle flickered behind. "Is the dragon thing a problem for you?"

"It's daunting," Cheron admitted.

Ekos placed the tip of his finger on Cheron's jawline and stroked its outline. "What can I do to comfort you, my fearsome rebel bear?"

"I—"

"Ekos!" Lion shrieked. Both of them jumped at the racket echoing down the hallway. "I'm lost!"

Ekos sighed deeply and offered his hand. "I'm going to assume you were about to say, 'I want you to suck my dick until I grow scales' before being cut off?"

"I'll never grow scales," Cheron teased and took the offered hand. "You'll be sucking for a *very* long time."

"That's my point, bear."

Ekos guided him down the path Lion had taken.

Soon, the darkness of the caverns forced Cheron to rely totally on Ekos's vision. He didn't mind. He knew it to be strong. But he did wonder why Ekos didn't light the place using his magic. In the end, he figured the other man enjoyed maintaining the connection, so Cheron squeezed the hand nested in his.

"Um," Ekos mumbled in pleasure.

The sound of running water overtook the clamor of blood flowing through his own body, but only barely. Light from crystals lining the cave walls, dim at first, eventually illuminated the hallways.

The first thing he saw wasn't encouraging. A skeleton, its bones yellowing and flaking, rested in the corner.

"Uh," Ekos said. "I have no idea how that got here."

"The body is old," Cheron said. "*Very* old."

"Okay, yes. It's the body of an enemy. Too disconcerting?"

"It does give the room a bit of a lair ambiance, yes."

"I'll get rid of it. *Later.* We're almost to my lai— chamber. Bedroom."

Cheron snorted. "At least tell me he did something nefarious."

"Came here to impale me on a spike. Bad enough, from my perspective."

"Did you give him a swift, honorable death?"

Ekos beamed. "I did! And here we are. Just in time."

They entered into a large room cut from the earth by claws. Above them, crystal geode formed an arch that stretched on like the horizon. The color was the same blue of Ekos's eyes. "Beautiful," Cheron said.

"Cozy, right?"

"Quite so."

Plush cushions covered almost the entire left half of the room. The fabrics were varied but exclusively in jewel-toned colors. The bedding was raised on a platform that overlooked a vast sea of treasure unlike Cheron had seen before. Beside all the other treasures, Ekos had placed the two thrones from the wedding.

"You could have left one of those," Cheron said, picking at the old wound to his pride.

"So you've said." Ekos chuckled as he led him to the top of the platform where a bed raised on a marble pedestal rose above the rest. Expecting a hard surface, Cheron was pleasantly surprised by a soft crib that cradled the contours of his body without sucking him into its folds. He held out his arms for Ekos.

"Stay here, I'm going to go get Lion settled," Ekos told him.

Ashamed his lusts made him forget about poor Lion, who was probably wandering aimlessly, Cheron flushed and said, "Go. But come back soon before something else disastrous happens. I can't take much more waiting."

Chapter Twenty-Four

NOTHING DISASTROUS HAPPENED, but Cheron did fall asleep. He woke to a soft hand caressing his cheek, blue eyes, and a rosy, half-tilted smile that hinted at mischief and perhaps a tad of playful villainy. It was the countenance of a beast who took the skeletons out of his closet and used them to decorate the halls of his lair. Why, then, was Cheron instantly erect?

"Ekos," he mumbled.

"Expecting someone else?"

"No, but...what's going on?"

While Cheron slept, Ekos had swapped out Cheron's clothes. He now wore a long, silk robe similar in design to his wedding garments. Only these were a thin, transparent white. The fabric was so fine, so delicate, it felt like spiderwebs sweeping against his heated skin.

Ekos, who straddled him, was naked except for a fur-lined brocade cloak. Magnificent, otherworldly, he dominated with a mere gaze.

Confused, and feeling foolish, Cheron realized he'd also been washed and smelled of raspberries and lilacs, which wasn't the manliest of scents but a great deal better than dragon slobber. He swallowed to wet his throat. He'd probably been snoring. "How did you manage all this?" Cheron asked.

"You hibernate, bear."

"How long have I been sleeping?"

"Awhile."

"Why didn't you wake me?"

"Hm, enjoying the show." Ekos traced the line of Cheron's mouth with his tongue. "And daydreaming about all the wicked things I'm going to do to you."

"What a coincidence. I was having a similar dream."

"Were you tied up in your vision? Because you were in mine."

Cheron tried to stretch but found his arms were bound above his head. To test their limits and his own, he gave the soft, velvety constraints a few good tugs. Solid. And an unexpectedly good butterfly knot. Wide awake now, Cheron regarded the situation with equal parts anticipation and confusion. "This is..."

"Going to finish that thought?" Ekos asked.

"Not quite what I expected you'd be into."

"Let me show you what I'm into."

Using the tips of his fingers, Ekos trailed a path from Cheron's pelvis to his throat, wounding him. Right after, he followed the same path with his mouth, gutting him. Pent-up frustration—the need to touch, stroke, kiss, conquer—had Cheron buckling against the bindings.

Ekos chuckled. "Honestly, I thought you'd be a bit more difficult to master."

Denying his lack of control ceased being an option as precome molded the fabric against his erection. Cheron made excuses instead. "It's been a long time."

"How long?"

"Two years."

Ekos whistled. The air from the expulsion grazed the wet tip of Cheron's cock. He struggled under the demands of his arousal, thrusting upward to simulate the maneuver his body knew by instinct. Ekos puckered his full mouth and blew again, and again, and again until Cheron moaned. "My rebel likes that."

Having Ekos's mouth so near him tantalized and tortured. Cheron shifted his weight to the best of his abilities to position his erection nearer Ekos's mouth. He'd settle for a nose bump, a brush against the cheek. Anything. But, mostly, he wanted to see if he'd grow scales as Ekos had promised.

"Do you think I'm going to stick that thing in my mouth by accident?"

"Hoping."

Ekos shook his head. Goddess, Cheron loved the way his eyes turned to black whirlpools. "Not likely, bear. Beg."

"What?"

"Beg me."

Absolutely not is what a proud warrior should have said. Raised to be tough, to stand strong, to trust in the goddess, Cheron's breed was bred to endure. He was a Northerner, not a simpering man from Wren Gardens. That's why he said *please* in his deepest, manliest voice.

"Please what?"

"Please suck my cock." Cheron angled his body nearer Ekos's mouth. "Have mercy."

"Why should I?"

"What!"

Ekos outright guffawed at Cheron's outrage. "Offer me something. Incentivize me to act in your pleasure."

Cheron couldn't quite decide if he loved or hated the game they were playing. Certainly, the torment heightened his fervor, but he wanted to make room for some tenderness in their lovemaking too. "You have all of me. Always."

Ekos tilted his head to the side as if to say *really*. "I'm a dragon. I love treasure, treasure like Hell's Echo."

"Sinnac has it."

"Yes, but he can't use the relic. Only the one who passed the test can."

"Then what good is giving it to you?"

His mouth drew nearer to Cheron's cock. "Symbolic."

The tone had a viper's bite, but then, Ekos's words always did, so Cheron didn't dwell on the request or on the sly smile peeping along the edges of Ekos's mouth. He was always clever, confident, unnervingly savvy. The bedroom version of him wouldn't be any different. Whatever game he was playing now was one they could enjoy together.

"Very well, dragon. My treasure, along with the rest of me, is yours."

An expression Cheron struggled to read vanished as Ekos's head dipped downward. He anticipated Ekos would remove the thin swathe of fabric first, but he used his hand to draw Cheron's erection toward his mouth and took the tip of him along with the silk, and sucked—gently at first, then with increasing force. Cheron's hips lifted to mimic the rhythm.

"I need to touch you," Cheron panted. "Please."

Ekos's response was to press the tip of his tongue inside the slit. He tugged at the base of the shaft at the same time. A broken moan escaped from Cheron. Abusing his goddess's gift of strength to eliminate his bonds might be an offense, but Cheron was starting to wonder how much he cared about blasphemy. The thoughts only intensified when Ekos took him entirely into his mouth.

Ekos broke away. "My poor helpless rebel."

Ekos's breathing came out in short gasps that undercut the illusion of discipline he was trying so hard to maintain. Seeing him that way—cheeks flushed, eyes bright, lips wet from giving pleasure—almost drove Cheron over the edge.

"Let me touch you. Let me hold you."

Eyebrow raised, smirking, Ekos told him *no*, which Cheron only hoped was a precursor to *yes*.

Since submitting worked before, he tried begging, "Please…"

Ekos continued to massage Cheron's cock. The wetness of the fabric pulled against his pubic hairs, creating pleasant tinges of pain that kept his nerves in a state of anticipation. Obviously relishing the control, Ekos pressed his mouth against Cheron's neck, nibbling the skin there. Still breathing hard, he said, "No, you're going to lie there and behave yourself. Say it, say you'll behave yourself for me."

Cheron resisted. This way of lovemaking felt foreign to him. Such time with Aethel had been brief, impassioned. They'd coupled moments after unclothing and spreading olive oil for lubrication. The battlefield had been the same. During the night, he'd hear men undress, ease their urges, then drift off to sleep.

This was better. But very different. Cheron wasn't sure if it was right.

Determined to have his way, Ekos whispered the command against his neck, all the while stroking, teasing, licking the hard parts of Cheron's body that yielded and turned tender. "Say it. Say you'll behave. Say you don't ever want me to let you leave."

"I want you to keep me here." Right be damned. The goddess was banished to another realm, and the North was very far away. No one, Cheron decided, would overhear his humiliated admission.

Right up against his ear, Ekos praised him, "Good. Now say you'll behave."

"I'll behave."

Strong without the aid of divinity, Ekos effortlessly turned him over so he was on his stomach. At last, he pulled the fabric away, exposing Cheron's skin to direct contact. Not quite knowing what Ekos intended to do, he contorted in surprise when Ekos parted his ass cheeks and thrust his tongue inside.

"What are you doing?"

Ekos didn't bother to lyricize. "Fucking you with my tongue."

And then he went right back to work. Cheron, feeling sinful, fought his own tide of desire at first, but then submitted fully, rutting against the bedding the way he wanted to take Ekos.

Finally, Ekos pulled away.

"Release me," Cheron said. "Let me finish."

"I'm going to finish for you."

Cheron gasped when he felt the tip of Ekos's cock press against his flesh. To highlight his intent, Ekos thrust against Cheron's butt. "Northern man too proud to be taken? Too kingly? Too majestic?"

Ekos's taunts roused more than his ire. He'd never received satisfaction this way, but Ekos wanted a show of trust, and he'd give it to him. "Take me, then. Claim me."

Ekos, given permission, wavered.

Cheron said, "That's your cue to jab that brutish, clunky thing inside the beast. You can pretend I'm a quivering maiden if that helps you along."

"That sounds familiar," Ekos laughed, giving the smile a rueful memory. "You and the basilisk related now?"

"Practically cousins."

"You insolent rebel."

"Punish me."

Ekos, over whatever had made him hesitate before, grabbed Cheron by the hips and ground their bodies together. The sensation of being penetrated overwhelmed Cheron. Willpower broke down and his self-reassurances that he'd hold out until Ekos sated his carnal needs were tested with each surge.

"Cheron," Ekos panted, sounding every bit as broken. "Hurry up and come already."

Cheron, surrendering completely, did as told.

Chapter Twenty-Five

EKOS REMAINED ASTRIDE Cheron long after they were both spent. Cheron, for his part, had nothing intelligible left to say. Had he opened his mouth, he probably would have babbled incoherently for the goddess's mercy. Would he have felt warmth or a stinging burn on his chest if he'd asked? Cheron didn't know. But he was content now, at home in his lover's embrace.

"Regrets?" Cheron asked.

"No," Ekos eventually said. "Confused. Also tired." To support the claim, he let out a massive, jaw-popping yawn. "Let's go get washed up."

Cheron followed Ekos toward the sound of rushing water. A natural spring trickled in the middle of the cave, flowing into a pool. Ekos got to the edge and dipped a toe; instantly after, he drew back, hissing and clattering his teeth in a way that was dramatic to the point of theater.

Ekos said, "People can't bathe in boiling water, I assume?"

"No," Cheron confirmed and laughed. "I'm afraid not. You'd have boiled bear for dinner."

"Drat. Well, you'll have to rub me to keep me warm."

Grinning broadly, looking forward to more intimacy, Cheron said, "Deal."

Tapestries, most depicting dragons, lined the walls of the bath. While they washed each other, Cheron studied the designs. The one Cheron stood in front of illustrated a village scene that would have been tranquil if not for the massive beast breathing fire over the sylvan landscape.

"Ah, Great Aunt Anna. She was a fearsome gal. Loved snakes and a good barbecue."

Cheron recoiled.

"Not barbecued *people*. We dragons have better taste than that."

"How did you manage to turn back?" Cheron asked.

"Hm?"

"Into a dragon. How did you get the collar off?"

The swagger returned. Ekos smirked and said, "I stole the key from Sinnac when he bound me in his chamber. I knew Isa would confirm the story about the diamond. I knew he'd take me to his chamber to torture me; it's the same as sex for him. I only hoped I could use his cruelty to my advantage."

"Bravo."

"Thanks." Ekos got out of the pool and gave the praise a slight bow, bending his knee and turning his hands up in the air. Water dripped from his hair onto the floor. Cheron enjoyed the way channels of water cut through the landscape of his body, sliding the length of his torso in a path Cheron wanted to trace with his tongue. Ekos, as if knowing his thoughts, said, "Come back to bed."

"Only if you insist," Cheron said with a wolfish smile.

"Not for that. A tattoo. I want to add to your story."

Pleased Ekos knew the function of his tattoos, Cheron beamed at the gesture, which was intimate on a new level. Much like the tapestries, his markings served to tell his history and to bind the significant people in his life to him. Ekos asking to make a contribution spoke of a greater affection than Cheron had previously dared hope for.

"Yes," he agreed. "Do you actually have supplies here?"

"I'm a dragon. My kind are known for our hoarding issues."

That meant *yes* Cheron found out later, as he lay flat on his stomach with Ekos perched on his back, tapping an iron needle against his upper shoulder blades. They'd been at it for some time, and Ekos still wouldn't give him so much as a hint regarding design. The pain was manageable only because the pleasure of the other man's nearness canceled out any discomfort.

Lion tried to spy for him, but Ekos hid the art from him too. "You'll see the tattoo when I'm done," he told the young man. "Until then, piss off."

"Okay."

Lion watched Cheron's face with keen interest. Uncharacteristic of him, his mouth was lifted in a knowing, secretive smirk. Occasionally, when Cheron grunted or clenched his fists, his eyebrow raised. He looked on the verge of saying something the entire time, like there were a million words caught in a breeze, and he was reaching up for the proper one. He drew back empty-handed each time, though.

"Something need saying?" Cheron asked him, prompting him to get on with it.

He bit his lip to keep the smile from spreading. He failed.

Ekos paused his work. "Lion, maybe you'd like to go pick out a treasure."

"Or two." The smirk spread to Lion's voice.

"*One.*"

"Three," Lion returned.

"One, you little devil."

Lion strolled toward Cheron and dipped toward his ear. "I want to tell you something," he whispered.

"Okay, okay. *Two*."

Clapping his hands, Lion left.

"Was he...extorting you?"

"No, no, no," Ekos said.

"Certainly sounded that way. Not to mention ominous for me. Are you going to eat me in a way I don't like now?"

Ekos sounded genuinely stung when he said, "I would never hurt you. I love...rebels. Also, I don't generally give my dinners elaborate, time-consuming tattoos."

Cheron's heart soared. He forgot the odd exchange between Lion and Ekos entirely under the strain of so much hope. "You love *rebels*? In general?"

"Yes. Dedicated lot. Very tenacious, not easily deterred, not even when you dislodge their grappling hooks and send them plummeting thousands of feet to their deaths."

Cheron tried to turn to scowl at Ekos's dark humor. It wasn't difficult to imagine him raising a supercilious eyebrow at some pour soul's climbing hook before dislodging the lifeline with his toe.

Ekos forced his head back down. "Hold still. You'll mess up the design."

Cheron mumbled into the bedding. "You're not as hard as you talk. Lion proves my point. You've been a father to him."

"Yes, well, the boy reminds me of myself. Did you hear him extort me a bit ago?"

Cheron laughed. "I thought you said he wasn't doing any such thing."

"Lied. But it's nothing you need to worry about. You're safe and I'm going to keep you that way."

Being taken care of was a new role for Cheron. He allowed his muscles, taut from a lifetime of being on guard, to relax and his brain to drift off to pleasant fantasies about his future with Ekos. Eventually, he'd have to go back out and reclaim the Echo from Sinnac, but for now, he enjoyed the novelty of someone else lifting his burdens.

"Bear," Ekos said. There was uncharacteristic hesitation in his voice.

"Hm?"

"Earlier, I said I loved rebels. Anything you'd like to say about—?"

"Dragons? Love them. Not a specific one. Just dragons."

"Um," Ekos said noncommittally, but Cheron heard pleasure in the slight noise. Ekos caressed the nape of Cheron's neck with the pads of his fingers, brushing aside a lock of hair before planting a tender kiss. The sensation aroused him despite the continual pricks of pain from the inking. His erection squeezed uncomfortably against the bed.

"Nearly done?" Cheron asked.

"Almost. A few finishing touches."

Normally, Cheron appreciated detail-oriented people, especially when it came to body art. Right now, he didn't much care about Ekos's craftsmanship. More than anything, he wanted to pin the other man to the bed, rip off his clothes, and tangle their bodies together. Today had already been a day of acting against Northern standards of decorum, so Cheron, keeping a dignified tone, said, "I look forward to the result."

Ekos didn't buy the feigned disinterest. "You know I can smell desire, a musty odor. I'm afraid you're going to have to wait longer. I promised Lion I'd let him see once I was done. Speaking of...plug your ears." Ekos drew in a massive breath. "Get in here, you little shit!"

The warning came too late. Cheron groaned at the racket.

"Coming, you loud-mouthed reptile!" Lion shot back, every bit as belligerent and loud. Cheron doubted he'd ever take either of them to a temple ceremony.

Soon after, Lion appeared, bright-eyed and holding a golden cup filled with several precious jewels. He tripped on the uneven ground, and a diamond the size of Cheron's knuckle rolled from the top of the cup.

"That's quite a bit more than two," Ekos told him, frowning.

"No, it's a *treasure cup*, which is *one* treasure, and I also took this..." Lion fished around in the pockets of his cloak, which Cheron noted with some wry amusement was also new, and pulled out a mirror with a golden frame. "Look, when I hold it up, I can..."

"Yes, yes. I know what it can do. Give it here."

Lion clutched the mirror against his chest.

Shaking his head, Ekos waved his fingers forward, signaling for Lion to hand it over, which he did but muttered darkly about the trickiness of dragons. Like most young men, he got over his disappointments quickly. He rushed up to Cheron to inspect Ekos's artwork.

"Wow, that's really good! Are you going to do one for me next?"

"If you can hold still."

They chatted, switching from topic to topic and ignoring Cheron. He didn't mind the familiar way the two bumped shoulders or sassed the other—he knew Ekos's feelings to be paternal—but he was dying to know what Ekos had given him.

"What is the tattoo?" Cheron asked.
"Wings," Lion said. "Dragon wings."
And Cheron did feel like he was flying.

Chapter Twenty-Six

THE NEXT DAY, Cheron woke wrapped in warm furs and tied to the bed, but Ekos was nowhere to be seen. Thinking he'd be back in due course, Cheron leaned against the soft cushions and prepared for another vigorous session of lovemaking. He hoped Ekos might trust him enough to untie him toward the climax this time. More than anything, Cheron wanted to earn the right to tangle his hands in Ekos's mass of golden hair and ride out their passions together.

At least a half hour passed. Cheron only knew because he got bored and began counting down the seconds.

Comfort wasn't an issue. The bindings were loose enough for Cheron to reposition himself had he needed. Indeed, he could have easily broken free. Impatience was another matter. Cheron enjoyed the games Ekos played, but straight-up fucking had its appeal too.

"Ekos?"

The stream trickled. Cheron strained to hear a response over the steady flow, which he was sure—despite its low volume—hid his lover's sharp retort. Ekos lingered nearby, probably laughing and waiting for him to beg. Cheron felt sure he knew his lover's game.

"Ekos. Come on."

Silence.

"Very well. *Please.*"

Still only the soft flow of water reached his waiting ears.

"Ekos!" he bellowed.

Footsteps—at last—pattered close to the entrance of the sleeping chamber. Soft brown curls, followed by worried brown eyes, peeped over the edge of the doorway. When he saw Cheron returning his curious glance, he slipped back behind the protective bulwark of the stone wall.

"Lion?" Cheron asked, befuddled by the young man's presence.

"H-hi," he stammered. "Not sleeping anymore?"

"No, where's Ekos?"

"W-well. He, uh, he. Well."

"Lion...?"

"Gone," he blurted. Equally rushed and loud, he shouted, "He's journeyed to get Hell's Echo."

"On his own!"

"Yes," Lion said, his voice a mouse-like squeak.

"Goddess on high! You let him!"

"H-he's a dragon!"

Cursing himself for a fool, Cheron twisted and turned in his restraints until they were loose. Without too much effort, which he found extra insulting since Ekos had clearly counted on Cheron's trust in him to keep him bound longer than the restraints, he broke free. Thundering in rage, he stomped across the room, pulling on his furs and searching the cache of treasure for weapons.

"You can't go after him," Lion said. "We're high up in the air."

Cheron growled in response. He yearned to get up in the young man's face the way he'd approach a disobedient soldier but stopped short. Lion's loyalties belonged to Ekos, not him. Directing his anger toward Lion wouldn't do him any good, so Cheron managed to give him a thin, humorless smile, and said, "I'll find a way."

Lion studied his feet like they were fine art. "H-he said you might get notions, and to tell you—"

"I don't care to hear his message."

Swallowing, Lion drew up to his full height and continued, "He said to tell you he did this so you two could be together."

Hearing what Ekos should have told him with his own mouth from a secondary source only enraged Cheron further. How could he care so much for a man who failed to make his own declarations of affection? Cheron launched a handful of gold coins against the wall and gritted his teeth to keep from screaming. His body heaved under his strain to keep his emotions in control.

"Thank you for telling me," Cheron said. "Now tell me how to get out of here."

"There is no wa—"

"Yes, there is. Ekos must have thought about his plan failing, of him dying. Perhaps he might leave me here to rot." The thought made the sour taste in his mouth thicken. "But you're his son. The nearest he can have to one, anyway. He'd tell you how to escape, should he not return."

Cheron determined by the way the young man's face blanched he had spoken true, but Lion lifted his chin in defiance and said, "He's trying to keep you safe."

"Yes. And I him. Show me the exit, Lion. He's facing down an entire army."

"He's a dragon. He can—"

"Isa is also a dragon. Before, Ekos had the advantage of surprise. That's gone. Tell me how to escape, Lion. Please. For Ekos's sake."

The rigid certainty left his features. His shoulders rolled forward in a slump, dispelling the illusion that he'd grown old and brave in the last few hours. Cheron had no doubt he'd one day be a fine man, but his years in captivity had stunted his development. He had little idea of who he was outside of being Ekos's chosen son.

Cheron had known many men on the field of battle. Being able to swiftly assess someone's personality was prerequisite to leading men. Lion might not know his place in the world yet, but Cheron had some sense of his measure. He doubted Lion would betray Ekos's trust, but he knew the argument he needed to make. Softening his tone, he said, "You love Ekos and would do anything for him."

Lion nodded.

"But you're worried for him?"

"He said he'd be fine."

"But you know Sinnac and Isa are cruel. You know what he faces and the consequences of him losing his battle?"

Lion flinched and chewed on the edge of his lip. "He made me promise. I gave him my word."

"He once told me honor is stupid."

"He didn't mean it," Lion said, smirking a little. "He says a lot of stuff he doesn't believe when he's worried."

"And he said he'd be fine before he left. Did he seem worried to you?"

Lion studied his feet again and rubbed the back of his head with one slender arm. That most certainly meant *yes*, but Cheron waited patiently for Lion to say the words out loud. "Ye—" Then, seeing Cheron's path of logic, Lion backtracked from the admission, practically screeching, "He's a dragon!"

This time, despite the volume of Lion's voice, the declaration lacked certainty.

"Dragons can die."

Twiddling his fingers, his eyes darting left to right, Lion considered his options. Cheron remained silent while the other man came to his own conclusions. Finally, Lion let out a massive gulp of air and said, "He'll kill me."

"He wouldn't touch a hair on your head."

"He told me you were more important to him than anything else."

Again, hearing such declarations from someone other than Ekos rankled Cheron's already wounded pride. Only Lion's own hurt at being sidelined kept Cheron from lashing out and punching a wall. "He said anything, not anyone. He would never hurt or forsake you, Lion. Defy him. I know it's difficult, that you consider it disloyal, but disobey him for his own sake. Let me go help him."

"Can you tell him you overpowered me?"

"I could. I doubt he'd buy such an account."

Lion kicked a nearby chalice and cursed, hopping in place when the metal hurt his toe. The thing clattered as it rolled along on the floor. "Okay, but if he abandons me, will you take me to academy? I want to study magic."

"Do you have the aptitude?" Cheron asked. He knew little of magic aside from the fact the skill was genetic. One couldn't simply learn magic as a trade; you had to be born with the innate ability.

"Yes." To demonstrate, Lion conjured a small flower in the palm of his hand. The plant bloomed, withered, and died. Smiling at Cheron's inhalation of surprise, Lion puffed his chest up and said, "Ekos said I need to learn better control before I do much else. He taught me some basic stuff, but dragon magic is different."

Fixated on the lingering effect of the dying flower, Cheron shook his head to clear it and then said, "I vow to take you to the academy."

"Okay, and also...please keep him from carrying me around in his mouth—it's gross! I prefer riding on top."

Cheron was about to say he preferred the same, but then he didn't want to speak of anyone's father in such a way.

Chapter Twenty-Seven

LION LED HIM through a series of twisting and turning caverns that Cheron couldn't have navigated on his own. Even Lion had his own assistance: a small, bouncing orb of light that darted in front of them, illuminating the passages.

Lion, when he saw Cheron's curious head tilt, put on a sheepish smile and said, "Ekos gave him to me after I kept getting lost. He told me I had the directional sense of a half-baked hog, and he was tired of me bellowing at all hours."

That sounded about right. Lion had a habit of bumbling through the hallways, scraping the jeweled rings he'd stolen from Ekos against the walls to mark his path. Ekos had joked about tying string to Lion's leg.

"I am grateful for its assistance," Cheron said. "I'd hate to vanish inside this maze."

"Same," Lion agreed. "And it's a he. His name is Vivi."

"My deepest apologies to Vivi."

The thing bobbled in the air.

Cheron wondered how much sentience the wisp possessed. Occasionally, the orb paused and swished back and forth—its light cutting a bright slash through the darkness—as if considering the next course of action. Then, it backtracked through caverns they'd already traversed. Lion would chat with him occasionally, encouraging the tiny light to continue forward by offering him a chance to sunbathe.

Finally, after he butted against a solid wall a few times, Cheron said, "Are you sure he knows where he's going?"

"Yes, Ekos said Vivi was addled after years of nonuse and to expect some wandering. He always gets me where I want to go, though."

Wander was a generous word. *Idle* fit the description better.

Lion stopped defending Vivi's abilities after the bright orb sat in one spot for over ten minutes. Worriedly, he chewed on his lip and said, "Vivi, take us out of here. The exit. Find the exit."

Vivi bobbed up and down like a fishing lure in still water but continued forward soon after. As they traveled, the air grew more stagnant, darker, and Cheron smelled the musk of mold. Whenever he put his hand on the wall, a slick slime coated the tips of his fingers. The stuffy, breezeless world of the cave had grown as stale as its air.

"We have to be close," Lion said. "We've been down here for forever."

Normally, Cheron thought youth exaggerated. Right now, however, forever sounded about right. Time didn't speed up as they traversed farther through the tunnel, which at points pinched into an impossibly tight passageway that Cheron had to turn and wiggle through to pass. Rock scraped his back, leaving the skin raw and stinging under a thick coat of sweat. Sometimes, when the claustrophobia became unbearable, Cheron swore Lion's panting breath seared his heated flesh like dragon fire.

"I think I feel a draft," Cheron said at last, hoping it wasn't wishful thinking.

"Maybe. Yes! I hear a gust! I hear the wind!"

They breathed a simultaneous sigh of relief when they heard the rushing waves of a powerful storm. Rain splattered against the outside wall. There were occasional crisp shatterings of ice, hinting at bursts of hail. Although the gales sounded fierce, Cheron would have welcomed being swept away with open arms.

Cheron let out a massive *whoop!* that doubled as a battle cry.

"Cut the celebration," Lion told him.

Cheron saw why when the wisp's light flickered where Lion explored with his hands. There were only small gaps of dark-gray sky between a very large boulder. Lion pushed his shoulder against the huge rock, testing the give. The slab didn't budge, not an inch. Lion dug his fingers in the cracks and said, "Maybe there's a switch of some sort."

"No, I doubt it," Cheron told him. "More like it normally takes a dragon to dislodge the boulder. Move."

"You're a big guy, but I don't think you can lift this thing. Ekos wouldn't tell me to come here if there weren't a way out."

"Goddess, if it is your will that I should join Ekos, give me the strength I need."

Lion snorted. Much like Ekos, he apparently didn't put much faith in the divine. If they lived through this, Cheron would have to teach Lion the call of service. A man with such loyalty and devotion would make a fine acolyte.

"She will not help if you slight her."

"Sorry," Lion said, sounding anything but. He leaned against the wall and held his hand out, open palmed, in invitation. "Please continue."

Sometimes he wondered if Lion and Ekos were truly blood related. Cheron hid his smile and forced a disapproving glower onto his face. Instinctively, he reached for the spot on his chest where the medallion once rested. It took him a moment to realize the talisman was no longer there. Would the goddess be able to heed his calls? Cheron didn't know for certain, but he had to try.

Closing his eyes, he willed Kalin to hear him, to feel him, the way he heard and felt her. The coldness throughout his body shook him. She wasn't responding to his pleas. There'd be no way out without assistance. Ekos would have to fight alone. He'd die.

"I'm not finding anything," Lion said, confirming Cheron's fears that Ekos had used his dragon's strength to move the boulder.

Helpless, Cheron balled his hands into fists and pounded against the rock. In his mind, he saw Ekos's body in the garden, his clear blue eyes lifted to the sky and his mouth gaping open. Until his hands bled and his body ached, Cheron spent his fury and pummeled the rock wall before him.

"You'll break your hands," Lion scolded him. "Then you'll be even less useful."

With effort, Cheron calmed himself. Lion was right. He couldn't afford such theatrics, not if he was going to save Ekos. "I'm sorry. I just cannot imagine life without him."

"Uh, I'll keep looking," Lion told him, giving him an awkward pat on the shoulder. "Maybe you should try praying out loud again. I won't bug you."

Yes, Lion was right. He had to try. "Kalin," he said out loud. "Please. I need you."

While Cheron prayed, waiting for the familiar incalescence of the goddess's blessing, Lion continued to search for some mechanism that would release them from their prison. Grunting and panting, he provided an odd sort of musical accompaniment to Cheron's prayers.

"Kalin, don't let Ekos die. He needs me. Please, let me go to him. Together, we can bring you back to this world."

"Working?" Lion asked.

Nothing so far. Not even an inkling, a vague tingle, to alert Cheron to the goddess's presence. Her absence stung. Surely, it couldn't be her will that Ekos complete the journey alone?

Desperate, once again seeing Ekos's life wilting in Sinnac's horrific garden, Cheron prostrated by resting his head on the floor and outstretching his hands before him. "Kalin, I beg of you. I live for your glory and enact your will. But I also live to love Ekos. I will remain here if that is what you ask, but have mercy on your servant. Part of my heart will die with him."

At last, she touched him. Heat spread through his muscles, which flexed of their own accord. The pain in his aching hands soothed as she healed his self-inflicted wounds. The blessing came with a warning, which cut through him, unspoken but loud as the thunder outside: *Do not put your feelings for him ahead of your service to me.*

"I will not," Cheron promised.

But his heart spoke otherwise. It said he'd rip apart the world to save Ekos.

Chapter Twenty-Eight

CHERON GENTLY PUSHED Lion aside.

"Hey, don—"

Lion's rebuke died on his lips. The cross expression on his face slid into befuddlement. Cheron didn't quite know why. He hadn't moved the rock yet. "What?" Cheron asked.

"You're, uh, glowing," Lion said. "She really does listen to you."

He'd never glowed before, but Cheron took the new blessing as a reminder of what he owed and said, "Yes, her grace binds me to her service."

A stab of guilt tangled his guts. Kalin's generosity had claimed him a kingdom, healed his wounds, granted him inhuman strength, but still he shirked her for the touch of a man, an apostate no less. He should feel more ashamed, but his love for Ekos felt as right and true as his love for the goddess. He only hoped time would prove the two could overlap. The goddess had a sense of humor at least. That would help.

"Do you have to quietly reflect after praying for help or..."

"No, sorry. Stand over there." Cheron pointed far behind him where he was reasonably certain he couldn't accidently crush Lion. The young man moved obediently to the side, a reverent expression on his face.

Cheron used his shoulder to leverage the boulder forward. Grinding, creaking, the massive rock slid from its casing and vanished inside the wall.

"Wow," Lion said in a breath.

Cheron grinned but sobered promptly when Lion started to leave the safety of the cave. Did he think he'd make the journey as well? Apparently so. He pulled the impractical silk cloak he wore tighter around his body and stepped outside into the rain. Instantly soaked, he sneezed and shivered.

"Lion..." Cheron began.

"Yes?"

The hope on his face made Cheron agonize over what he needed to say next. The young man was at the age where grand adventures were appealing, and when wounded pride was a life-or-death affair. Cheron doubted the young man would challenge him to a duel if slighted, but he couldn't discount Lion setting out on his own.

Cheron opted for the direct, honest approach. "You can't come with me."

Brows pinched forward, Lion demanded to know, "Why not?"

"Because you're green. Life at the palace didn't prepare you for fighting."

"I'm not weak," Lion told him. His eyes were fierce, dark brown and broiling with anger. Cheron didn't doubt for a second that, if trained, the man would make a worthy opponent.

"I know you're not. But you're not schooled."

Chin cocked to the side, Lion considered this information in a scholarly way that indicated at the type of man he might eventually become: cautious, analytical, dedicated. Admirable traits, all.

Sensing Lion's reasonableness, Cheron continued, "I can't push you back inside and seal the passage shut. If we fail, you'll die in there. Ekos depended on me to move the rock had he not returned. You have to make your own decision. You're not ready for battle. Go with me now, and you'll be of no use. You might even be a detriment. Stay here. Please."

Cheron determined by the way Lion flinched and looked at the ground that the word *detriment* stung. He felt sorry for it, but he didn't have time to coddle or tend to the young man's ego. Lion needed to hear the truth without ornament.

Cheron continued, "You'd be most helpful here where we don't have to worry about you."

Lion nodded. Swallowing his pride, he straightened and said, "Bring him back home. I miss that churlish lizard. And take Vivi." To the wisp, Lion said, "Help Cheron find Ekos."

The light bounced and went to hover behind Cheron.

Cheron yanked Lion in for a hug, which he returned after a lengthy pause. Cheron wasn't sure how he'd made his way inside this odd, makeshift family, but he praised the goddess for the good fortune and hoped to be able to return to its embrace.

JAGGED ROCKS CUT through the earth, pointed like the teeth of a massive animal. Sheets of rain poured down, making the surface beneath his feet shift. His steps cut deep grooves in the ground. Cheron angled his body and slid to what flat bits of land he found on the hill's steep slope. He forced himself to move slowly, to make sure each foothold took, before continuing. One wrong move and he'd tumble off the side, and—if he were lucky—he'd instantly snap his neck. If not, if he just broke limbs, he'd be in for a long, agonizing death.

Selfishly, and foolishly, he often wished for company to keep his thoughts from focusing inward. The lingering effects of the goddess's blessing reminded him of his disloyalty. Ever since childhood, he'd followed Kalin, but hadn't he betrayed her in his heart?

Upset, but knowing he needed to clear his head and move forward, Cheron dug his fingers into the soil and slid to a ridge. Beneath him, the hillside broke way to a headwall. He could traverse along the edge, which extended as far as his eye could see, but that would add days to his journey. Ekos had likely flown, which meant he might already be at the palace.

Vivi agreed. The wisp ran along the steep incline, illuminating footholds on its path down.

"Okay," Cheron told him. "That's the way I'll go, then."

Throwing his shoulders back, Cheron prepared to climb. All around him, the air swirled. The sting of cold even cut through the layers of clothes he wore and chilled his sensitive skin.

His furs, heavy from rain, would only weigh him down. He stripped and tied each article of clothing around a heavy rock, which he let fall to the ground below. Later, he'd get to a shelter where he could dry them and wear them again. For now, he had to abandon them for the sake of agility.

"Okay, show me. Where do I start?"

Vivi bobbled and darted to the left. The rocks flattened on one part of the crag. Cheron tested the sturdiness with part of his weight before fully settling down in the groove. He swallowed the lump in his throat when the wind tore upward and he heard the small pebbles crash to the ground. Cheron hated high places.

Cold rock pressed against his face. Directly above him, the top of the cliff beckoned. Below him, where Cheron refused to so much as peep, the light-colored rocks of the scree waited to gash and cut slits through his body. They'd turn red with his blood. In time, brown.

"I love Ekos," he told himself. "I love that stupid son-of-a-bitch dragon who could have flown me over this nightmare." He turned his head toward Vivi and asked, "Where next?"

Vivi hovered near his left side. Cheron, trusting the strange creature, stuck his foot out and found another hold.

Things progressed that way for what seemed like hours. Fear had stolen his endurance. His lungs burned; his chest ached; his breathing came rapidly, and sometimes it felt like it wasn't going to come at all. Cheron's muscles, taut from fear and exertion, wobbled with the strain of keeping himself in place. Oddly, the small cuts on his hands gave him the most trouble. Sweat trickled into them, stinging and itching in an unbearable harmony of nuisance. To scratch was to die, and so Cheron groaned and bellyached, hoping no one—including the goddess—heard him.

"Are we almost down?" Cheron asked, still refusing to check. He dared a glance where the light shone, then, only briefly.

The wisp illuminated the next stop in response. Cheron opted to take that to mean yes and clung to what little hope there was to be had in this dismal world.

"Stop being dramatic," he said. "You're not some green boy."

Had he been able to see himself, he was fairly certain that was the exact word to describe the coloring of his face. He decided to find that image funny and barked a short laugh.

"Where next?" he asked again.

Vivi didn't move. He stayed positioned right where Cheron rested, waiting for instruction.

"Where to?" he asked again, thinking the creature might be resting.

Again, the orb stayed where it was, floating and entirely indifferent to the pleading note in his voice. Sighing tiredly, Cheron used his toe to prod the landscape. The ground was much more uneven, rocky. He risked a glance at his feet. He was standing on top of a large pile of smaller, chunky rubble. The cliff's scree, he realized. He'd reached the bottom.

"Praise Kalin," he said and touched the spot on his neck where the amulet normally rested.

He heard the rattling of rocks before the loose pebbles beneath his feet slid, and then Cheron tumbled.

Chapter Twenty-Nine

THE SLOPE OF scree beneath the cliff face was unstable. In retrospect, he should have guessed as much. Loose rocks weren't dependable perches, but he'd been too preoccupied with the aches of his body and his fears to notice his footing.

Too late now.

Cheron hit the ground with a thud. Since he was surprised, he'd forgotten to close his mouth. The fall did it for him, snapping his jaws together on the tip of his tongue. He didn't have time to register the pain, from that or any of the other cuts and broken bones along the way. The world spun—one moment a hazy gray sky, the next a blur of white rock, and then a half-blotted-out blend of both. Blood, Cheron realized dimly, obscured his vision.

Beside him, Vivi trailed his descent, zipping along faster than Cheron had ever seen him move. The occasional flashes of light brought an odd sort of comfort: at least he wouldn't die alone.

As suddenly as he'd begun to fall, he stopped. Groaning, Cheron tried to rise up, but a sharp, stabbing pain in his chest stopped him. A broken rib at least. In a haze, too exhausted and resigned to panic, Cheron waited for blood to seep up through his throat, drowning him. None came. There was still a lot of hot liquid in his mouth. Cheron, not daring to turn, spit upward. Blood rained back down on his face from where he'd bitten off part of his tongue. Luckily, he'd only severed the very tip; the wound would gush, but he wouldn't lose his speech.

He also understood his injuries were too severe for the goddess to heal. Only the priests of Atyx had power over death, and their gift came at a great cost.

Vivi hovered above him.

"You made it," Cheron said. "Good for you."

The strange creature scanned him head to toe, then buzzed in a horizontal line as though shaking his head.

"You're right. I probably don't look too good. Not that I ever did, but I'm probably worse off than before."

Vivi jumped up and down, as if nodding.

"You didn't have to agree with that. Spare a dying man's feelings."

Instead of giving another vague, questionable response, Vivi flew off toward the horizon. Cheron couldn't fault him for abandoning the helpless scene. There wasn't anything an ethereal ball of light could do. Afraid to move, Cheron lay on his back awhile longer, wondering if this was punishment from Kalin. Perhaps she'd heard his internal voice that said Ekos's life meant everything. Goddesses and gods were jealous creatures. Although Kalin was more reasonable than some, she was no exception to that rule.

"Forgive me," he prayed. But even that was meant for Ekos.

Cheron closed his eyes and tried to decide on the next course of action. One rib, at least, was most certainly broken. If he moved, he'd puncture a lung, his heart, or—for an especially painful death—his stomach. Staying on the ground wasn't an option either. Starvation would claim him, then. It seemed he would die alone after all. His soul would drift forever, a ghost in a strange land.

Feeling every last ache, Cheron sat up. If the rib punctured something, he hoped the sharp bone would go straight for his heart. Otherwise, a roving hungry beast might be his only shot at mercy.

"Take me to Yellow Sky," he wheezed at the pain.

Bursts of light exploded behind his eyelids. It took a moment for his vision to clear. When he could see again, the glow of campfires caught his attention. Judging by the radius, the settlement was small, perhaps even only a few hundred souls.

He was about to meet one of them. Nearby, soft footsteps disturbed the loose rocks. Cheron couldn't scamper off fast enough, or at all, to avoid detection, so he hoped his blood might hide his tattoos, which marked him as a foreigner. Otherwise, they might kill him on sight.

"Hello?"

Cheron didn't answer. Perhaps the woman who called out would overlook him. Her voice sounded old, tired. It had the gravel of a smoker, the grainy stops and starts of poor use. The rocks were steep and unfriendly to aging feet, as he had learned.

No, the woman climbed toward him with the ease of a goat. When she saw him, she stopped in her tracks and stared. Her mouth hung open. "What in the twin moons happened to you?"

"Fell climbing down the cliff."

"Why would you go and do a stupid thing like that?"

"Love," Cheron answered simply and truthfully.

She nodded. Hands on her hips in a way reminiscent of his mother, the woman regarded him through narrowed eyes. Coated with dirt, which Cheron assumed was the result of poverty, her features remained mostly hidden. She wore a long brown robe, unembellished by any form of decoration. Her large stock of hair stood straight up on her head, held up by the nest of tangles. She touched the base of her neck as though tracing the outline of an object beneath. Then, she slapped her hands together and said, "You're King Cheron Ashborne?"

Denying it seemed silly. What was he to say? No, he was *another* giant Northern man with a jagged scar from temple to chin? "Yes," he said.

"I went to your wedding."

Cheron winced at her declaration, which also served as an admonishment. "Sorry," he said.

She smiled at that answer. "I actually kind of enjoyed the ceremony. I despaired when the dragon didn't eat a few of the nobles." She gave the thought a rueful, gap-toothed smile. Her teeth were uneven and yellow, but Cheron found a great deal of charm in her presence, anyway. "Is it true you worship Kalin?"

"Yes."

"Not Atyx?"

She sounded doubtful. Cheron couldn't very well blame her. He had the look of a follower of the war god with his scarred body and battle-ready physique. His history was also one of strife and civil unrest. None of that could be denied if she knew who he was.

"I went to war as a young man," he admitted. "Battle was never what I wanted."

"Then why did you go?"

"To overthrow a cruel, violent man."

"You married one of those. Perhaps you'd like to serve the war god now?"

Startled by the woman's denouncement of her ruler and her sudden fervent tone, Cheron failed to respond in a timely manner. The sweetness left the woman's features.

The mass of wrinkles on her face contracted around her pug nose, giving it the appearance of a snarling dog's muzzle.

"I will never serve Atyx," Cheron told her. "He requires endless war, sacrificial human misery, strife, and conflict. I want none of those things."

"Not a fortuitous night for you, then, Cheron Ashborne."

He didn't need her to tell him that. Shooting pain articulated his lack of luck better than words. Instead of answering, he closed his eyes and waited for her to grab a rock and bash his skull. That was what he expected her to do all along. He started to think it was the fate he deserved. She was an instrument of Kalin's displeasure.

"Open your eyes," she commanded him.

There was authority in her voice. Cheron did as she asked. She'd brought an amulet out from under her long, dung-colored cloak. The obsidian was formed in the image of a fierce griffin with its talons outstretched. In each claw, it held a crumpled body. In its beak, a spear. Even from a distance, Cheron felt the power of the god she served. The red rubies of the creature's eyes flared when she faced them toward Cheron. Recognition. Anger. The fiery condemnation of a vengeful god.

Chapter Thirty

HE'D PASSED OUT from the pain during his transportation from the bottom of the cliff. Torture was what he expected when he woke. When he instead felt a soft bed, Cheron couldn't get his bearings. He thought he was back home with Ekos. He whispered his intimate thoughts only to hear the high tittering of a young woman afterward. Not Ekos. His niece, then. He flushed in embarrassment. She was old enough to know such things but not to hear them from her uncle.

"Saran. I'm so sorry. I thought... I thought you were someone else."

"No, no," she responded in a singsong voice. "I'm no one you know, Northener. Not this Saran. Not Ekos."

Cheron rose but was instantly drawn back down with equal force. The restraints he wore felt loose enough until he tried to escape. Then, somehow, they tightened to the point of agony until he gave up. It was as though they could guess his intentions.

"Shush now, hold still," the same woman with a high voice told him. "You'll rip your bandages."

People tended to his injuries, healing the worst of them with their strange magic that felt like fire searing his veins. Feeling the power of their healing enchantments made him realize where he was and whom these people served. Priests of Atyx. Under the war god's cruel finger, mending spells were accompanied by a blistering pain.

Such a price was a reminder of debt to the god, that he would inflict so much worse if his good favor was squandered.

Cheron didn't quite know what to expect after his revelation. Anxieties ramped up, turning his dull acceptance of his fate to dread. Why hadn't they killed him? What did they have planned?

"Comfortable?" The woman who found him spoke. She hovered nearby. Her face blurred, coming in and out of focus. He knew her by voice, which had the same bumpy texture as dirt.

"Can you hear me, Cheron Ashborne?" she asked.

"Yes," he answered. "I hear you."

"Good. Good." The genuine delight in her voice further confused him. She was amiable for someone who would most likely disembowel him and string out his innards as tribute. Normal people made for the worst sort of monsters. "You're safe for now. Be at rest and welcome."

"Welcome? I'm a prisoner, not your guest."

She gave his venom a dry chuckle. "Things could change. This might be your lucky night yet. Atyx smiles on you."

"I don't smile back."

She only laughed.

Candles illuminated the hovel, giving the faces of the priests around him an eerie underglow. Gathered in a tight circle, they wore the same dung-colored robes and chanted and prostrated themselves.

Atyx demanded subservience in everyday aspects of life, including manner of dress. His priests showed their devotion by forsaking finery and covering their faces with a layer of thick dirt, obfuscating their features. Cheron should have guessed at the woman's identity when he first saw her, but he assumed poverty made her filthy, not faith.

Atyx was not equally humble.

In all depictions, the god dressed resplendently in silver armor. Crimson plumes cascaded from his helm. Jewels lined his knuckles and pinned the long, flowing white cape to his shoulders. War for glory, blood for sport, bodies for hunger. Atyx's philosophy left a dying world in its wake.

Kalin's world lived. Her followers thrived.

"Atyx promised me your arrival," the woman who found him said. "But he said you'd come on the wings of a dragon. Wouldn't it be better if gods were literal?"

After saying this, she poked his tattoos and grinned.

Cheron glared, refusing to engage.

Her smile broadened. The mud on her face cracked until chunks fell off, merging back into the dirt floor. Beneath the mask, her face was a silky, pale white and near as translucent as a fly's wing. She spoke to the rest of the community in a language Cheron didn't understand. Two men bowed and vanished.

If possible, the woman's grin got wider, fiercer, more feral. The yellow of her teeth reflected the light of the flickering candles. Atyx also had other restrictions on personal hygiene. It showed.

Cheron failed to imagine what made her so happy until the two men returned. They had someone between them. Although he had a bag over his head, Cheron instantly recognized Ekos's frame. He struggled against his captors, kicking and twisting to free himself. Around his neck, he wore a collar similar to the one he'd had in the palace, only the new one lacked the grace and sophistication of the old. The metal was roughly beaten into a round shape, and there were no jewels or precious stones embedded to decorate. Functional. Crass. Punitive.

"At first, I thought the god meant this one, you see," the woman said, pointing at Ekos. "But he wasn't satisfied. He made that known."

The woman pulled back the sleeves of her robes and extended her arms. Dark purple lines extended all the way up her forearms. Cheron, from his position, couldn't quite see the significance, so the woman crept up and nearly pressed her flesh against his face.

Creatures wiggled beneath her skin. Cheron saw them twist and turn. It must have been excruciating. Indeed, the woman's fierce smile now appeared more like a grimace. But pain wasn't the use for the creatures. Before his eyes, the strange things rearranged themselves in traditional Northern tattoos similar to Cheron's.

"You see," she said. "The god speaks."

"Cruelly."

"Such is his way. It sharpens our hearing."

Ekos hopped at the sound of Cheron's voice. He renewed his struggles and began to scream. The noise was muffled, but Cheron was fairly certain he heard a slurry of curse words.

The woman smiled at his commotion and let her sleeves fall over her arms. She walked up to Ekos and removed the bag from his head and then the gag.

Ekos spat on her.

Rather than anger, as Cheron expected, the priestess laughed and wiped the spittle from her face. She licked off her hand afterward, closing her eyes in a manner similar to a grooming cat. Practically purring, she said, "Delicious, the mark of a chosen one."

"And this is why I'm an apostate," Ekos said in disgust.

The woman's eyes snapped open. Once again, she smiled. "Among other reasons, yes. Have you told your lover these reasons? He's over there if you'd care to share or I can do it for you?"

When Ekos saw Cheron, his eyes widened and then his nostrils flared. It was a look Cheron knew well—anger, but also a strange, contradictory relief. It was what Cheron had come to interpret as gratitude. Ekos didn't want Cheron to be in danger, but he didn't want to face his trials alone. There wasn't any comfort to offer, so Cheron kept things simple with a "Hello, love."

"Hello, you stupid bear," Ekos said sweetly.

Chapter Thirty-One

NONE OF THE cheerfulness evaporated from the high priestess's demeanor. No matter how much salt Ekos poured over her, the old snail wouldn't dry up. In the end, this earned her a sort of grudging admiration from Ekos, who ate the meal placed before him in large, noisy gulps. Cheron had forgotten his voracious appetite. Entire chickens vanished down his throat as if by magic. As far as mystical talents went, it was a rather lackluster one.

"What if the food is poisoned?" Cheron whispered fiercely.

Ekos hiccupped a small laugh, which immediately morphed into a belch. "Then I'm going to be slightly more pissed off when they stab a dagger into my stomach."

Although Cheron got the point—they were in a dire situation regardless if the food was poisoned—he still grumbled at Ekos's lack of concern. Ekos grabbed his thigh under the table and gave it a slight comforting squeeze. Then, he let his fingers trail upward until Cheron's grumble turned into more of an uncomfortable cough. Ekos grinned and ate another chicken leg.

He was sure the high priestess noticed the exchange, but she kept her eyes focused on her food and made polite conversation with everyone around her.

Once again, Cheron was struck by how normal the town seemed on the surface. Children played with dolls; grown men and women who weren't attending dinner saw to their daily chores, such as chopping wood. Followers of Atyx were known for cruelty and cunning, not for braiding their hair with wildflowers and scrubbing pots.

"Not what you were expecting?" the high priestess asked.

"No," Cheron admitted. "I expected…much worse."

"Even the evil must live daily lives." She clucked at him and stuck a large wad of meat into her mouth. "The wicked must sup."

"Yes, it's what else you dine on that concerns me."

She gave his dry comment another big-toothed grin. This time, there was bite to the show of teeth.

Under the table, Ekos's light squeeze became a pinch. When Cheron looked at him, his brows were knitted together and his full mouth squeezed in warning. With that look, he said, *Stop antagonizing our captors*. Had they been talking in the open, Cheron would have pointed out Ekos's several examples of blasphemy. At least five in the last hour alone.

There wasn't any sense in keeping score. Ekos worried for Cheron's safety, not his own. He put on his sweetest smile and said, "My apologies for King Cheron, High Priestess. And thank you for the lovely dinner."

Cheron picked at the food, eating mostly for show more than anything else. Whenever he thought he could get away with a quick scout, he scanned the area for weaknesses in their defenses. Despite the fact that many of the citizenry were engaged in common chores, making it appear every bit a community, fierce warriors suited up in heavy plate armor guarded the perimeter. One of them saw Cheron glance in the direction of the city gate. She smiled and raised her spear.

"Our god has great plans for both of you."

Cheron snapped back to the conversation and realized he'd missed a chunk of it and was about to be missing a chunk of his leg as well. Ekos pinched him again. Hissing softly, Cheron pulled away. They were like two callow youths at a wedding festival, and it drove him mad in two ways.

"I have no interest in Atyx's designs," Cheron said. "Why haven't you killed us yet?"

Ekos slammed down his ale mug.

The high priestess didn't don one of her fierce grins. Her lips twisted into a thin line that reminded Cheron of a blade's edge. She had the type of wit that cut. "My, you are quite artless for a follower of the wisdom goddess."

"Isn't he, though?" Ekos agreed.

The priestess ignored him. This seemed to rankle Ekos, who probably thought he—a dragon—was the main attraction. "Very well, Cheron Ashborne, we will get to business. You are spared by the god's mercy. He wishes to conscript you in his services."

"No."

The thin line of her lips vanished inside her mouth. When she brought them back out, they were wet and their natural flesh color, free from the mud. "Consider," she said. "Atyx does not make offers lightly. He chose you for a reason, for a great purpose."

"No," Cheron said again. "I will never abandon Kalin."

She chuckled at this and looked to Ekos as though they shared a joke. Under her knowing, piercing gaze, Ekos flushed and went back to his dinner. This time, he didn't eat with the same good cheer. He picked at the meal, all the while darting his eyes in Cheron's direction.

The high priestess continued. "Again, shall I tell him or will you?"

"There's nothing to say. He knows I'm an apostate."

Yes, Ekos had told him that much, but the goddess still favored him. Cheron had felt her blessing when they were trapped together in the dungeons. She'd wanted Cheron to give Ekos the amulet, for him to know her love again. Such a gift meant she favored him despite whatever he'd done.

"Tell me," Cheron said. "Kalin forgives you, as can I."

Ekos's eyes sharpened. "She doesn't forgive anything. No god does. She wants me to atone through blood. My blood."

"She favors—"

Ekos slapped his hands on the table. Suddenly, he shot up, his sides heaving and his face red from rage. "She loves you, my bear. That much is true, but she does not hold me in the same esteem. I am sure."

The high priestess twirled a fork in her hand, clearly enjoying the show. Her yellow teeth covered her bottom lip; she bit down as though to keep from laughing. "Tell him. Do it or allow me."

The fine white cotton tablecloth bunched in Ekos's fists. Head hanging low, he relented to her request, never once meeting Cheron's curious, worried gaze. "I am the one who betrayed her and ensured her descent to Yellow Sky."

The lump in Cheron's throat was going to choke him. He managed to squeeze words past, but each one hurt. "She forgave you. I saw her do so in the dungeons."

"She was warning me away from you. I didn't heed it. How could I?" He gave the last question a helpless laugh. Eyes watering, he savagely clutched the fabric of the tablecloth to his chest and repeated, "How could I?"

"No," Cheron said. "Why would you do such a thing?"

Sadness melted from his features. Anger scorched it away. "Those poor souls in the garden are my people. Kalin allowed them to be slaughtered to ensure she'd be the only god left in this world. Cheron." Ekos said his name like a plea. "I trusted her, loved her, worshiped her, and she slaughtered my kind for her glory. She gave me death and enslavement. And then you came and set me free."

"So you see," the high priestess began. "You cannot have your goddess and your love. Atyx gives you both, and a kingdom to rule in his name. Sinnac's kingdom," she added with a smile. "He has displeased the god and failed him for the last time. You have Hell's Echo. With it, you have the love of the god."

The absence of the goddess's talisman disturbed Cheron now more than ever. He needed answers, some sign that Ekos's words weren't true or that he'd somehow confused the goddess's actions. Immortal beings required sacrifice, but such disloyalty was beyond Kalin's grace.

"Well," the high priestess prompted him after a long period of silence. "What will you decide, Cheron Ashborne?"

He imagined himself as a servant to the war god, as his hand in the world. Nearby, Ekos held his breath. Cheron heard his heart racing. The pounding in his chest drowned out all other sensations. It wasn't difficult for him to remember when they'd shared the same pulse. One night. He'd always have one night.

"I choose Kalin," he whispered. "Her grace binds me to her service."

Pale, trembling, Ekos slumped back in his seat. When Cheron tried to touch his leg, he twisted out of Cheron's reach and flew away as best he could without wings.

Chapter Thirty-Two

THE HIGH PRIESTESS let him run to Ekos, perhaps thinking his lover could change his mind and win him for Atyx's collection of earthly tools. That was her indoctrinated way of thinking. Cheron planned to reclaim Ekos for Kalin's glory, not the other way around.

He found him sitting on the floor, his legs drawn up to his chest and his head resting on his knees. He picked small clumps of dirt, ground them between his fingers, and let the fine dust fall.

"Ekos," Cheron said to get his attention.

Ekos twisted his head away, trying in vain to hide his emotions from Cheron's concerned eyes. Cheron's words caught in his throat when he saw the tear tracks streaking Ekos's proud, high cheekbones. Maybe coming here was a mistake. Perhaps he wasn't strong enough to resist the torment of his lover's misery.

"Ekos," Cheron said again. This time the other man's name was a curse, his own.

"My heart belongs to rebels," Ekos said with a small smile that was a mere shadow of his former defiance. "It belonged to you. It's not fitting so neatly back in my chest right now. Please leave."

"Kalin—"

The mention of the goddess's name sparked a flame of anger. He shot up to his feet and closed the distance between them in seconds. Finger jabbing against Cheron's broad chest, he spat, "Your goddess slaughtered my entire family. Do not think my love for you transcends that memory."

"We are the total of our scars," Cheron said quietly.

"My kind can grow new skin," Ekos spat back. Some of his former defiance flashed in his eyes, which shone with rage, anguish, and—yes—love. Although he tried to hide the last behind a protective sneer, Cheron knew his moods too well by now. There was no real malice in his words, only hurt.

Giving his bravado a small smile, Cheron grabbed hold of Ekos's finger, still sharply digging into Cheron's flesh where his heart rested, and pulled it up to his lips for a kiss. Ekos resisted at first but then allowed his hand to be curled against the scruffy line of Cheron's cheek. Seemingly of their own accord, his long, delicate fingers stroked a tender line from ear to jaw. "My bear," he whimpered. "Don't abandon me as she did."

Keeping things simple between them, Cheron said, "I won't leave you, but I must—"

"Serve the goddess? Yes, I *know*. You don't care for me enough to choose us."

Touching Ekos gently under the chin to force their eyes to meet again, Cheron said, "Not enough to let the world turn to ash, to wither, to die. Ekos, I would give my soul for you, but not the souls of everyone else. Whatever her reason for letting your people suffer, I believe Kalin meant it for the greater good. She—"

Ekos snapped out of Cheron's embrace. Whatever lingering tenderness there was before vanished under the compulsion of his fury. "The greater good! You saw what Sinnac did to them!"

"Yes." Tears came to Cheron's eyes. Ekos's pain was his own. "I saw."

"How can that be for the greater good?"

Ashamed, Cheron turned away. He didn't know the goddess's will, but he knew himself guilty of her crime. "I watched my lover burn," he confessed. "I could have tried to save him. I could have intervened. Perhaps, I would have even succeeded, and we'd be living tucked away someplace safe, clinging together for our lives but both of us breathing. But I let him die alone, leaving his body unattended so his ghost is forced to roam the world seeking vengeance."

Ekos waved his hand at the story, dismissing it. "He betrayed you."

"Yes, but that's not why I abandoned him."

"For Kalin, then?"

"For her vision of the world. One where men aren't burned to death, so there is no call to intervene."

Ekos sneered. He probably saw himself twisting on the same pyre, Cheron watching him die but doing nothing. No doubt he thought something similar was happening now.

"Ekos, I want to be with you, but I cannot abandon the vision of a world where everyone gets to live peaceful lives for my own desires. We might be safe for a century or two, but Atyx demands a world on its knees. We'd be the ones to bring them there, our feet on the necks of children like Lion, forcing them to the mud. That can't be what you want."

Cheron determined by the way Ekos suddenly jerked his head away to hide his eyes that such a world was not what he desired, but he wasn't willing to say it. He couldn't forgive Kalin for what she'd done. Voice gruff, he said, "I understand. Now go serve your goddess."

"Ekos. I know you are not gutless."

He clenched and unclenched his fists. Shoulders tense, his entire body pulled into a tight, rigid edge, Ekos appeared on the verge of transforming to his true self. Had the collar not prevented the shift, he probably would have. "Damn me for a coward. I damn you for a fool. The world she wants you to win for her will be another version of Atyx's. At least the war god is honest about wanting senseless slaughter. You might be lured by Kalin's false promises of harmony, but I am not. I have known the touch of the *mercy* goddess."

"Believe in my vision if not hers."

He snorted. "You need spectacles."

"Don't do that. Don't treat me like I have no sense. I'm not stupid, Ekos. I choose to serve a purpose higher than myself."

"You're right. You're not stupid. You're honorable, which is just as bad."

It was like fighting a current of water surging over a cataract—hopeless and tiring. Surrounded by a large wall, trapped with his greatest enemies, facing a foe who had a loyal dragon as a pet. Cheron had a very long swim ahead of him. And a lonely one. His heart, already tired, constricted. He had to believe the goddess had brought them together for a purpose.

"Help me," he said again. "If you love me, help me."

That broke Ekos the same as being on a rack. Almost immediately, the anger dissipated, leaving his features smooth, touchable, kissable. "Cheron, I..."

The voice of the high priestess cut in, "That's quite enough. The notion either of you has a choice is laughable. You are here to serve Atyx, willingly or by force. I thought you had him in our pocket for a second," she said to Ekos. "But it seems he's the more persuasive. Pity."

She lifted her hand, and two armed guards entered the room. One of them took Ekos, the other Cheron. Briefly, before they were ripped apart, Ekos met his eye and donned a secretive, plucky smile that warned of brashness to come. Seeing the look gave Cheron hope he might share the future with Ekos. Together, they'd bring Kalin back and undo the harms caused by her absence.

Then something hard and heavy cracked the back of his skull. Lights flashed behind his eyes, and he pitched forward to the hard ground.

Before he totally went under, he thought he heard Ekos say, "Why do I have to do everything myself?"

Chapter Thirty-Three

WAKING UP BOUND was becoming familiar to Cheron, who had only found it pleasant once. This time he was cinched to a long pole stuck in the ground. His legs—tied at the knees—bent at an unpleasant angle. Movement beside him caught his attention. Someone else was there and struggling with all his might.

"Ekos?" Cheron asked, but the sound of his voice was muffled by a gag.

"Do something!" Yes, it was Ekos. Like Cheron, he was gagged, so the words came out muffled.

Panic had never sounded in Ekos's voice before. Hearing the emotion there now spurred Cheron to action, even though he had no idea what danger they currently faced.

He tried to pray to the goddess to give him strength, but his senses—clouded by a strange, thick fog—couldn't formulate the thoughts or the words.

"You're enchanted," the high priestess explained to him. "As I told you, you will serve the war god in one way or another. His desire was willing, but..." The woman shrugged as though the rest were of no consequence.

Ekos buckled against his constraints, which pulled Cheron's tighter. Blood ran down his wrists from where the ropes were digging into his skin. The one around his neck constricted on his Adam's apple, pushing against the delicate bone with such force Cheron feared it might snap.

When Ekos struggled even harder, Cheron cried out in pain.

The high priestess laughed. "You'll kill him before Sinnac arrives."

Ekos stopped. Cheron heard the panting gulps of his labored breathing. He kicked toward her, cursing. Without too much thought, Cheron imagined the dark glower gracing Ekos's fine features, the way his proud head tilted to the side as he inspected the other woman with open disdain.

The priestess gave his fury a wry arch of her brow and a soft, puffy laugh. "Yes, yes. Your fury is great. I see that. I do. But not as great as my god's power."

She cut the bindings holding Cheron. Two guards wrestled him down and brought him to his knees in front of the priestess. No matter how hard he tried, he couldn't lash out. He failed to even manage an angry word. She said he'd been enchanted, but he'd never heard of magic that prevented mere thoughts. It was an even stronger, more unnatural version of what Isa had done to compel his confessions.

"Yes, Atyx's power has grown since his exile. From Yellow Sky, he has learned new means of ensuring his followers' subservience. Your enchantment is temporary, but we will fix that now."

A young woman, possibly the one who'd treated his wounds, was brought forward. The expression fixed on her face was serene. When she saw the priestess, her mouth split open in a wondrous, trusting smile. Her voice was young, far younger than her age allowed. "Mama! Do I get to ride on the dragon now?"

"Yes, child. It's time."

Gleeful, her eyes dancing in merriment, the young woman bent forward and wrapped her arms around Cheron's neck as though there were nothing amiss with his bindings. As she pulled away, Cheron saw her eyes more clearly. Pupils wide, the blackness overtaking the white, they had a glassy shine to them. Her dirt-covered face didn't give any other hints, but Cheron knew an enchantment when he saw one.

"Yes, she's been with us for a long time. Waiting for you. Waiting to serve her purpose," the priestess said, confirming his suspicions.

At the mention of her destiny, the young woman's hands clapped together. Childlike, she jumped up and down in anticipation. "I get to ride a dragon!" she said to everyone in attendance.

The priestess, along with the rest of the priests of the god Atyx, gave her antics an indulgent smile.

Cheron studied the rest of the villagers. Like the ensorcelled woman, their eyes were vacant, dull, listless. Enchanted. All of them. Except the priests of the god: their focus was razor sharp.

The priestess bent and removed Cheron's gag by roughly yanking it down around his chin. "Will you serve the god by choice?" she asked.

"What is that poor woman's destiny?"

The priestess lifted her lips in a cruel smile. "To ensure Atyx's ascension and your cooperation in the matter. I ask you again, will you reconsider serving the god? His reward for you is great. He will even grant you use of your dragon pet."

"Never. I serve only Kalin."

Tsking at his stubbornness, the high priestess turned her back to him to face the rest of her congregation. Eager for whatever was to come, they shuffled their feet and pressed forward until they were nearly at her toes. "Servants of Atyx," she began.

"His glory binds us!" they shouted back.

"Today, we witness the rebirth of our god!"

"Glory, glory, glory!" they cheered back.

"Today, we undo the work of Kalin, the miserable bitch who bound him to the Yellow Sky!"

"Glory, glory, glory!"

"Today those who defied us will bend the knee! They will bleed upon our weapons, submit to our fury, and then they will die by our hands!"

"Glory, glory, glory!"

"Before you kneels the servant of the bitch god, brought low by our god's wondrous magic. He has refused to renounce his worship and join us in the battle ahead!"

The rest of them didn't boo as Cheron expected. Instead, they pinched their mouths shut in mute fury, as though his refusal were an unspeakable act. A man spit in his direction, but none of the saliva made it any further than the tips of Cheron's leather shoes. The high priestess narrowed her eyes at the man and pointed. A blow to his stomach, delivered by a close companion, brought him to his knees.

"Do not profane his chosen!" she admonished the crowd. "Soon, he will understand his glory through our beloved Atyx."

"Glory, glory, glory!" The crowd chanted as the castigated man crawled toward the priestess and kissed her feet in repentance. Without pausing in her sermon, she shrugged him off, and he wiggled back to the crowd.

The priestess continued, "Come forward, child. Fulfill your purpose."

The young woman's smile broadened. Teeth cut against her lips under the fierce pressure of her bite. Cheron wondered if part of her mind remained and if she knew she was about to die. If so, she shook off her fear and came forward, practically skipping.

"I'm here to serve, Mama," she said. "His glory binds me."

"Excellent, child. He will rise from your blood."

The woman shuddered. Lips, wet with her own blood, parted, and her mouth opened wide.

Almost tenderly, the priestess cupped the young woman under the chin, inspecting her features one last time as though to commit the face to memory. Something like sadness, or perhaps grief, crossed the priestess's features, making the mud around her eyes moisten and the mud on her cheeks crack.

"This is really your child?" Cheron asked.

The priestess gave a short nod in acknowledgment. Gently, she stroked the hair back from the young woman's face, tucking the loose strands behind her ears. "Bring me the flask!" she demanded.

Another priest came forward carrying a sublime golden cup encrusted with jewels that winked. Light radiating from the chalice nearly blinded Cheron, who had to squint to maintain focus on the spectacle before him. The priests bowed low to present the gift to the priestess, who took it with equal reverence.

"His glory!" she shouted.

Once again, the crowd chanted along with her.

Then, she tilted the cup against the woman's open mouth and poured. A black, congealed liquid spewed forth. Sour-smelling, the goop made Cheron retch. Ekos as well. The servants of the god, however, stuck their noses in the air and breathed in deeply.

Chapter Thirty-Four

CHERON TRIED TO rise from the ground to save the young girl. Lumps of the black goo continued to ooze into her mouth. Eyes wide, tears running down her cheeks, she begged for mercy in silent appeal. None was forthcoming. Atyx's followers only spared those with strong enough backs to toil in the mines or those who could somehow serve his war efforts. Everyone else was expendable.

"Let her live," Cheron said. "She's your own child."

The high priestess didn't listen. She didn't even flinch as her daughter's face began to puff up and turn an ugly shade of red. She was suffocating. She locked onto Cheron's gaze, turning her eyes but not her head. In that final moment, Cheron saw a glimpse of who she actually was—a young woman on the verge of death and full of hatred. For him. Then that light dimmed. Her eyes were once again glossed over in death.

She slumped to the ground. For a moment, the high priestess stared down at her, lips twisted in what Cheron wanted to say was regret. Intractable in her service to the war god, she overcame whatever guilt she experienced, and quickly. Using the tip of her foot, she turned the corpse of her daughter so her face met the sun.

Cheron felt his facial muscles twitch at the sight of the dead woman. He'd seen men's faces after they'd died in battle—their eyes milky white, their mouths wide open, flies buzzing around the open wounds. Often times, they evacuated their bowls before expiring, and the stench of human waste mingled with the metallic odor of blood. The field of battle was a place where man was his most base, both in life and death.

This was a different level. The black slime wiggled around in the veins under the young woman's skin, making the dead muscles contract; her mouth appeared to open and close with a ventriloquist's dummy's precision. Bubbles of the ooze popped, splashing her face. Eventually, the sludge invaded all her muscles and veins, overtaking the host. Her body contorted as the thick substance bound itself to her.

And then she stood.

"Glory, glory, glory!" all the priests chanted.

The creature sneered at them and focused on Cheron. "Give me the Echo," the risen woman said. "Serve me."

Overcome, the high priestess fell to her knees and then to her belly. She crawled around in the dirt, rubbing a new coating of dust all over her body. The other priests followed her lead and dropped to the ground, hiding their skin behind a veil of thick brown soil.

Face-to-face with a god, Cheron's knees trembled. Had he been standing, he would have toppled over. Resisting the urge to hide from the deity, to cover his body in a thick layer of dirt as his followers did, Cheron lifted his chin and met him as he would a man in battle. "Atyx," he said.

The god frowned at his insolence. "You will serve me. You will give me Hell's Echo."

"No." Cheron denied,even as his willpower slip. "Never."

The god tilted his head and bared his teeth, but he turned his attentions away from Cheron and to his high priestess. "Where is it?"

"King Sinnac travels with Hell's Echo as we speak, my master. Soon, your body will be born anew, and we will all bear witness to your glory."

"Glory, glory, glory," the others chanted, softly this time.

The god ignored them and redirected his steely gaze back on Cheron. This time, Cheron flinched away from the heat in the eyes, which were endless in their depths. He heard the footsteps approach before he felt the searing fingers dig into his body, biting at him with the precision and sharpness of a surgical instrument. Atyx forced him to stand. At first, Cheron thought he might collapse back to the ground in an undignified heap, but then he saw Ekos—so fierce and struggling against his bindings, doing what he could to save Cheron—and found his courage.

"I will never give you what you desire," Cheron said. "You may as well kill me and spare yourself the humiliation of my refusal."

The war god laughed at him. The hollow sound carved out a spot in Cheron's guts, where dread twisted and churned. Atyx's fetid breath had a hint of acid. Where the spittle landed on his cheek, it burned and hissed. A small tendril of smoke rose upward, momentarily hazing Cheron's vision.

"Servant of Kalin," he said. "The mercy goddess. Where is she now?"

"In the Yellow Sky where is she banished with the rest of the gods and goddesses."

"I am here, mortal!" Atyx held both arms in a victory pose while his followers chanted, "Glory, glory, glory."

"This isn't your true form. You borrowed a feeble human shell that will break."

Atyx's nose wrinkled in a feral snarl, making him appear more rabid animal than god. In a fury, he placed his hand on Cheron's chest and uttered words in the same foreign language the priests spoke. Molten pain coursed through Cheron's body. Refusing to be cowed by the display of force, Cheron gritted his teeth and withstood the god's wrath in silence. He prayed to Kalin to give him the strength to continue, but his mind was filled with the same fog from before. No matter how hard he tried, he couldn't even think the goddess's name, let alone ask her for a blessing.

Unable to withstand the onslaught, Cheron screamed out in agony. But Atyx would not relent, not even when Cheron fell to his side and began to convulse. Spittle flung from his mouth in long, wet strands.

"My master," the priestess said tentatively. "You will destroy him before he can use the Echo for your journey back to our world."

Seeing the sense in her words, but infuriated by the correction from a lesser being, Atyx switched and used her as an outlet for his pent-up violence. Cheron watched as he placed his hand upon her brow and said the same strange words.

"No, my master. I beg you," the priestess whimpered. "I have sacrificed for your glory."

"Glory, glory, glory," his followers echoed.

This time the high priestess didn't seem equally caught up in the revelry. She darted anxious glances toward her peers, who licked their lips in anticipation. Bloodshed excited them. It didn't matter whose as long as it wasn't their own.

"My master," the high priestess began again. But it was too late. White sparks arched from her sides, looping back down in a white torrent of power. Without anything to bite down on, her teeth were left to chatter until they broke off, falling from her mouth in broken fragments.

Atyx's followers writhed in ecstasy.

While they were distracted, Cheron risked a glance in Ekos's direction. Sickened, his already pale skin blanched, Ekos set his jaw and observed the death of the forsaken priestess. Then, as if sensing his eyes upon him, Ekos turned to Cheron and mouthed, *You're free when she dies.*

It took a moment for Cheron to catch the meaning, but then he understood: the priestess was the one to enchant him. Her death canceled its effect. Cheron hated anticipating someone's demise—ignoble, to say the least—but he made an exception in this instance.

Evil undoes itself. That's what his mother had told him each night before lighting a candle beneath the statue of Kalin. *It's jealous, petty, unlawful. It's easy to find loose threads in such a poorly woven tapestry.*

He saw the truth in her words now. The vengeful god, without any consideration of the consequences, exercised his vast power to his own destruction.

"My master...please," the priestess begged one last time. And died.

Cheron's mind was free.

Chapter Thirty-Five

THE PRIESTESS'S BODY crumpled to the ground in a heap that smelled of piss, vomit, and burning hair. Bodily liquids, and their familiar stench, were the only remaining vestiges of her humanity. Otherwise, she'd be easily confused for a steaming pile of rags.

The war god towered above the corpse. Fist clenched, he let out a massive, bellowing roar, which his followers greeted with another chant. Cheron shook his head at the exhibit. Only the war god and his followers celebrated such one-sided victories. There was no honor to be found in slaughter.

Still, everything changed for Cheron in that moment.

A familiar and comforting name made its way back to his mind: Kalin. Once released from the enchantment, Cheron prayed to his goddess and sought her assistance. For now, though, he contented himself with feeling her presence once more. He'd wait until the time was right to tip his hand. And this wasn't a good moment.

Above them, the massive shadow of a dragon blotted out the sun. Isa and Sinnac. The high priestess had said they were on their way with Hell's Echo.

Atyx's lips lifted in a half smile. Cheron had no doubt the god saw victory sweeping in from above, carrying his key to the world of mortals. As the dragon and her rider landed, dirt swirled in eddies around the massive wings. Sinnac dismounted without waiting for the dragon to dip her neck or fold down a wing to ease his descent. He sprang from the saddle to the ground, landing much more elegantly than Cheron anticipated.

"My master," Sinnac said and bowed low. Instead of his fine silk robes, he wore natural, dung-colored garments. No embellishments, save for Cheron's amulet at his throat, cluttered his attire. He'd turned Kalin's eyes, the eyes of the dragons, inward toward his chest.

Atyx received his worship the way drunkards grasped at a new bottle of wine. Cheron heard his inhalations and watched his taut, angry features relax into some semblance of contentment.

"You have brought me Hell's Echo."

"Yes, your glory binds me."

Sinnac lifted the necklace and gave it to Atyx with a flourish. The priests chanted in the background. The familiar hum of their words lulled the rest of the townspeople into an odd slumber. They fell where they stood. Those lucky enough to collapse onto a nearby building, or who had their fall broken in some other way, were spared serious injury. Others weren't so fortunate.

Steam hissed from the god's fingers when he took Kalin's amulet in his hands. Gritting his teeth against the pain, the god tried to loop the relic around his neck. Some force Cheron couldn't see or fathom prevented the war god from wearing it. Enraged, the god flung the relic from his grasp. On his hands, dark blisters formed. Before Cheron's eyes, they popped and seeped out a foul-smelling liquid.

The amulet fell to the ground. The dragon's eyes caught the light and twinkled.

Atyx's followers studied the relic, but they'd learned the lesson not to correct or even try to guide the god. They let him come to his own conclusions as he stared at the pus-filled wounds on his hands. Eyebrows drawn in a tight *V*, he seethed at the inconvenience of needing a mortal to materialize in the world. He said, "Only the chosen can activate the magic."

"Yes, my master," Sinnac agreed. He gave Cheron a nervous, bitter glance.

Atyx whirled and headed straight for Cheron, pushing Sinnac aside in the process.

"Use it for my glory!" Atyx demanded.

Cheron shook his head.

The same white light that had enveloped the high priestess crackled around the god's body. Thunder boomed. Intended to bully Cheron into submission, the display had the opposite éffect. Cheron lifted his head higher, defying the god with all the rebellion in his heart.

Atyx bared his teeth and said, "There's another candidate. I saw it in a vision."

"Perhaps his lover, my master. The dragon." Sinnac pointed to Ekos, who said something that was most likely an insult.

Isa, her reptilian eyes narrowed to slits, watched her counterpart struggle against his bindings. Her massive jaws worked up and down, as though she were breaking his bones, rending his flesh, and tasting his death on her tongue. In the face of her fury, Ekos gave her a crooked smirk, partially hidden by his gag but visible enough to make the she-dragon huff in anger. Smoke billowed from her nostrils. When she opened her maw, Cheron saw flames swirling in the black cavern of her mouth. He remembered the heat of the fire.

"Ungag him," Atyx commanded Sinnac. "Let us hear what he has to say."

Sinnac did as his master commanded, roughly jerking the gag down around Ekos's neck. "My favorite pet has been fitted with a new collar," he said and grinned. When he tapped the thing with his finger, the choker made a dull thudding sound.

"Twat," Ekos said. Apparently, he wanted his last words to be vulgar.

Unbothered, Atyx strolled up to him. Hands outstretched in a friendly pose, he said, "My immortal brother, can you release the magic of Hell's Echo?"

"No," Ekos said. Then added, "Twat."

The god's brow furrowed again. Cheron sensed the rage he was trying hard to conceal: the tension in his muscles, the pop of his jaw, and the swirling blackness of his eyes. He needed someone to unleash the magic of the relic. Killing his only two candidates, or torturing them to the point where they may as well be dead, might have a certain appeal, but the plan left him without a way to fully materialize in the world.

"I will reward you," Atyx promised Ekos. "The goddess would banish you to the Yellow Sky for your transgression against her, but I will allow you to stay. I will even give you the human as your pet. What say you, my immortal brother?"

"Twat," Ekos said again. He *really, really* wanted his last words to be vulgar.

Atyx, even if he needed Ekos, wasn't about to endure such insolence. Lightning crackled from his fingers. Ekos, in response, tightened his body to prepare for the onslaught of pain.

One of the priests came forward, crawling forward on his belly like a worm. "M-My Lord."

"What is it?" Atyx snapped. Power surged around him, making it clear whatever the man interrupted for had better be important.

The priest swallowed and continued, "The high priestess enchanted King Ashborne. He is malleable to your will. Perhaps if you applied more pressure on his weak mind?"

After speaking, the hollow-cheeked man scuttled back to the crowd, hiding among the numerous men and women who were dressed as he was. Atyx watched him leave. The white light coiled around his hands, making his intent to use violence clear to everyone. The other priests stepped aside, leaving the helpless man susceptible to the god's wrath.

But Atyx stopped.

Confident once more, his cruel smile appearing easy, he bid his followers to bring Cheron forward. They grabbed him under his arms and dragged him until they flung him down at the god's feet. Atyx placed his hand against Cheron's stomach and spoke the words of the enchantment. "Now, my disciple, unleash the magic for your master."

"Yes, my master," Cheron said. The priests allowed him to pick up Kalin's amulet. The metal against his skin had the familiarity of a lover's kiss. Reverently, Cheron lifted the chain around his neck and closed his eyes as warmth flooded his body. Kalin was with him now, and he wouldn't fail her.

Chapter Thirty-Six

CHERON HOBBLED FORWARD as though fighting off the spell the deceased priestess had cast upon him. He forced his muscles to constrict to the point he was sure the veins in his neck stood out in stark contrast to his pale skin. He gritted his teeth, moaned, thrashed. He had to appear as though he were struggling for his very soul; anything less and the war god might become suspicious.

Although he wasn't sure why Ekos knew the enchantment had been broken and they didn't, Cheron assumed his additional knowledge had something to do with their connection. If they both lived, he'd have to ask Ekos later. Until then, he'd take the advantage for what it was—a blessing.

"Cheron..." Ekos's voice drifted past him.

Cheron forced all other thoughts out of his mind and focused on closing the gap between himself and the war god. Atyx's human shell, frail and crumbling, would break easily enough. Grabbing a weapon was out of the question, so Cheron would have to make do with his hands, which twitched in anticipation.

Kalin give me strength, Cheron prayed. *Let me strike true with one blow.*

On his chest, the familiar warmth of the amulet flooded him with vitality. The goddess answered his call.

Atyx, who must have seen the amulet glow, spoke in a cajoling whisper. "Yes, good. You'll unleash its power for me. You'll bring me back to the world."

Even if he wanted to obey the god, Cheron had no idea how to activate the relic. Continuing the theme of his journey, he failed to have a goal beyond obtaining the damn thing. But his lack of preparation had been by design. His was a quest of faith, and he depended on the goddess to guide him through the details of *her* plan. Such had been his challenge in his journey.

By the time he reached the feet of the war god, sweat dripped from his forehead into his eyes. The salt stung, but he couldn't risk wiping away the liquid. He needed to appear completely spellbound, unable to act without Atyx's permission.

"Kneel," Atyx commanded once Cheron was within touching distance.

Cheron fell to his knees before the god, resting the base of his forehead against the deity's slippers. Enjoying the supplication, Atyx took in a deep breath and tilted his head back.

"Good, good. This is as it should be," the god said. "Now release me."

Cheron stared at the ground. Dirt stirred with the force of his breathing, bounding up and sticking to the layer of sweat on his face.

Atyx's voice boomed, "Why do you not obey my command? Release me!"

Cheron forced himself to stammer and answered honestly. "I... I don't... I don't know how, my master."

Sinnac and Isa guffawed. The war god sneered down at him, one lip upraised above his black teeth. "You savage fool. You expected to test yourself against me without even understanding the power you hold?"

"Y—Yes, my master."

Behind him, he heard Ekos struggling against his bindings, but he couldn't afford to check on his lover. Ekos would have to keep for another few minutes while Cheron waited for his opening.

"Very well, then you must take it in your hands and—"

A crash behind them, the sound of a clay pots splintering on the floor, jarred the god's attention, along with everyone else's. Cheron didn't bother to turn in the direction of the new threat, if that was what it was. Instead, he took advantage of everyone's distraction and leaped to his feet.

Hastily, he grabbed hold of the god's soft human shell by its neck and twisted. He kept his eyes closed, trying to forget the face of the dead woman who'd lived her life bound to her mother's will. As the god struggled for his life, his shrieks high and oddly human, Cheron willed himself into a stoic state where all that mattered was his duty. He'd often done the same in battle. Men died all around him, some stuck in a half state of pain and misery. They'd reach out to him and beg for mercy. Just as their screams haunted him later, so too would the girl's.

The god, in his new form, proved more durable than Cheron imagined. Although he twisted and pulled with all his might, the head would not release from the shoulders.

"Seize him," Atyx bellowed, snapping Isa's and Sinnac's attention back to Cheron.

Sinnac sprang into action first. Sword drawn, he lunged directly at Cheron's exposed side. The cold metal of the blade pierced flesh. The cut was a shallow wound but one that would bleed out swiftly if left unbound.

"Do not kill him! I need the Echo!" Atyx shouted.

But Sinnac was already in the middle of another attack. Cheron watched the direction of the man's blade and turned so that the sword went straight through Atyx's gut. The god bellowed his rage and twisted in his grip. The black liquid the girl had been forced to swallow spilled from the wound, flowing to the ground below and eating the earth away like acid.

Sinnac withdrew his blade slowly, his face etched into lines of disbelief. He stood perfectly still, jaw hanging and eyes bulging as he stared at his dying god. Atyx looked back. The promise in those molten red eyes was one of an eternity of pain. Forgetting himself, Cheron knew a moment of pity for the doomed man.

"What have you done?" Isa's voice thundered, cutting Cheron and Sinnac both out of their dumbfounded states.

Cheron didn't stick around for the answer. He knew from reputation that Sinnac was a fine swordsman, and Isa was a motherfucking dragon. He had to reach Ekos and release him from the enchantment of the collar if he were to stand a chance.

"Stop him!"

Without looking back to check, Cheron knew Isa was midtransformation. He heard it in the growl of her voice, but, mostly, he sensed her power by the electrical charge in the air as her power coalesced.

But Ekos wasn't tied up where Cheron had last seen him. Frantic, he arced his head left to right, searching for some sign of his lover. Not seeing any, Cheron whirled and prepared to face his foes alone—weaponless except for his faith. The goddess's warmth flowed through him, reassuring Cheron that—no matter what—he had a home in her.

Wings unfurled, Isa's body stretched from one end of the small village to the other. Her massive neck craned upward, and she inhaled. Perhaps his imagination ran wild, but Cheron swore he felt the air stir around him and then go still in anticipation.

"Don't kill him!" one of the priests shouted. "We need him for our master's glory."

Isa considered the man's words. Fire boiled in her maw. Electricity jumped around the contained ball of gas in a manner reminiscent of a volcanic eruption. There was a beauty to the display that Cheron couldn't deny, despite the terrifying heat. It was no less glorious when she unleashed the energy, spewing the fire directly toward him.

Priests in the way of the blast were swallowed whole. Cheron heard their agonized cries, only briefly, before the thunder drowned out all other signs of life. There was no structure sturdy enough to absorb the blast, only the mud huts of the common townspeople. Those turned to glass before his very eyes, shattering as the air swept in behind the fire.

Chapter Thirty-Seven

THERE WAS LITTLE else to do besides pray, so Cheron grabbed hold of Kalin's talisman and muttered his offerings under his breath while the world around him disintegrated in a torrent of fire and ash.

Expecting to feel the heat of the blast at any moment, Cheron forced himself to be dignified and embraced his fate believing that his purpose, whatever it was, had been served. Otherwise, he'd feel the goddess's sharp disapproval and not the warm rush of love flowing through him now.

He thought he heard Ekos's voice amidst the chaos. He hoped not. *Please, let him be safe*, Cheron prayed. *Let him go to Lion, let the boy go to school, and let them both live in a world where neither will be slaves again.*

The fire didn't touch him. He heard the rush of heated air whistle in his ears, which popped as though he were climbing a peak rather than standing in one spot clutching his faith to his breast. In wonder, he gaped as the smoke billowed around him in a dome; fire cracked against an invisible barrier. The amulet glowed a brilliant white.

"Cheron!" Ekos yelled. "Cheron!"

A hand on his shoulder shook him. Blinking a few times to clear his vision and his head, Cheron willed himself to come to his senses. Ekos didn't want to wait. He got up in Cheron's face and yelled, "Grab that thing." Ekos pointed at a nearby sword. "And go stab something. Now!"

The sharp tone woke Cheron from his trance. Then, pain followed. The injury on his side pulsed like another heartbeat: faint, fluttering, sharp. "I won't last long. I need to bind this."

Smoke clouded the air around them, hiding them from view. Soon, the sky would clear, and they'd be exposed to another attack. Quickly, Cheron showed Ekos where Sinnac's blade pierced his flesh, and said, "It's not deep."

Ekos's eyes widened when he saw the wound. "Hold still," he said and ripped at what remained of the tattered brown robe they'd dressed him in. An instant later, he wrapped Cheron's injury in a tight binding. The wound stung like the devil before it numbed. That was good, though. The improvised bandage would hold. At least for now.

"There, that'll have to work."

"What are you going to do? You need to hide or…" Cheron's voice trailed off when he saw Ekos no longer wore his collar. There were two branded red welts where the metal had dug into his skin, nothing else.

Ekos gave his curious stare a lopsided, toothy grin that was more dragon than man. "I told one of the priests I wouldn't bludgeon him to death with a rock if he released me. And then I stabbed him, keeping to the letter of my oath if not the spirit."

Cheron groaned at the somewhat dishonorable bargain, but his anger couldn't hold. Then, he asked, "How did they even catch you?"

Ekos's face turned bright red. "They may have put a bunch of gold coins in a pile."

Cheron balked at what he'd just heard. "By the twin moons, you're jesting?"

The red deepened and spread up to the very tips of Ekos's ear. "I couldn't help myself. They were so *shiny*."

Cheron had nothing to say to that.

"What! You probably headed this way for some *honorable* reason or another."

"To save you," Cheron said.

Ekos scratched his belly, as if contemplating. "We're both flawed. What? You keep staring at me."

Rather than answer, Cheron leaned forward and brushed their lips together. Before he died—if that was to be the outcome—he wanted one more touch, one last feel of his lover's smooth skin against his. Expecting a protest, and perhaps a sharp retort, Cheron was surprised when Ekos leaned into the embrace and wound his fingers through Cheron's thick and tangled mass of brown hair.

Who was he kidding? He needed so much more than a mere light touch. Throwing away caution, he pulled their two bodies together. There was no dignity in meeting his maker fully erect and seething with frustration, but Cheron found he didn't care so much about his dignity when he was with Ekos. Not when his heart beat so rapidly that his mind couldn't keep up.

"We need to kill stuff," Ekos panted. "Or we may as well jump in Isa's jaws and get it over with. Let's not be those idiots."

"Yes," Cheron agreed, his breathing ragged.

"Go get the sword. Cover me while I slip into something a bit more scaled."

Cheron darted to the weapon. He sensed Ekos's transformation. It had the same signature as Isa's, the staggered pulse in the air, except Ekos's metamorphosis to his dragon form filled Cheron with pure excitement, instead of dread. Cheron knew relief the moment he heard the golden wings unfurl. The sound of a sail. The promise of adventure to come.

"Good battle," he shouted the encouragement to Ekos. "Her mercy binds us!"

Up ahead, Isa's head rose through the smoke. Through the fog, her yellow eyes glowed a brilliant orange. A mix of awe and terror assailed Cheron, momentarily rooting him to the spot. He snapped out of his reverie in time to dodge as the dragon slammed down her massive paw. The tremors from the impact caused him to teeter backward, but he anticipated the quake this time and recovered his footing swiftly.

Overhead, Ekos's golden wings circulated the air. The florid mesh of white veins glowed in the sunlight. Cheron reached up and ran his hand along the smooth scales of the dragon's underbelly. For luck. Mostly for love.

Isa's eyes widened when she saw Ekos. Abandoning her assault against Cheron, she flew up higher, keeping the other dragon at a disadvantageous lower height. Cheron feared she'd dive at any moment. If she did, Ekos would crash to the ground.

Although he wanted to keep track of the aerial battle, Cheron couldn't watch over his love. Ahead of him, Sinnac stood, blade drawn and ready.

"Husband," he said.

"Soon-to-be widower," Cheron returned.

The man's wisp of a mouth pinched into nonexistence. If Cheron didn't know any better, he'd say Sinnac actually regretted things hadn't worked out between them. He playacted the part of the bereaved, jilted lover with the high color in his cheeks and watery eyes. When he spoke, his words barked and had equal bite to them. "My god wants you alive. I serve his will."

"Your blade ended his hopes to reenter the world. Maybe you should reconsider your allegiances?"

"Give me the Hell's Echo. I will spare you."

In response, Cheron snorted at the false offer.

Sinnac's eyes narrowed. "Reconsider."

Cheron pulled the blade to his right in a defensive posture and waited for the battle to begin.

Sinnac guffawed. "Is this how you imagined it would be? Two men facing each other one-on-one, each battling for his respective god?"

Cheron nodded. "Let us settle the matter with honor."

"Dear me, no. My god requires your submission, and I see only one way to procure it."

Something sharp pricked the side of Cheron's neck. After, Cheron wobbled, seeing the world through waves that stretched and constricted. His eyes watered. And he fell.

Chapter Thirty-Eight

AT LEAST HE wasn't tied up. That was the best Cheron could say of the sight that greeted him when he awoke.

The world smoldered where it had previously burned. Blackened husks that were human bodies crumbled in the wind, taking to the air like petals. None had been spared, not even Atyx's own faithful. The glass huts had melted into clouded glass. The dragon's fire destroyed every living thing within eyeshot.

Groaning, Cheron forced himself to sit up. "Ekos! Ekos!"

Last he remembered, his beloved had been preparing for a battle with Isa. They had climbed higher and higher into the blue sky. Their dark shadows blotted out the sun, making the ground beneath colder. A chill took hold of Cheron. Against his will, his limbs trembled.

"Ekos! Ekos!" No answer. He didn't expect one. By now, he'd come to the realization that his lover was either dead or taken. Quite possibly both. But his heart couldn't accept what his brain knew. "Ekos! Ekos!"

A light popped out from behind one of the incinerated shacks. Cheron thought the flickering orb might be a trick of his eyes, but then it headed his way, and he recognized Vivi. The wisp hovered above his face, bobbing up and down in his familiar pattern.

"Do you know where Ekos is?" His voice broke in his desperation.

Vivi nodded.

"Can you take me to him?"

Of course, the thing couldn't speak, and there was only so much one could glean from a series of motions—some jerking, some fluid. Cheron did his best with the information the strange creature provided.

Vivi swung, his light blurring with the motion. Once, twice, three times—each to the left.

"Ekos is this way?" Cheron asked, uncertain. The creature pointed back in the direction of the cave. "You're certain?"

Vivi performed his version of nodding again. Perhaps the wisp knew the location of Ekos's body, not Ekos himself. The thought took hold and wouldn't let go. Swallowing down the terror threatening to undo him, Cheron trailed, walking on legs that lurched. Walking on water would have been easier.

Sweat dripped down the grooves of his back. Each charred husk grabbed hold of his heart and made it palpate in wild abandon. Did the deceased have a graceful face, a smooth brow perfect for kissing? Was the corpse's eyebrow tilted upward in a sardonic, mocking line? Cheron studied each soul's frozen face, searching for his beloved.

"He's not here," he said. "He's alive. He's a dragon."

Releasing his breath became as painful as taking air in. The muscles of his chest ached under his efforts to slow his inhalations. There was no one to witness his unmanning, only Vivi, so Cheron allowed himself to wheeze and make small cries. When the sobs came, he didn't stifle them.

His steps faltered. Cheron doubled over, placing his hands on his knees while his head buzzed, his vision swam, his guts twisted.

Vivi stopped and began circling.

Cheron thought he heard a voice over the sound of his own labored breathing. Soldier's training kicked in, overriding his grief. His ears pricked, acutely aware of everything.

"Ekos! Cheron!"

Lion?

"Ekos!"

Yes, it was him. His voice sounded hoarse, as though he'd been crying out the names for a very long time. There was also an edge of determination, as if he'd go on forever if necessary. "Hello? Cheron? Ekos!"

Vivi zipped toward the sound. Seconds later, the two emerged; Lion followed along after Vivi at a full sprint. He flung himself into Cheron's arms, wrapping them nearly all the way around his massive torso. The warmth of the greeting overtook him. Tears pricked the backs of his eyes. Wetness against his chest indicated Lion was similarly affected by their reunion.

"I thought you were dead," Lion gasped between sniffles.

"There, there," Cheron said, patting Lion's slim back.

"What happened here?"

Quickly, Cheron told him of the skirmish between him, Sinnac, Ekos, and Isa. What little of the battle he remembered.

Eyes wide in fear, Lion listened attentively. He interrupted when Cheron described the looming fight between the two dragons. "Where is Ekos? Is he safe?"

"I don't know. I could not find him among the bodies."

"Vivi, is Ekos here?" Lion asked.

The thing moved side to side. Its version of no.

"Do you know where he is?"

Vivi nodded.

"Where is he?" Cheron asked. "Did Sinnac take him?"

Vivi nodded again.

Both Cheron and Lion flinched at the news. Before he passed out, Cheron remembered Sinnac saying there was one way to force him to use Hell's Echo to free Atyx from his prison. He must have meant Ekos.

Cheron swallowed his outrage, his grief, and said, "He'll remain alive until I serve my purpose in their plans. I have to make it to the palace."

The how of it eluded an explanation. The palace was at least five days' journey on foot. Sinnac's men would have plenty of time to prepare for his arrival. Scouts would be posted at every trail. They'd know of his every step, right down to what might be his last.

"I cannot divine a way to gain an upper hand."

He spoke mostly to himself. Venting his frustrations was the luxury left to him after all else had been taken.

Lion shifted from foot to foot. He ran his fingers through his thick nest of curly hair, nervously pulling on the longer strands.

"Is there something you'd like to say?" Cheron asked him.

"I traveled here using sorcery." Lion licked his lips and stammered. "Uh, dark magic. I found a book in Ekos's library. When Vivi came back, I got worried and decided to do whatever I needed to help you guys. I won't use it again unless you want me to now. I promise. I…"

Cheron ignored the rest of the rambled explanation, which came fast from Lion's lips. He asked, "Why did Ekos have a book of dark magic?"

"Dragons are hoarders. He has a lot of stuff."

Cheron touched Kalin's amulet, which rested in its rightful place against his chest. Using sorcery broke with her basic tenants. Magic, the type that came from Kalin and her twin moon consorts, was allowed.

"Is there a way to get me there using magic?"

Lion flushed and looked away. "None that I know of. My skills are limited. It was by luck I found this transportation spell. It's all I have. I'm sorry."

He wanted to keep fighting honorably, to wage war in the goddess's light, but not as much as he wanted to win. He had to concede that Kalin demanded of wisdom as well as honor, and so far, his strategies only ended with him flat on his back and trussed up like a principled goose. It was time to embrace the reality that his foes were dishonorable and skate the line between scoundrel and knight himself. It was time to embrace his inner Ekos.

"Use your sorcery" he said to Lion. "And then stay here. Wait for us."

Chapter Thirty-Nine

LION VANISHED INSIDE the forest's shadow, reemerging again when the sun had set, casting the entire world into darkness. When he came back, he carried so many herbs he had to cradle them using both hands. Various doodads, which he'd tied to his waist, bounced against his thighs. Cheron had no earthly idea where he'd found any of the magical paraphernalia. He decided not to ask. He didn't really want to know the answer, not if the explanation involved more sorcery.

"Welcome back," Cheron greeted him.

Huffing, his cheeks flushed from his exertions, Lion gave him a winded hello and plopped his pile of herbs onto the makeshift table he'd asked Cheron to construct. He gazed at all the items, counting them off silently but moving his lips to form the words. Then, he said, "I need a blood sacrifice."

Cheron balked at the demand. Then, fearing the answer, he asked, "What did you use last time?"

Lion held up his arm and showed Cheron a jagged cut down the length of his arm. Whatever magic he'd used to travel here had sealed the wound. A scarred stretch of white skin ran up the length of his arm like a cord of rope. Around the laceration, an ugly red rash branched through, connecting like a mesh of veins. His real veins stood out in stark contrast, bloated and purple.

"It is a wonder you didn't bleed out!"

"I thought I was going to die," he confessed. "I thought my ghost would help you two."

The thought shocked Cheron into an uncomfortable silence. That Lion was willing to die only to check up on them, to confirm his suspicions that something was amiss, humbled him and quashed his previous ungracious thoughts about the use of sorcery. He forced his tone to be severe when he said, "Never do anything so reckless again."

"Sure, Dad."

Both of them knew the title, despite the sarcastic tilt he placed on the word, was spoken true. Cheron grabbed hold of Lion and gave him an awkward hug until the moment passed.

"You better find him," Lion said. Like Cheron, he playacted at being harsh, even pointing a slender finger at Cheron's face. "You and him are all I have in the world."

"I'll do my best," Cheron said. "And when I get back, we're both taking you to the academy. Will you accept the one in Broken Maw?"

"What's the curriculum? Fighting bears?"

"*And* ax throwing."

Lion laughed, truly laughed. Cheron had only seen him do that once before with Ekos. It bolstered his mood to see Lion happy after everything he'd been through. There was hope for the future.

"So is that a yes to the academy at Broken Maw?"

Lion nodded. His grin stretched the length of his face, cutting much deeper than his scar ever could.

"What do we need for a blood sacrifice?" Cheron asked.

Lion's face fell into its pinched and worried lines, and Cheron momentarily regretted bringing up the subject so abruptly, but he had to leave soon. Ekos depended on him.

"I saw some squirrels," the young man eventually said in a hushed tone. "The spell says blood. The text in the book doesn't specify a source. But I hate to kill anything. I..." He flushed, embarrassed. "I like animals. They're *good*. Usually."

"What can we use, then?"

Mouth trembling, Lion held out his uninjured arm and considered its clean, smooth surface. He grabbed hold of a rock he'd sharpened to cut and pressed it against his flesh. Blood pricked up around the welt.

"No," Cheron said. He took the boy's hand and gently drew it back. "You're not going to harm yourself. If the spell needs blood, I'll give mine."

"You have to be in fighting condition when you get there," Lion said. "The spell is draining. I had to sleep off its effects for a day, and you don't have that much time."

"Then a squirrel. I'll give it a soldier's death."

The attempt at humor fell flat. Lion made a valiant effort to lift his lips in some semblance of a smile. "Can you go into the forest to find one? I...kind of already named the ones in town."

"Sure," Cheron said, and gave him a slight clap on the back.

True to his word, Cheron walked far out into the forest, wielding a bow he'd found in the nearly destroyed town. Luck was with him. A squirrel jumped up on one of the tree stumps. Tail twitching, its ears rotating to catch every noise, the critter considered him through black, beady eyes, with an odd calm.

"Are you offering this creature for my use?" he asked and touched Kalin's talisman. Warmth flooded through him. The goddess answered. "Thank you. Your grace binds me."

The animal didn't run when Cheron approached or when he bent to grab hold of it. "Sorry, little guy," Cheron said and snapped the creature's neck. He drained the blood into the small wooden cup.

By the time he traveled back to the dwelling, Lion had prepared the rest of the spell. Strange symbols unlike Cheron had ever seen painted the walls. Most of them were straight, intersecting lines. He'd drawn a series of circles on the ground, tracing the pattern in the dirt.

"Watch out!"

Cheron had nearly stepped on one of the lines. "Sorry," he said and carefully made his way toward the center circle where Lion stood.

"Do you have the blood?" Lion asked.

Cheron nodded and handed him the cup.

The grim expression on his face when he took the offering warned of a more odious task ahead. Lion spread the offered sacrifice over the herbs, mixing them together with his hands until the leaves were saturated. Nose wrinkled in disgust, he stared off to the side, never looking at his hands. Killing was never easy. Using the life force of a slain foe to power a spell was nothing short of brutality. Cheron felt his heart pinch for the sensitive young man.

"I'm sorry," Cheron said. "Hopefully this will be the last time."

"I hope so. Here, you have to eat this. And you have to *chew*."

Lion handed him a clump of the mixed herbs. The bundle smelled like coins, and Cheron knew the taste would match, if not the consistency.

Cheron put the mixture into his mouth and chewed as instructed. The slimy texture stuck in the crevasses of his mouth. Plant fibers slipped between his teeth, digging into his gums. Although the notion was absurd, Cheron resented this the most. It wasn't enough for the offering to be absorbed; it had to weave its presence throughout his body, scarring him as a user of dark magic.

"Okay, now we have to mark where we are on the map."

Lion used a stick to place an *X* where they stood.

"Think of where you want to go. Get a really good mental picture, and then use this stick to trace a straight line forward. Make sure to connect it to the third circle or you may...uh...arrive in pieces or get stuck between ports."

Clearing his thoughts, Cheron conjured a vision of the royal dungeons. Their cell had been small and barred off by polished silver bars. The hole they made in the wall crumbled. A fine dust coated the rim. The unbroken walls were a smooth concrete with no markings. On the floor, their discarded chains took in the chill of the room. They'd be frigid to the touch.

The picture was as clear as possible. Cheron heeded the warnings and connected the line directly to the third circle.

Chapter Forty

PRISON WALLS CLOSED in around him. He and Ekos had been the only captives when Sinnac had confined them here. No guards had been posted to ensure they wouldn't escape because Sinnac had wanted them to. He needed them to procure the Hell's Echo. Luckily, the same held true now. Cheron emerged from the spell to a cold, empty room. He was alone.

He crawled through the same hole he'd created before. Once he was through, he dusted off the fine powder that rubbed off from the crumbling concrete.

Using only his memory to navigate the twists and turns of the catacombs proved to be more difficult than he imagined. Ekos had guided him last time, which made the passageways seem more straightforward than they actually were. Without assistance, Cheron quickly lost his way, and it didn't help that the halls only became darker the farther he progressed.

He stopped to think out the problem. He didn't dare risk talking to himself, not even to break the oppressive silence. Out of nowhere, a light appeared before him.

"Vivi?"

The wisp didn't bother to nod. Cheron determined that meant something close to *How many other floating balls of light do you know?*

"I'm glad to see you," Cheron said. "Can you get me outside?"

The wisp gave his greeting a slight dip and then swooped off until his solid light became a long blur. Cheron trailed after him the best he could, as running was difficult for a man of his bulk.

Soon, the stagnant air had a crisp edge. A slight breeze fluttered the loose hem of Charon's brown robe, cooling his legs but mostly reminding him of his vulnerability should he have to fight right away. They were getting close. Cheron, galvanized by the rush of air, picked up his pace. As he came up on the rounded staircase that led to the gardens, he managed a full run. He broke free from the catacombs in a burst, and the world transformed from a monotone slate gray to one of bright eruptions of yellow, orange, red, and blue all adrift on a sea of green grass and black sky. The flowers were in full bloom, as was the night.

Warning bells chimed. Expecting battle, Sinnac was warning his people to stay inside.

"Do you know where Ekos is?"

Vivi nodded.

"Take me to him."

Cheron held his breath and waited for Vivi to leave the garden. To go somewhere, anywhere, other than deeper into what Cheron knew to be a hellish nightmare sustained by profane black magic. But Vivi didn't divert his course. He drifted amongst the flowerbeds, eventually stopping to hover over a long patch of weeds in the garden paradise.

Slow, lumbering legs that weighed a dragon apiece carried Cheron forward. Every limb weighed him down; every breath stung; each footfall reached his ear as a thunderclap. And then Cheron was at the end where the face of his beloved blurred in his vision and imprinted itself onto his mind.

Crystal-blue eyes, now clouded over by a thin white sheen, met his brown, pleading in mute agony for a swift death. His crown of golden hair had turned into a brittle brown, the color of the wilting husks of corn. Cheron forced himself to view the rest. Witnessing the horror was the least he owed Ekos. Choking thistle, a noxious weed as common as crabgrass, spilled out over Ekos's flesh from his chest cavity, which was pried open and flayed like a gutted fish. Whatever dark magic kept him alive removed the necessity for his internal organs, which were pushed off to the side.

Cheron fell to his knees and took hold of Ekos's limp hand. Too defiant to simply slip away, to become one of the motionless, drained souls around him, Ekos used his thumb to weakly stroke Cheron's rough skin. The small thread of contact brought him to tears.

"I'm going to free you," he said, trailing kisses over Ekos's forehead. "I'll find a way. I promise."

Ekos gave his declaration a slow blink.

"I have to go now," Cheron said, the lump in his throat muting his voice. "I have to find armor and a weapon."

Ekos let him loose. The lingering contact tingled along Cheron's flesh. He longed for a deeper embrace, to pull Ekos into his arms and hold him there until they both lost themselves in the comfort of their love. "I'll free you," he repeated. "And I love you. Not just dragons. You."

Ekos gave the declaration a small smile and another slow blink.

Necessity dictated that Cheron focus on the battle ahead. Under dim moonlight, he made his way to a nearby guard tower. It would certainly be staffed, but Cheron hoped Sinnac had diverted some of his forces to keep track of Cheron's progress on the road to the palace. He kept his footsteps light, his breathing even but deep enough to keep his blood pumping.

"How many guards are there?" he whispered to Vivi. "Get ahead of me and check."

Vivi zipped off and came back a minute later. Cheron held up his hands and spread out his fingers. He twitched his right pinky. "One—" And then he twitched his left. "—to ten. Float next to the correct number."

Vivi fluttered to his second finger.

"Armed?"

Vivi nodded.

"Attentive? Alert?"

Vivi flitted side to side to indicate no.

The last bit was the only good news. As he'd hoped, the palace was not expecting him yet, so no one was too worried. Two armed soldiers were better odds than four or five, but still daunting for an unarmed man wearing a brown frock.

As a battle veteran, Cheron knew how to get into the proper headspace to kill. He took a moment to pray to Kalin, reveling in the instant warmth, and then closed his eyes and envisioned the battle ahead. Then, when he felt ready, he moved forward, sticking to the shadows and once again concentrating on keeping his naturally boisterous footsteps light and delicate.

They were talking about women they'd wooed. High and young, their voices were nearly as crisp as the air. The mercy goddess frowned on slaying the young, especially those who'd been conscripted into the armies of the corrupt.

Cheron sighed at the inconvenience of encountering two green boys rather than veterans, but he had no choice but to adhere to the tenants of the goddess, whose grace bound him in service.

Hastily, he revised his plan.

He burst through the door with a loud, disorienting roar.

One of the young men, his jaw down and his eyes wide, dropped his weapon, which clattered on the floor with a rattle of steel. The other's reaction was more precise, more seasoned. He lunged forward, using the blade of his sword to put distance between himself and Cheron. Smart.

"Halt!" the guard shouted at him.

Cheron dodged the boy's next lunge. The boy, believing he was about to thrust the blade through Cheron's body, put more force behind his charge than necessary. His momentum carried him forward right past Cheron into the wall. His sword stuck inside the wood, embedded nearly to the hilt. Cheron cracked him in the back of the head. He fell to the ground in a heap.

"Halt. Stay where you are," the other guard said. The order sounded like he was asking a question rather than giving a command.

"Put down the weapon," Cheron said. "You've lost."

In response, the boy lifted his blade higher and fixed his expression in the fiercest war glower he could manage.

"Put the blade down. The goddess asks that you accept her mercy."

"You can't get to a weapon. I'll run you through the moment you bend to pick it up," the boy said.

"Don't you know who I am?"

"Yes, the savage from Broken Maw."

"Then you know you cannot kill me. Your order will be to take me alive. Do you think you can subdue me?"

Cheron was taller than the boy by a few feet and heavier than almost anyone by a hundred pounds of pure muscle, a difficult discrepancy to overcome for an untested low-ranking guard. Uncertainty showed in the dip of the boy's sword. The adrenaline rush he was too inexperienced to control shook his hands. Memories of his own youth told Cheron that the boy's hands sweated. He'd drop his sword before he ran Cheron through.

Cheron walked forward and put a hand on the boy's shoulder. "I'll make it look like you put up a hell of a fight."

The blade dropped to the floor. The boy fell soon after.

Chapter Forty-One

ARMED WITH A sword and dressed in a rather hodgepodge suit of armor he'd crafted from whatever gear fit, Cheron made his way to Sinnac's chambers. His heart raced, his chest heaved, and his fists clenched and unclenched. Cheron wore down the jagged edge of his rage by focusing on each breath, counting them out silently until his limbs stopped shaking.

He couldn't think about Ekos. Each time he did, the anger and grief crippled him. And so he cleared his mind and moved forward.

Cheron wanted to avoid detection for as long as possible, a difficult task. Anyone who saw him would know who he was, and the narrow, straight-line paths of the hallways made sneaking impossible. Honor demanded he make every effort to minimalize casualties, so he took extra precautions to avoid other living souls.

Vivi came back from another scouting mission.

How many? Cheron mouthed the words and held up his hands.

Vivi hovered next to Cheron's second finger.

Armed? Cheron mouthed.

Vivi indicated that they were not.

Citizens? Cheron mouthed, dreading the answer.

Vivi nodded.

Any way around them? Cheron asked.

There was not.

Swearing softly under his breath, Cheron leaned back against the hard marble wall and considered his options. Realistically, there were only two: kill them or walk past and hope they didn't sound the alarm.

The soft patter of their footsteps rushed his decision. Much like the young men who had guarded the tower, they were caught in a mundane conversation about everyday life and palace gossip. Their melodious, feminine voices carried through the narrow hallways, echoing with an ethereal resonance.

His earlier ruse, where he'd playacted being under the influence of the god's spell, had been adequate to fool a god. Perhaps the ruse might also work with common palace folk.

Cheron removed the helm and mussed his hair until he was certain he appeared disheveled. He knew his body was already covered in grime, his arms and legs with cuts. He'd appear broken, beaten.

He'd seen the faces of men in the village caught up in one of the enchantment spells. Their big, listless eyes, dry and unblinking, fixated on nothing. Slack-jawed, as though continually caught by surprise, they meandered the world on their master's word alone.

Cheron mimicked their countenance. Praying to Kalin, he stepped into the hall in front of the two women and walked toward them as though guided by forces beyond his control. He jerked his limbs to indicate an inner struggle and twisted his head side to side in denial.

"It's the Northern savage!" the older woman shrieked. The younger clutched her heart as though it were about to burst from her chest and scamper down the hall without her.

Cheron forced himself not to respond emotionally to the disgust. Expression blank, his features taut as though he were fighting against a magic force stronger than anything he'd encountered, he said, "I'm here to serve my master, King Sinnac of Wren Gardens."

The two women visibly relaxed.

"Oh, they caught him," the younger one said.

"Thank the twin moons!" the older echoed the relief. "What a hideous outfit they dressed him in."

"I must serve my master," Cheron repeated, but he felt heat rush to his face.

The older woman waved him away. "Well, he isn't here. Shoo."

Obediently, Cheron bowed his head and stumbled down the hall. Since he was going for totally mindless, he bumped into a couple of walls along the way. Behind him, the two women tittered into their hands and made fun of his strange accent and mismatched armor.

When he was out of sight and earshot, he indulged in a smirk and a satisfied chuckle to celebrate the success of his ruse. For people who prided themselves on their cleverness, the servants of Atyx were easy to dupe. Their arrogance made them so. That's why, despite his successes, Cheron approached each corner fully alert and ready to fight.

Vivi flew up to him and bobbled up and down excitedly. Whenever Cheron tried to move forward, he zipped directly into his face. He couldn't risk any vocalizations, so Cheron held up his hand, hoping the wisp might clarify and tell him how many guards were ahead.

Vivi swung back and forth.

No guards? Cheron wasn't sure what else to expect, but, trusting Vivi, he backed up and retraced the corridors they'd already traveled. Eventually, they ducked inside one of the many rooms that—when his eyes adjusted—Cheron realized was a library. He glanced at a few of the titles and hoped one day he'd be able to travel back to the palace and peruse the shelves under better circumstances.

Are we good? he mouthed to Vivi.

No, Vivi signaled back.

Soon after, Sinnac, flanked by Isa and three guards, strolled past. Oddly confident for someone who had run his god through, he held his head high. One of the robes he favored, this one threaded with silver and gold, trailed behind him in a long train. Cheron's lip curled at the display. The man probably heard *glory, glory, glory* in his own wake.

"What are the reports? Is the savage near our gates?" Sinnac's voice boomed the question.

"No, Your Excellency. Our scouts report no sightings. He vanished."

"Find him or I'll have your heads."

The guards broke away and ran toward the door. Their armor rattled.

When Sinnac and Isa passed the door to the library, the dragon's nostrils flared, and she stopped in her tracks. Eyes narrowed, she turned her head in Cheron and Vivi's direction and stopped.

Bloodlust overtook Cheron when he thought about Ekos in the garden, his chest ripped open and delicate heart beating alone. Cheron put his hand over the hilt of his sword and prepared to fight everyone at once in the cramped room. He visualized running Sinnac through on his blade, the blood raining down on his face. His limbs fell naturally into a battle posture—legs spread apart, shoulders squared.

But she moved onward.

Vivi gestured for Cheron to follow once the procession vanished down the hall.

Cheron ignored the ball of light. Seeing Sinnac, detecting wafts of the sweet raspberry perfume he wore, sparked the fires of his rage. Although he knew the odds were overwhelmingly against his favor, he wanted to fight now. Each step away from his foes made him snarl in frustration.

Pent-up energy taunted his muscles. Veins stuck out along his arms. Sword in hand, the naked steel winking in the light, Cheron stalked through the halls. He lashed out at the first inanimate object he encountered: a pedestal holding a crystal vase. Swinging wide, Cheron splintered the fragile display. As if rebuking him for his temper tantrum, a shard embedded itself in his forearm. Cheron pushed the embedded fragment in farther, welcoming the pain as relief from his despair.

Kalin's amulet warmed uncomfortably on his chest.

"Yes, I am sorry. I...just..."

He pinched the bridge of his nose and thought of Ekos and his pleading eyes. Would any of this even matter? In the end, could he save his love?

In sympathy, the amulet thrummed on his chest. The sensation calmed and simultaneously reminded him there was more at stake than his love affairs.

"Yes, your grace binds me still."

Cheron moved forward, forever bound in service to his goddess.

Chapter Forty-Two

"HIDE," HE TOLD Vivi. "Only come out if needed."

Sword laid across his lap, Cheron waited for Sinnac to return to his chamber. Had the other king thought of Cheron as an equal rather than a stupid savage, this course of action would have easily landed him back in the dungeons, back in Isa's cruel clutches and the war god's thrall. But Sinnac's contempt would prove his undoing. At least, that's where Cheron placed his bet.

"Tell me what I plan is right," he prayed to Kalin.

Her amulet warmed on his chest.

And so he waited. A light breeze fluttered the thin chiffon curtains. Sometimes, they grazed the side of Cheron's cheek and a cold shiver ran down the length of his spine. The smells of the garden—lavender, jasmine, and the sweet tang of honeysuckle—had delighted him earlier. Now, each floral fragrance reminded him of Ekos. Pushing his lover from his mind was an impossible task. Cheron embraced his dark thoughts and allowed his rage to build, storing the energy. He'd need it soon.

Alone, with no guards in sight, Sinnac entered his chamber. Seconds later, his valet knocked on the door, a timid, apologetic series of taps. "Your Excellency..."

"Not now," Sinnac barked back. "Leave!"

Cheron slunk into the shadows of the room and waited until the echoing footsteps of the servant faded. Then, he revealed himself. "Your Excellency."

Sinnac whirled. The fabric of his long cloak swished on the floor, creating a soft flow of air that disturbed the curtains. His jaw muscle twitched, and his eyes widened slightly, but he mastered his features like the warrior Cheron knew him to be. Brow arched, he said, "Will a servant of Kalin slay an unarmed man in his bedchamber under the cover of night?"

"No," Cheron said. He pointed at the armor he'd laid out near the bed. "He would deny you the chance to stack the odds and use your dragon pet. Equip yourself."

Cheron examined each and every movement the other man made as he donned the armor, searching for any sign of trickery. Servants of Atyx often rubbed poisons on their armor. Any slight brush of skin against the metal and the unwary opponents would find themselves groggy and sometimes—if the follower were especially cowardly—completely immobilized. Kalin demanded her servants to behave honorably. Atyx demanded his servants win at all costs.

"Did you like the addition to my garden?" Sinnac asked as he pulled on his gloves.

"Release him," Cheron said. "He's no longer of use to you."

Sinnac gave his order a breezy laugh, barely enough air within it to blow out a dying candle. "Delightful. My goodness, you never change. I don't think I shall ever trim back the weeds inside him. Ten years from now, his entire body will be grown over. You'll have to imagine the gruesome beauty of the exhibit since you won't live to witness my creation's evolution."

"My anger is already stoked. You waste time."

Sinnac gave that another short laugh, then settled his face into grim lines. He positioned his sword so that the point aimed right at Cheron's heart. "I'll plant my blade where I already pierced you."

Their blades crossed. The familiar clank of metal centered Cheron and put him in the moment. His muscles, finely tuned to the rigors of battle, worked on instinct to heave his blade to the level of his shoulder. As they circled, Cheron's feet moved in time with Sinnac's. Neither man flinched in the face of the other's stare.

"Have you figured out how to use the Echo, Cheron?" Sinnac asked him. The edge of the man's lip, as sharp as his sword, lifted in a smirk. "Or are you still awaiting the call of your goddess?"

"Her grace binds me," Cheron answered simply. He wasn't going to allow himself to be goaded into a verbal fray or other such distractions. Sinnac's throat, his thigh, his chest—Cheron's attention was already as divided as his blade was hungry.

"Our journey doesn't have to end this way. My god wants a union and his ascension. The world is ours for the taking, but you have to stop being a fool. I could release Ekos if you bend your knee."

In response, Cheron started the fray by lunging forward. Sinnac fell back, blocking the thrust with the edge of his sword. Cheron pushed forward again, recklessly putting himself in range for an easy kill. Sinnac did not capitalize on any of the opportunities. He kept falling farther back to the wall, only blocking—with expert precision—each of Cheron's attacks.

While Cheron kept himself exposed to lethal wounds, he guarded against injuries that might incapacitate him. When Sinnac went for his upper leg yet again, Cheron countered and scraped the tip of his blade along the contour of Sinnac's cheek. An insult.

Blood, only a thin stream, ran down Sinnac's cheek. Sinnac's nostrils flared at the feel of it on his skin. Enraged, his pupils dilated, he growled his frustrations, but he still didn't lunge and pierce Cheron's exposed flesh.

Cheron said, "Your god wants me alive. He needs me alive. You're already outside his favor after the debacle in the village."

Pale and trembling, Sinnac pursed his lips but said nothing. His sword arm trembled. No doubt the burden of the sword's weight was growing heavy and his muscles would be tired from countering all of Cheron's fierce attacks. Neither the man nor the blade had the same sharp sheen.

Cheron continued, "My goddess asks her followers to embody her virtues. I offer you her mercy now in exchange for freeing Ekos, her servant."

Sinnac snorted, but Cheron saw the slight flick of doubt as his eyes darted back and forth and he licked his dried, cracking lips.

"Do you think Atyx will reward you, or even let you live, if you fail to subdue me?"

"Do you think your goddess will forgive you if you fail to free her and save your lover instead?"

"Yes. And she can forgive you as well."

The certainty of Cheron's declaration stunned Sinnac, who collapsed backward against the wall. The point of his sword fell toward the ground. Half-heartedly, he raised it again and pointed the blade at Cheron's stomach.

Cheron held up his arms, giving his opponent a clear opportunity. "Strike me down if you dare cross your god. Impale me on your blade and quash his chances of ascension."

"He punishes his defectors," Sinnac stammered. "An eternity of torment."

Unsympathetic, Cheron shrugged. "Kalin is honorable. If you commit yourself to her service, she will protect you from your vengeful god."

Although he knew what he said to be true—Kalin's grace applied to the undeserving as well as the truly virtuous—the words felt like clumps of clay in his throat. His plan hinged on his opponent's cowardice, his willingness to betray anything and everyone for his own benefit. Such a man earned his death on the end of the blade. But he had to be humble where his foes were arrogant. The other man's fate was not his to decide.

"I will free Ekos," Sinnac said.

True to his word, Cheron sheathed his sword.

Chapter Forty-Three

BETRAYAL HUNG IN the air between them. Whenever anyone approached, whether it was a commoner or a guard, Cheron held his breath and readied to fight his way back to the garden. As they passed yet another patrol unit without incident, Cheron released the tension in his body, allowing his shoulders to roll backward in a relaxed position. The breath he'd been holding in escaped in a ragged huff.

Sinnac chuckled at his discomfort, but when he spoke, his voice was serious. "If we wish to maintain the illusion you are under my control, you'll want to stop calling attention to your weapon."

Cheron moved his hand away from the pommel of his sword.

"There now. You appear subdued as well as refined."

Once again, Sinnac had dressed Cheron in the attire of Wren Garden. Silk rather than cold metal shivered across his cool skin, which was scrubbed and scented with sandalwood oils.

While he felt naked without his protective gear, Cheron admitted to the sense of the attire. Suspicions, and uncomfortable questions, would have followed them had he been fully decked out in battle gear. This way, passersby accepted his presence without quarrelsome remark. A few gave their leader an elated *huzzah* for capturing the Northern savage.

"Excellency," a woman greeted them.

"Don't you hear the bells?" Sinnac asked. "You should be indoors where it's safe."

"Of course, Excellency. And thank you for bringing this beast to heel."

Sinnac's imperious smile blew from his face like dust in the wind the moment the woman hurried away. His scowl persisted until they stood in front of Ekos, who rolled his eyes upward to meet Sinnac's. Through his pain, Ekos managed to mouth the words *Fuck you*. Sinnac crept forward, a dark grin once again twisting his already narrow face.

"Release him as you promised," Cheron said. "No tricks."

Ekos gritted his teeth and tried to rise from the bed.

"Your pet doesn't think your plan is very wise."

Cheron knelt by Ekos's side and gently tucked a loose strand of hair behind his ear. Using the flat of his finger, he traced the tender line of his chin. He used the lover's gesture to smuggle a whisper. "I need your help. I can't fight Isa alone. This is my only chance."

When he pulled away, Ekos gave him a slow blink to let him know he'd heard and understood.

"All right, fulfill your oath," Cheron said.

"Of course."

Sinnac knelt in the exact spot where Cheron had. For added measure, he repeated the sweet gesture, even planting a light kiss on Ekos's furrowed brow after smoothing down the loose strands of his hair. Then, he grabbed the weeds springing from Ekos's chest and pulled upward with brutal force. Using a small dagger, he dissected the tangling stems from Ekos's chest cavity.

Ekos's slender fingers clutched the side of the flowerbed. The white of his knuckles contrasted with the dark brown of the wood, mimicking the white of his teeth standing out against the bright red of his blood.

In horror, Cheron watched the minor fluctuations of Ekos's ever-changing expression. Pain, although he tried to hide his agony behind a brave smirk, contorted his features. Blood oozed up from his mouth when he moaned. The noise, while squeezing Cheron's heart, gave him hope. Ekos hadn't been able to vocalize before.

"Help me lift him," Sinnac said. "Keep him level."

"His organs..."

Ekos's innards were still shoved off to the side. The sight of his lover's beating heart tangled in the remains of rotting weeds, which shriveled and dried instantly after being cut from the chest cavity, made bile rise in his gourd. Cheron swallowed it down.

Cheron bent to take one of Ekos's hands in his. "This will be over soon. Be strong awhile longer."

"Keep your sweet nothings for later. He'll bleed out if we don't snip him from the ground," Sinnac said.

Fighting down his rage, Cheron gripped Ekos where Sinnac indicated he should and lifted in concert with the other man. Together, they sat Ekos on the hard stone tiles. Sinnac stood and cocked his head to the side, studying his handiwork like an appraising artist. The smirk came back, drawing ever upward as Ekos writhed. "Aw," he said in mock sympathy when Ekos let loose a massive shriek.

"Remember your promise," Cheron spat through gritted teeth. "Should he die, you get no protection from Kalin and your god collects his due from your excuse of a soul."

Sinnac tsked his severe tone, and his face fell into a moue. "We are friends now, I thought."

"Save him."

Shrugging in the face of Cheron's animosity, Sinnac knelt back beside Ekos and whispered in the same spidery language that Cheron remembered from the village. A moment of panic assailed him. If the magic worked on the will of Atyx, then Ekos would die at his feet and their journey together would be over. Cheron should have considered that. Ekos was right. He was a shit planner.

His worries turned out to be unfounded.

Sinnac placed each of the organs back in Ekos's chest, muttering magical words over each one, before closing the cavity. The fragile bones of the rib cage cracked when Sinnac pushed the two sides together. Cheron hissed out air when Ekos whimpered and arched his back into an impossible angle.

"Careful."

"Yes, yes," Sinnac said. "He's almost done."

By magic, the jagged cut sealed, leaving behind a light scar that resembled Cheron's. That too vanished.

Ekos's breathing evened. His eyes lost the milky-white sheen and once again became a clear crystal blue. The color and texture returned to his sunken cheeks. Golden again, rather than the dry, brittle color of harvested straw, his stunning swath of hair shone in the lamplight.

Cheron took off the decorative cloak he wore and wrapped it protectively around Ekos's naked, shivering body. Ekos entwined their fingers and pressed his head against the massive expanse of his chest. Cheron cradled him and tried to keep from weeping in relief. Wetness against his cheeks told him he'd failed.

"These big hands of yours are suited for tender burdens after all," Ekos whispered, his voice rough.

The laugh Cheron released was half sob. He wanted to say something in return, to console his love, but he only managed a light kiss on his sweet brow.

Isa walked from the shadows. "Quite a scene."

"I was touched," Sinnac agreed. "Love is grand."

"Keep your head on your shoulders. Literally," Ekos said, his voice weak. "I need time to recover."

Cheron laid Ekos back on the ground and stood. Isa came in behind him and grabbed hold of the chain of Kalin's amulet. She pulled him backward against her body. Knowing it was useless to struggle against her superior strength, Cheron kept his dignity and mutely accepted her embrace.

"Your god needs me," Cheron reminded them both.

Sinnac clucked his tongue. "Just so. Just so. But you gave the power of the Echo over to your sweet love, didn't you? Now that I have him, you're redundant."

Isa plunged the blade deep into Cheron's back. Only the chain, the metal digging into his neck, kept him from collapsing forward as the sword severed his spine. It went through his stomach. The point emerged where his belly button once was. The sharp pain, followed by the odd numbness of death, stole the air from his body. And then he realized he couldn't breathe because his lungs were quickly filling with blood.

The world blurred, contorting into vague shapes and a loud, primal cry he dimly realized came from Ekos. Isa removed the talisman from Cheron's neck. Triumphant, a smug expression on her face, she looked into the eyes of the twisting dragon figures of the banished goddess.

Sinnac's voice drifted in through the confusing chaos of his dying. "He gave you dominion over the Echo. Use the relic to release Atyx from Yellow Sky. The god will reward you both with Cheron's life."

Chapter Forty-Four

CHERON COLLAPSED ON the ground where he coiled in on himself. He didn't feel pain, not anymore, just a dim sense of his own mortality and the aching realization that Ekos was in danger and he couldn't do anything.

Coldness seeped straight to his bones. The sounds of the world muted. He disconnected from everything except the loud rush of his life leaving his body. No, not *everything*. An odd sensation cut through the haze. His back itched. Horribly. Cheron wanted to laugh at the absurdity..

"Save Cheron," Sinnac said to Ekos. "Release my god from his prison. Share in his glory."

"Yes, save your pet," Isa crooned. "We know you'd do anything for him. Only Atyx can save him. Only he can heal a fatal wound."

"You are right. I would do anything for him. Give me the amulet," Ekos said. He held out his hand. Isa placed Kalin's talisman on his palm. The chain dangled between Ekos's slender fingers as he curled his fist around the metal.

No, Cheron wanted to scream, but when he tried to talk, he spat up blood.

"Better hurry," Isa said. She nudged Cheron with the tip of her foot, flipping him to his back. "He'll drown or bleed out."

Ekos took the amulet in his hands and broke it in half. The sound of the snap, like a thousand tree branches breaking in a fierce storm, reverberated through Cheron's chest cavity. In his mind, he screamed out in frustration. He tried to reach up to Ekos, to snatch the amulet from his hands and reconnect the two parts into a whole, but he couldn't move an inch.

Dark mist arose from the halves. Cheron remembered the odd substance from the test, and it had the same strange, indefinable power. As the cloud ascended to the sky, it took the shape of a golden dragon, its long neck coiled upward toward the heavens, and then it vanished.

Cheron twisted on the ground, trying in vain to speak.

"I think your lover is upset," Isa said. "Perhaps Atyx will make him more amenable as well. Control spells can last a lifetime."

"Maybe so," Ekos said. "Guess we'll have to wait and see."

The itching on Cheron's back intensified. The pain, starting as a mere poke on his shoulder blades right where Ekos had tattooed him, intensified. It was the feel of someone resting a finger against his flesh and pushing lightly. Then, that same finger kept pressing, digging until it cut through the first layer of skin and into muscle. Cheron screamed. Blood sputtered from his mouth, dropping back down onto his face.

"Hang in," Ekos shouted down at him. "Fight."

An explosion pitched Sinnac and Isa to the ground, where they rolled on top of each other and got tangled in the long fabric of Sinnac's robe. Ekos stumbled as well, hitting the side of the wall with a heavy thump, but he regained his footing before tumbling to the ground.

Taking advantage of the chaos, he began his transformation.

Above them, the sky opened up. Clear blue gave way to a sickly yellow, the same color depicted in all the drawings of the realm where the gods had been banished. Enraptured, Cheron stared upward, both dreading and anticipating what was to come. Witnessing the return of a god, even a hated enemy, was a sight few mortal eyes would ever see. Cheron was drawn in by the spectacle.

Spasms of pain on his back traveled from his shoulder blades to the small of his back where Isa's blade remained embedded in his flesh. Unable to hold back, Cheron cried out. Sound, actual sound, came from his mouth. Filled with air, not his own blood, his lungs ached as he belted out another cry.

"What's happening?" Isa's voice rose above the din.

"Our god's glory!" Sinnac responded. "Glory, glory, glory!"

The dragoness clearly didn't agree with Sinnac's assessment. Hissing, Isa followed Ekos's path and began changing into a dragon. Cheron observed as her human hand sprang claws, her hair became long tendrils, and her skin became scales. In her fury, her human frame vanished under the weight of her reptilian one.

A black figure emerged in the sky, the train of a cloak trailing out behind. Kalin, haloed in a brilliant white light, appeared. Tears of joy came to Cheron's eyes, momentarily blocking out the sight. It was too late for the goddess to heal the wound draining his blood, but in time, she would heal the one draining the world. Ekos had done the right thing. He'd saved everyone.

"What is this?" Sinnac demanded. "You've killed him. You killed your lover. Your goddess can do nothing for him!"

Instead of lobbing a sarcastic response, Ekos fanned out his wings, expanding their golden length across the plaza. Lightning crackled in his maw. He inhaled sharply, and the air around him crackled with energy.

"Isa!" Sinnac called out. "Guard me!"

The dragon heeded his call. Bellowing out a war cry, she stepped between the charging Ekos and her master. Her long tail sliced through the air, hitting Ekos in the flank right before he discharged his blast.

Helplessly, Cheron watched his love topple to the ground with a thundering crack. He slid across the cobblestones and hurled straight into the flowerbeds. Dirt and rock shot high into the air along with the corpses of Ekos's kin. Limbs rained down along with the rich soil, coating the area in grime and desecrated body parts.

The sword that had been embedded in Cheron's back lay off to the side. Cheron blinked a few times to clear his vision. After each blink, he was still whole, the sword was still removed from his back, and he still wasn't in pain. It wasn't a trick of his mind. He'd somehow been healed.

Sinnac shouted, "We must combine the relic fragments before Kalin fully materializes! Stop her before she coalesces!"

Isa took her attention off Ekos long enough for him to right himself. After shaking debris from his scales, he charged a lightning blast. Isa flung her tail at him, but Ekos was prepared for the maneuver this time. He took to the air as she swiped, raining down an electrical current to her body, which jerked in twisted as if caught in marionette strings.

The smell of burning flesh, accelerated by Ekos's flapping wings, blew toward Cheron. He gagged.

Sinnac was similarly affected. He'd doubled over, one hand braced against his knee, and let loose a series of hacking coughs that shook his body.

"The amulet!" Sinnac shouted between coughs. "Get it!"

Cheron looked to where he pointed and saw the two halves of the relic on the ground. Hurriedly, before Sinnac realized Cheron's injury was no longer incapacitating him, Cheron grabbed hold of the sword.

Chapter Forty-Five

KALIN HOVERED ABOVE them, still only half-visible but quickly solidifying. All around her, the dank yellow sky surrendered to a clear blue one. Cheron swore he saw the brown of her eyes and the dark hue of her skin. Radiant, glorious—she'd stand before them soon and then usher in a new world where the just and merciful ruled.

In front of him, Sinnac screamed at Isa to fight, to destroy their enemies for Atyx's glory, but Ekos wouldn't allow the injured dragoness to move even a step toward the relic. Whenever she tried to crawl forward, he'd flick his tail to send her reeling.

"Must I do it all myself?" Sinnac roared.

Fatigue from his injury made him sluggish. The sword, heavy in Cheron's hand, dragged on the ground. Breathing deeply, he lugged the blade upward and positioned himself between Sinnac and the two broken pieces of the goddess's talisman.

Sinnac's nostrils flared when he saw Cheron. A practiced warrior, he mastered his emotions with a dismissive wave of his hand and a roll of his shoulders. When he drew his blade, his hand was steady.

"You're beaten," Cheron said. "Lay down your weapon."

"You're halfway to Yellow Sky already."

"Perhaps, but you won't send me all the way before Kalin is reborn into this world."

Their blades met, clanking loudly in the open garden. Reverberations from impact traveled all the way down Cheron's arm; he swore he felt the force of the blow in his toes. This time, Cheron knew the fight would be to the death. Atyx no longer needed him alive. Indeed, the war god would most certainly want him to suffer an agonizing death.

"Your luck ends, savage," Sinnac said. "The garden will be a pleasant memory in comparison."

Cheron didn't taunt his foes. He fought as he lived—simply. He forced their blades together again, noting how the other man's arm quivered. Sinnac probably hadn't recovered from their last duel any more than Cheron had recovered from his injury.

Honor compelled Cheron to say, "Surrender and you'll know the goddess's mercy."

Sinnac barked a short laugh. Then, he lunged forward. Cheron easily countered and fell back into a defensive position as Sinnac's blade cut harmlessly through air. Catlike, the other man laughed and acted as though Cheron had unwittingly stepped inside a master scheme.

"You're a predictable fool."

Cheron only grunted and thrust his blade forward, nearly impaling Sinnac on the tip. He caught the tail end of his cloak. The thin fabric sliced down to its hem. Snarling at the tear, Sinnac yanked the garment from his body and flung it to the ground.

"That was worth more than you'll ever be."

"Goddess keep you, Sinnac."

Rage drove Sinnac's attacks. He kept a manic gait, trying to catch Cheron off guard long enough to run him through or at least cripple him. His eyes were always on the two halves of the medallion or on the sky. Time conspired against him. More importantly, it made him panic. Carelessness would eventually be his undoing. Cheron only need keep his head and wait for the right moment.

Their blades clashed again. Skilled, possibly more so than Cheron, Sinnac wove in and out, testing and retesting his defenses. Cheron kept with the pace but never went on the offense.

"Strike, you coward."

Cheron shook his head and kept his blade poised and ready to defend.

"Coward!"

Sinnac drove straight at Cheron, extending his body well within Cheron's lunge range. Cheron seized on the opportunity and brought the blade down on his opponent's arm. It carved through flesh and bone the same as it did fabric. Twitching, the fingers on Sinnac's detached arm continued to move as if by memory.

At first, it didn't seem like Sinnac realized he'd been injured nor did he understand the severity. Face screwed up into tight lines, his teeth bared like an animal's, he continued to stare at Cheron as if he were going to kill him.

Blood spurted from Sinnac's wound, running down the side of his body. Finally, he turned his head to behold how his life would end. Disbelieving at first, he touched the stump and withdrew his fingers, gawking at the blood with an open mouth—jarred and set for screaming.

"Goddess go with you," Cheron said as Sinnac crumpled to the ground. "Her mercy binds."

There was no time to give the body its last rites. That would have to keep for later. Cheron grabbed hold of the two halves of the medallion and shoved them into the folds of his clothes. They'd be safe enough there.

Ekos still struggled with Isa. The badly injured dragoness let out a massive bellow when her master fell. Renewed in her fury, she lashed out at Ekos with her tail. Fire broiled in her maw. The heat of her looming attack electrified the air, charging the air heavy with potential energy.

Ekos didn't give her time to complete the attack. His massive jaws tore into her shoulder blade. To deepen his hold and open the wounds, Ekos dug into her thick hide with his front talons and twisted his head back and forth. Gore welled up from the wounds as scales peeled away from her flesh.

The roar Isa bellowed shook the loose dirt that had been flung from the planters. Rocks vibrated on the remaining cobblestones. Cheron covered his ears to block out the high-pitched shrieks. Despite everything, hearing the creature cry out in pain carved a hollow pit in his stomach.

"Ekos," Cheron called. "Offer her the goddess's mercy."

Both Ekos and Isa turned their eyes toward Cheron.

"Please, Ekos. Being a servant of Kalin requires compassion."

A sound an awful lot like a sigh escaped from Ekos's maw, but he eased his hold so that Isa collapsed on the ground in a bloodied heap. Her massive sides heaved in and out. A thin blood drizzled out of her flaring nostrils. Her eyes shut, and Cheron feared she might already be dead.

Ekos left the grizzly scene behind him and transformed to his human form. He gathered Cheron in a spine-cracking hug.

"You forget how strong you are, my dearest," Cheron grunted.

Ekos let him go. "I'm sorry. I'm sorry. It's just I'm so glad to see you."

The two stood rapt as the goddess continued to descend.

"She won't let me stay with you," Ekos said. A single tear rolled down his cheek. "Not after what I did. Not after banishing her along with Atyx."

"She will."

Ekos shook his head. "I'm just glad my magic saved you."

"The tattoo?"

"Yes."

"Thank you," Cheron said. Emotion choked his voice. "But next time tell me."

Ekos gave the command a dry chuckle that told Cheron the surly dragon regretted nothing. What he said next confirmed Cheron's suspicion. "Kalin has a rule against sorcery. I knew you wouldn't allow it, so I made the smart decision for you."

Cheron sniffed at the tone. "I traveled here using dark magic."

"I wouldn't say that too loud just now."

Kalin materialized. She was even more beautiful than Cheron imagined. No painting had ever captured her grace. Her thick silver hair fell in a long braid over one slender shoulder. White eyes, luminous like the stars, fixed on him. As she moved, the world moved with her. Trees swayed, plants dipped their heads. Even the air conformed to her gait, blowing gently as she drifted toward them.

"My servants," Kalin said.

Upon hearing her melodious voice, Cheron fell to his knees. Ekos did the same, bowing his head as though laying his head across the executioner's block.

In a way Cheron knew in his heart to be forgiving, Kalin gazed down at her fallen servant. "Ekos," she said. "You came back to me."

"I'm not the one who left."

Cheron inhaled sharply at the blasphemy, but Kalin only tilted her head to the side and rested her hand on his head in sympathy. "Your people suffered for me, and I was unable to save them. I am sorry. Can you forgive me?"

Blue eyes swimming in tears, Ekos met her gaze with a boldness Cheron admired. He said, "Can you end their suffering?"

"Yes. And yours. But you must come with me."

Ashen-faced, Ekos stood and squared his shoulders. When he saw Cheron, he plastered a crumbling smile on his face and said, "Goodbye, Cheron."

The goddess and Ekos vanished, leaving Cheron to his myriad of emotions and an aching sense of loss he feared would never abate.

Chapter Forty-Six

"I THOUGHT I'D never see you again," Cheron said. The tip of his index finger tilted Ekos's face toward his own. He brushed their lips together to confirm the reality of his lover's existence. Flesh, living and warm, pushed back against his. For a moment, they stayed that way, each exploring the contours of the other's face. Cheron broke away first. "I thought she'd banished you."

"She...she forgave me. But I can't serve in her council, not until I prove myself. I have to go back to my lair...er...home."

"No," Cheron responded. "No, no, no."

"Come with me," Ekos said.

Cheron's heart beat faster. "I must stay and serve my people and the goddess."

This time Ekos's voice sounded less confident as he tried to lace it with his familiar brash sarcasm. "You can come with me. King or dragon, Kalin said. Easy choice. Dragons eat kings for breakfast."

All his life Cheron had served the goddess. As a child, he had felt her call. He had answered the moment he found his own voice. Now, he wanted to walk away and live in his lover's embrace. Was the desire selfish? Perhaps Kalin tested his worthiness with such an offering.

"I..." Cheron stammered.

"She expects you to worship," Ekos said dryly. "You just can't rule alongside her. She's asking you to step aside."

The trial to obtain Hell's Echo came back to him. The relic had used the exact verbiage. Cheron found he didn't mind. Leadership didn't offer him any thrills. It had been a burden he accepted because no one else was suited to the task. He found no fault in letting his goddess rule. His people would be in safe hands.

Ekos seized on his hesitation. "Stay with me. I love rebels. Not in general. *You.*"

The naked vulnerability of Ekos's declaration brought stinging tears to Cheron's eyes. He hadn't realized how long he'd been waiting to hear the other man express his affections. Now that he finally had, Cheron felt lifted to the sky.

"I choose dragon," Cheron decided. "Let Kalin lead."

"If you choose me, take me."

Cheron lifted Ekos into his arms and carried him to a patch of clover, where he lay him down. Only the robe from earlier covered his body. Loving the way the garment both revealed and hid his lover's flesh, Cheron took a moment to appreciate the elegance of Ekos's features, the taut flex of his muscles, the delicate hollow in his throat.

He nuzzled the smooth line of Ekos's neck while his fingers stroked the exposed nipple. The nub there instantly puckered under his touch. Thrilling at the response, Cheron dipped down to lick it. Ekos moaned at the light flick of his tongue and then inhaled sharply when Cheron nibbled the sensitive bud.

"More," Ekos said.

The fabric of the robe fell away as Ekos lifted his body off the ground. Already hard, his cock jutted from a nest of fine golden curls. Cheron ran his fingers through the coarse hair, barely grazing the side of Ekos's shaft with the side of his hand as he caressed the inner thigh.

"Put me in your mouth. Taste me."

"You're going to have to beg," Cheron laughed, enjoying the way Ekos's normally controlled voice broke.

"Dragons don't beg bears."

"We'll see."

Before Ekos retorted, Cheron sealed their mouths together. Ekos's lips parted, allowing access to the warm inner cavern of his mouth. But he didn't give any other quarter. Demanding, his lips pushed back as his fingers tangled in Cheron's thick brown hair to pull him forward. They licked, sucked, and nibbled until their ragged breathing synchronized and they tasted of each other.

"Cheron," Ekos panted between kisses. "My sweet one, my honorable rebel?"

"What?"

"Suck my cock."

"Say please..."

Snarling his frustrations, Ekos ground their bodies together so that the friction from their rubbing shafts sent them both into a frenzy. Refusing to give up, to once again be the one who begged for pleasure, Cheron matched rhythm while he caressed all the other tender, engorged parts of Ekos's body with his tongue and hands. He found his love had a particular weakness for ears. Whenever he kissed or nibbled a lobe, he felt Ekos's cock jump against his stomach.

"Your body pleads even if your mouth doesn't."

Ekos had no retort, just a small, dissatisfied moan.

"My poor dragon needs a sample, I suppose."

Using one hand, Cheron grabbed the base of Ekos's shaft while the other fondled the smooth ridge of flesh between balls and anus. The small, strangled noises Ekos made were obviously stifled cries of pleasure, so Cheron continued his assault on his lover's defenses. "I can do this until you sprout scales," Cheron told him.

"Cheron, my dear heart. My most darling treasure."

"Yes?"

"Please suck my cock, or I will literally eat you."

Such an appeal was probably the best he'd get from Ekos, whose teeth had indeed taken on a sharp quality. Laughing, Cheron trailed kisses from neck to navel, stopping along the way to torment him further. By the time Cheron reached the cock, Ekos's breaths came out as pants.

He'd suffered enough.

Cheron took the head into his mouth, working the base with his hand until Ekos lifted his hips and forced the rest of his shaft inside his mouth. He accepted the length with a satisfied murmur, enjoying the taste of salt and the way Ekos moved his body to take his pleasure. Over and over, Ekos simulated the movements of lovemaking while Cheron sucked the cock to the back of his throat.

With a whimper, Ekos pulled out of Cheron's mouth. "Make love to me," he pleaded. "Please. Now."

"There's nothing to ease the passage. I can finish you with my mouth."

Cheron licked the head of Ekos's cock again and prepared to swallow it to the root, but Ekos stopped him.

"Dragons don't need it. Naturally slick."

That was all he needed to hear. Cheron thrust inside Ekos with one fluid motion. Back arched, heavy lids partially concealing his crystal-blue eyes, he let loose a long moan that Cheron swallowed with another kiss.

"Did I hurt you?" Cheron asked, licking the tender curve of Ekos's ear. He kept still, allowing Ekos a moment to adjust to his bulk.

"No. Harder. You can't hurt me."

Cheron pulled almost all the way out before entering again, this time burying his shaft deeper inside his lover. He angled so that he brushed against the prostate with each thrust and drove harder and harder.

"Faster," Ekos begged him until his words broke away into sharp cries. In his climax, Ekos spread his arms as if he were flying and cried out as if he were falling. Cheron came soon after, pulling out to release his seed on Ekos's chest.

Cheron collapsed on top of him. Enjoying the sensation of their two hearts beating side by side, Cheron closed his eyes and pulled Ekos tight against his body. He buried his nose in the golden crown of hair and took a deep breath, creating a memory from the scent that would forever be associated with deep contentment.

"Cheron," Ekos muttered into his chest, his eyes half-closed.

"Yes, my love?"

"Is this what you truly want? It's not too late to change your mind and rule your kingdom."

"Kalin knows where to find me should she need my blade," Cheron said.

Ekos cuddled closer against him. Absentmindedly, his slender fingers brushed through the fine hair on Cheron's abdomen. The light touch brought goose bumps along his arms. Cheron knew that, had he not been already spent, he'd be aroused.

Ekos yawned, his jaw popping, and said, "I just don't want you to have anything less than what you desire."

"Having you is more than I ever imagined."

And that was true.

Cheron had journeyed far from his homeland and fought an impossible foe to bring his goddess and her mercy to his kingdom. For his reward, he got to hold the sky and the sea in his hands. In return, the sky and sea held him too.

Epilogue

THE PEACEFUL CAVE became a war zone. Ekos had been threatening to send Lion off to school, but he was finally following through.

Although they both griped at each other nonstop, Cheron felt the underlying sadness. Ekos didn't want to part with the boy he considered to be his son. Lion didn't know anyone or anything outside of Ekos or his life as a concubine. Learning the arts of magic, while it had been an exciting prospect in the abstract, now threatened to undo the only sense of normalcy the young man knew.

Lion said, "I don't need school! I'm plenty smart enough."

Ekos snorted and tossed a series of heavy tomes inside a satchel. All of them had leather bindings and a flourish of letters up and down the spine in a language Cheron couldn't decipher.

"You guys need me," Lion said, trying a different strategy. "What if something else bad happens?"

Ekos snorted at that too. "Finish packing."

Grumbling, Lion sat in a corner and pawed through his stuff. He picked through the assortment of clothes and treasure without really looking at what he had in his hands. At some point, he shoved an actual rock inside the already bulging suitcases.

"There, that's the last of my stuff," Lion said. "You can get rid of me now."

Ekos harrumphed at that last line. He riffled through Lion's packed bags, pulling out gold coins, purses filled with jewels, lavish clothes, and all manner of riches. Pursing his lips, he yanked out an elongated fake penis. Waving it at the young man, he yelled, "And what do you need this for?"

"What did *you* need it for before he showed up? Not all of us have a giant from Broken Maw to scratch our sweet spots!"

Cheron flushed at the mention of their lovemaking, which was almost constant. They couldn't last more than a few hours without touching. Once they touched, they were soon undressed. And once they were undressed. Well...

Ekos yelled back, "You need an education, not a...fake dick."

"Give that back, you old lizard!"

Ekos grabbed him by the collar of his shirt and pulled him backward. At first, Cheron assumed they were about to bicker more. Certainly, both of them had that same stubborn look to their face—their lips pursed, their brows furrowed in a fearsome angle over their big eyes. Instead, Ekos wrapped his arms around the younger man, hugging him from the back, and said, "Okay, it's time to go."

"No," Lion said, sniffling. "You guys need me."

Ekos rested his head on Lion's shoulder. "Yes, it's time. You're going to go learn how to shoot fireballs and open portals to goblin rooms. You'll meet some cute boy with a real dick, and I'll threaten to eat him if he ever hurts you. If he does hurt you, I'll incinerate him for real."

Cheron cleared his throat.

"But before I do that, I'll offer him the goddess's mercy. Of course." Looking directly at Cheron, Ekos simpered, his full mouth playfully pouting, and whispered in Lion's ear, "And then I'll incinerate him."

Lion grinned and grabbed hold of Ekos's dangling hand and squeezed it. "Can I have the fake dick back?"

"You wouldn't want it if I told you where it had been. There isn't a cleaning spell powerful enough to undo the things I've done."

"Okay. Buy me a new one?"

"You'll have plenty of money to buy your own. Now come on, it's time."

"I get to ride up top!" Lion shrieked.

Ekos's smile somehow managed to grow at that remark, stretching the expanse of his face. He gave Cheron a conspiratorial wink and said, "I think our Northern man here can give someone else a turn up top. Also, that reminds me. Come here, lover," Ekos beckoned Cheron with a sweet smile and a wave of his hand.

"I'm going to go wait outside," Lion said with a roll of his eyes. "Keep it short."

CHERON STAYED BEHIND while Ekos dropped Lion off at the door of the school. From a distance, he watched them hug and cry. Although their faces remained hidden, he knew they wept by the way their shoulders lifted up and down. Ekos rubbed his hand in a circle on Lion's back. They swayed as if caught in a light breeze.

Hours later, they broke apart. Ekos transformed before he got to Cheron, no doubt to hide his tear-streaked face. Showing emotions was something they'd need to work on later. For now, Cheron acted as though everything were normal and admired the way the white veins of Ekos's wings caught the light.

"He'll be fine," he said while climbing up onto Ekos's back. "We can visit him during holidays."

Ekos gave his massive reptilian head a shake that was meant to convey lack of concern. Cheron chuckled at the gesture and said, "Ready to go."

They flew until the sun set, dipping on the horizon before sinking under the curve of the earth. Ekos sat him down in a field much like the one they'd made love in not too long ago. The memory had the lower half of Cheron's body tingling.

He took Ekos into his arms, kissing the long line of his neck. "This place is perfect."

"I need to ask you again. Am I what you want?"

Cheron cradled the side of Ekos's face and gave his nose a tender kiss. "Stop asking me that. I love you."

"I love you too. Always."

"Lion is going to be fine," Cheron said, responding to the sadness he heard in his love's voice. "One of my best friends is looking after him."

"I know. Just hold me."

It was no burden to do as he asked. Cheron loved the feel of him in his arms, the smell of his hair, and the way the smooth lines of his body responded to Cheron's lightest touch.

"Hold me closer, Cheron."

"Any closer and I'll crush you."

"Then do that."

Cheron hugged him as tightly as he dared.

Ekos whispered strange, soothing words that Cheron took for another hidden love confession. Liking where the encounter was going, he pressed their bodies together to feel Ekos's erection against his own. Something pinched him. Startled, he jumped back and searched for the bug—

or, Kalin forbid, the scorpion that had bitten his chest. All he saw was Ekos, who grinned ear to ear in his familiar, mischievous way.

"Did you...did you bite me?"

"Maybe..."

"Why?"

"So we can go flying together."

"I can't fly, dearest."

"Tell that to your wings."

Cheron looked to his sides to see there were indeed two small wings, the light cream of the moons highlighted by a mesh of white veins, unfurling from his back. "By the goddess's grace..."

"Kalin said I had to offer you three chances to leave me. She now offers you the reward you chose—dragon. Is being with me still what you want?"

Laughing in wonder, Cheron said yes and watched as the wings grew. Dark-brown scales spawned around his belly, crawling upward to his neck. He didn't realize he'd grown taller until he looked down and saw Ekos, a tiny white dot on the endless black landscape.

"Jesus, you're massive," Ekos shouted. "And somehow you still sort of look like a bear."

Cheron shouted back, "Join me!"

The familiar yet different electrical charge of Ekos's transformation traveled the length of his spine down to his tail, which thrashed in anticipation.

Ekos took straight to the air. Roaring a challenge, he beckoned Cheron to follow. Cheron lifted his wings for the first time. The air beneath them lifted him upward into the sky, toward Ekos, toward home.

About the Author

Jacqueline Rohrbach is an asexual living in windy Central Washington with her husband, two dogs, and two cats. Writing has always been a passion of hers, and when she decided to pursue her dream, she wanted to tell stories of people who are often left out or relegated to secondary character status or put in the villain box. She likes unconventional, even absurd, stories, sweet romances, dark fantasy, and horror. Really, she'll write and read pretty much anything.

Email: Jackeeroh@gmail.com

Twitter: @JackeeRohrbach

Website: www.jackeewrites.com

Other books by this author

The Worst Werewolf

The False Moon

The Soulstealers

Just in Time

Speak with the Dead

Parallel Larry

Also Available from NineStar Press

Connect with NineStar Press

www.ninestarpress.com

www.facebook.com/ninestarpress

www.facebook.com/groups/NineStarNiche

www.twitter.com/ninestarpress

www.tumblr.com/blog/ninestarpress